ARLENE McFARLANE

Murder, Curlers & Kites

A Valentine Beaumont
Mini Mystery

ISBN-13: 978-1-9994981-1-5

Published by ParadiseDeer Publishing
Canada

Cover Art by Sue Traynor
Formatting by Author E.M.S.

Praise for
Murder, Curlers & Kites

"Arlene McFarlane seamlessly blends fashion, fun, and a frenzied murder in her breezy beach read, *Murder, Curlers & Kites*! If you're looking for a fabulous stay-cation escape this summer, I highly recommend it!"

–*New York Times* Bestselling Author, Gemma Halliday

"Fresh, sexy, and original! Valentine's inventiveness and sharp wit dazzle in this hilarious, clever romp!"

– *USA Today* Bestselling Author, Diana Orgain

"*Murder, Curlers & Kites* will have you on the edge of your salon seat with mascara running from laugh-crying while fanning yourself from the heat—and I don't mean from the hair dryer!"

–*USA Today* Bestselling Author, Traci Andrighetti

"A clever mystery and a loveable heroine who looks great while hunting down bad guys. A perfect summer read!"

–*USA Today* Bestselling Author, Sam Cheever

Acknowledgments

My humblest and warmest thanks to *New York Times* and *USA Today* Bestselling Authors Gemma Halliday, Traci Andrighetti, Diana Orgain, and Sam Cheever for your kind and witty endorsements. I'm honored that women with your talents and high standards found delight in my story.

As always, when I have questions regarding police protocol, I turn to people in law enforcement for clarification. To that end, I'm deeply grateful to Constable Karl Baumann for graciously answering my questions. If any mistakes have crept in, they are mine alone.

Karen Dale Harris, Noël Kristan Higgins, Amy Atwell, and Sue Traynor: I am continually amazed by your efficiency, wisdom, and professionalism. When I publish a book, I know it's ready, thanks to you.

My treasured family: This journey would mean nothing without you. You are my world, and I love you! xoxo

Lastly, thank you, God, for Your many blessings and for filling me with the desire and skill to write the Valentine Beaumont series.

To my devoted readers:
Your love for Valentine motivates me daily.

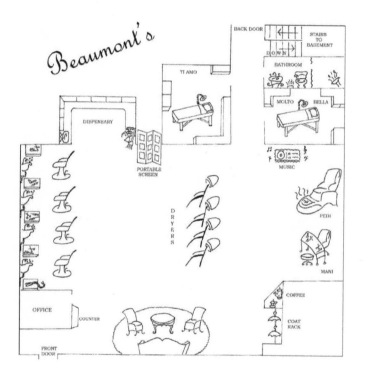

Chapter 1

May had never looked cheerier. Skies were blue, buds were blooming, my smile was wide, my mood buoyant. I could feel it. Today was going to be one of those days where everything went right. Lady Luck probably figured I'd had enough misfortune lately to warrant a carefree Friday.

My name is Valentine Beaumont. My surname comes from my French side, my coloring—think Kim Kardashian—from my Armenian side, and I'm not sure who's to blame for my impulsive side.

I own and run Beaumont's, a full-service salon in a charming section of Rueland, Massachusetts, minutes north of Boston. I'm also a part-time sleuth with a tendency to unearth dead bodies, which is what I meant by the *misfortune* part.

There's been considerable controversy over my involvement in solving homicides, mostly because I use my beauty tools in ways most people wouldn't imagine. I'd once brought a murderer to his knees by whacking him with a hot three-pronged curling iron, then using it to melt a hole in his bag of cocaine, spreading the drug everywhere. Not ideal uses for a beauty tool, but desperate times call for desperate measures.

The fact that I'd had a sizzling, albeit exhaustive, night with Michael Romero, the hot cop in my life, may have had something to do with my cheery mood, my ridiculous smile, and the reason I felt nothing could go wrong today. Even the bird poop that seconds ago had landed on the windshield of my yellow Daisy Bug wasn't going to bring me down on this glorious morning.

I swerved into the parking lot I shared with Friar Tuck's donut castle and pulled up beside a shiny silver sports car that by its sleekness alone warned away the breeze and rustling debris. I'd never seen a car like this in my part of the lot before, much less knew who could own it.

My smile waned, my twitching nose telling me something was up. Who was booked this morning? Off the top, I knew Mrs. Benedetti was my first client.

Mrs. Benedetti was in her seventies, Italian to the core, and wouldn't think twice about slapping someone upside the head if they needed sense knocked into them. Though her Mafia-linked sons went around town in flashy cars, flaunting wads of cash, Mrs. Benedetti drove a big old boat with long fins at the back. And there it was, right half of the car perched on the curb ten feet from Friar Tuck's rusty revolving donut pole.

I clutched my ever-present black beauty bag, angled out of my Bug, and gave the sleek car another suspicious look. I didn't want to keep Mrs. Benedetti waiting, so I skipped buying a box of Tuck's Tidbits and darted past the Dumpster behind our buildings.

Friar Tuck's back door creaked open on the other side of the Dumpster. A second later, a paper coffee cup was pitched on top of the bin's overflowing trash. The cup tipped toward me, and I watched in horror as coffee sprayed onto my trendy white mini dress.

"*Aaah!*" I yelped, arms and legs spread wide as brown spots saturated the patterned yellow daisies on my dress.

Silence ensued, followed by a croaky voice I recognized as Austin's from the donut shop. "Valentine? Is that you?"

The pimply adolescent poked his head around the Dumpster in his Robin Hood uniform and gawked at me from head to toe. I gawked back, in too much shock to answer.

"Hey, cool retro outfit." He nodded in approval, coming into full view. "I especially like your poufy hair and go-go boots. You look like a Barbie doll. Or that Twiggy chick from the sixties I saw in one of my grandma's old magazines." He pushed back his felt crown and leaned in, brows knit together. "But you should know you've got coffee stains all over."

Restraining myself from clobbering him for ruining my dress—not to mention lumping me in with the grandma reference—I lowered my arms and took a deep breath. "Yes, I know, Austin. Thanks for pointing that out."

He shrugged. "Glad to help."

He plodded back into Friar Tuck's, and I hitched my bag over my right shoulder, accidentally tearing out my glittery hooped earring with my thumb. *Youch.* The hoop dropped to the ground with a *clink*, and I squeezed my eyes tightly, massaging my ear from the sharp sting.

Exhaling in frustration, I scooped up the earring, cleaned it off, and speared it back through my ear lobe. Then I marched my stained white go-go boots into the shop. These mishaps would not spoil my day. Thankfully, the pleasing smell of bergamot essential oil soothed my jagged nerves while Andrea Bocelli's version of "O Sole Mio" echoed down the hall.

Since Mr. Worldly, a.k.a. Jock de Marco, began working in the salon, the music had shifted from jazz and rock to pieces that, as Jock put it, were drenched in emotion. With his mysterious, vast connections, I wouldn't have been surprised to see the tenor Bocelli himself singing in the salon.

Secretly, the music had begun to soak into my skin. It was one of the things I looked forward to every morning when I came to work. Usually it went downhill from there.

"Jocko! Jocko! Jocko!" Mrs. Benedetti chanted in her husky, accented voice.

I rounded the corner into the Mediterranean-styled salon and saw the Italian matriarch, plumply filled out in typical black, reach up past Jock's mammoth washboard chest rippling under his tailored blue shirt, and squeeze his cheeks.

Another one bites the dust, I thought, adding my first client to the harem that idolized Jock. My smile faded another notch, but not because of Mrs. Benedetti's gushing display. A nagging feeling needled me that something was off in the salon.

Clients in the waiting area chatted, mini lights to my right above the four cutting stations twinkled through grapevines on the stucco wall, and Maximilian Martell, my second-in-command, was at his station, dazzling his own first client of the morning with her haircut.

"Valentina!" Mrs. Benedetti extended her hand toward me, her purse dangling from her arm. "This man"—she beamed from Jock to me—"he is truly a god."

"Oh?" Derailed from whatever was pulling at me, I turned down the volume on Bocelli and joined the others. "What did this god do that was so amazing?"

I didn't dare look at Jock, but the heated tension was there. Thing was, the guy was loved by everyone. Men. Women. Cats. Dogs. If there were such a thing as a real-life Hercules, it'd be this gorgeous, enigmatic Argentinean.

"He's a-going to fit in my daughter, Carla, tomorrow, for the works." Mrs. Benedetti bobbed her head at me. "Carla needs help, no? You've seen her, Valentina. She doesn't hold a candle to you with your lustrous burgundy hair, your beautiful skin, and *Mamma mia*, those amber eyes!" She elbowed Jock, his arms folded in front. "My sons…they say they'd swim the Mediterranean for a chance with a sensual woman like Valentina."

Jock grinned. "I hope they have good lungs."

She whacked her purse across his biceps. "You must-a be blind not to notice this girl's beauty."

I knew I was blushing, but no way was I going to look up and catch Jock's teasing eye. Truth was, not only was this god well loved, but he'd also succeeded at everything from navy firefighting to ranking as a master-at-arms to stunt-doubling. Why he'd resumed hairstyling and chosen to work for me was something I'd never understand.

To say I enjoyed working side by side with this intriguing hero was an understatement. Our day-to-day banter was stimulating, witty, and at times, sexy. But I also reminded myself he was an employee, not a lover. The lines blurred from time to time—we'd had our moments—but he knew where things stood.

I squared my shoulders, pleased at how in control I felt. "Your daughter simply hasn't found her style yet, Mrs. Benedetti. But I'm sure this god's the right person to *give* it to her."

Jock raised a suggestive eyebrow at me, then took a second to appraise me in my newly stained dress. He slowly grazed his finger across my neckline and put it to his tongue. "Mmm. Cappuccino. When did you start drinking the java?"

My breath caught in my throat from his touch, and I patted my dress, double-checking it hadn't gone up in flames.

"Aha!" Mrs. Benedetti piped. "You see? You *do* notice this beauty."

Jock hadn't taken his eyes off me. "I notice a lot more than Valentina thinks."

I swallowed thickly, ignoring the way he mimicked Mrs. Benedetti's pronunciation of my name. "I didn't *start* drinking the java." I shook the hem of my dress, airing out the damp spots. "I was merely the target of a flying coffee cup. Nothing that's going to ruin my day." How many times had I already thought *that* this morning?

I gave Mrs. Benedetti a gentle nudge toward the hall. "Why don't you make yourself comfortable in Ti Amo for that wax job? I'll be there in a minute."

She slipped out a tiny flask from her purse, steeling herself. "This time, I come prepared. And I pay for Carla's treatment today. You name the price. This is my gift to her."

Jock ushered her down the hall to the treatment room, and I aimed for the nine-by-nine dispensary—our supply room and nook between customers—coming an inch from bumping into Phyllis Murdoch, employee #3, shuffling out in her latest handmade getup.

Uh-huh. The *something* that was off.

Phyllis was packed into a yellow satin kimono like those delicate geishas portrayed in Japanese paintings. Unfortunately, *delicate* wasn't a term used when describing Phyllis. Her face was unevenly powdered white, her mahogany hair was swept up and dyed black, and her lips were painted like two maraschino cherries. Plus, she was wearing white socks and two-inch wooden-based flip-flops on her feet.

She click-clacked past me in her tapered kimono and squirted a huge glob of the new setting gel I'd ordered last week onto Mrs. Wozniak's head. The tube wheezed, signaling it'd almost been emptied, and the glob streamed down her client's face.

"What the *heck*?" Phyllis smeared gel off Mrs. Wozniak's cheek and flapped her wet hand in the air like a dog shaking its fur after a bath.

Max and I ducked, narrowly missing being slung with goop.

It was clear Phyllis hadn't read up on the product, and my heartbeat quickened at the thought of poor, hard-of-hearing Mrs. Wozniak walking out of the salon, hair spiked like a blowfish.

"Phyllis…" I lowered my voice, edging closer. "You're only supposed to use a dime-sized portion of that gel, and you need to warm it in your hands first before applying it to wet hair."

"*Pff.*" She gave me a flippant wave. "That's how *you* apply it. I have my *own* technique."

"Also known as the lamebrain technique." Max had sent off his client and was scribbling in a notebook he'd grabbed from his station, eyes on Phyllis making a mess of her lady's hair.

For obvious reasons, I kept it a secret that Phyllis was distantly related to me on my mother's side. She remained in my employment because it was easier to face her ineptitude every day than it was letting her go and risk being put in front of the firing squad made up of my mother's aunts.

"*Eek!*" Mrs. Wozniak clutched her scalp with a bony-knuckled grip.

Phyllis tore a comb through the hardened gel on the woman's hair, and Max whipped out his phone, clicking pictures of his co-worker in action.

"Phyllis," I said, pulse hammering, "you need to wash out the gel and start over."

She swept away the flowery things dangling from the chopsticks in her hair, then jerked Mrs. Wozniak back into the sink. "It's not *my* fault the stuff hardened so fast. If she had hair like mine, this wouldn't have happened."

I was trying hard not to stare at Madame Geisha's patchy dye job and the ornate chopsticks holding up her saggy bun, but ignoring Phyllis's hairdo was like turning a blind eye to an ogre with three heads. "Speaking of, why is your hair tinted black today?" Not the only thing I was wondering.

"To go with the outfit," she responded, unaware of the water trickling down her client's neck. "Do I ask *you* why you poufed up *your* hair today and dressed like a sixties replica?"

Her remark didn't faze me. Piecing together an outfit was one of my God-given gifts, and my aim *was* to look like a sixties hipster, minus the coffee stains.

She flung Mrs. Wozniak upright, nearly ejecting her from her seat. "I'm amazed I colored anything at all. You know you need another tint bottle? That one with the white lid is a loose cannon. Squirts tint everywhere but on the hair."

Max, who has been in my employ almost since day one, rolled his eyes in a full circle. "Like how you just sprayed water everywhere but on your client's hair."

Phyllis slapped a towel around Mrs. Wozniak's neck, sneering at Max. "I would've asked *you* to color it last night," she said to me, "but you had that date with Romeo, so I did it myself."

"It's Ro-*mero*," I emphasized, my insides boiling from her lack of courtesy, "and I would've delayed the date in order to help you." I gaped from her to the floor. "What's this black stuff we're stepping on?" As if I didn't know.

"Huh?" She leaned over and ogled the black smudges on the ceramic tile circling willy-nilly around the stations, into the dispensary. "See? That bottle's the pits. Must've left a trail to the sink when I went to wash it out."

"A *trail!* Hansel and Gretel would've needed a GPS to follow this path. How do you suppose we'll get these marks off the floor?" My patience was wearing thin, and it was only 9:15 in the morning. So much for starting the day in a great mood.

"I'll clean it up," Phyllis said, unbothered by the steam whistling out my ears.

"You don't have enough spit in your mouth to clean the *whole* floor," Max volunteered.

"Hardy-hoo-hoo." Phyllis swung her head from Max to my bag squashed under my arm. "Enough about the floor. Where are the Tidbits?"

"Who cares about Tidbits?" Mrs. Wozniak squawked at us. "I want to know where Phyllis is today. This nitwit doesn't know a curler from a comb."

Max smiled and patted Mrs. Wozniak's shoulder, enunciating his words crystal clear. "That nitwit, darling, *is* Phyllis. But you're right. She doesn't know a curler from a comb."

I repeated today's mantra that everything was going to go right, when the tension in my neck reminded me I'd been wrong before. "I didn't have time to buy Tidbits, Phyllis. Feel free to get a box from Friar Tuck's when you're done here."

Leaving the scene before I strangled someone in a kimono, I carted my bag into the dispensary and plunked it on the counter, giving a routine glance at the appointment book. I was looking for clues as to who owned the sports car when Max wandered in with his notebook. "The queen of day-old donuts buy a box of fresh Tidbits to *share?* That'll be the day."

I gave up studying the appointment book and eyed Max in his sharp dress shirt and perfectly fitted pants. Choosing not to discuss Tidbits or Phyllis's cheapness any further, I motioned to his hand. "What's with the notebook and picture-taking? All you need is a fedora on your head, and you'd have the whole reporter look down."

He tossed the book on the counter and crossed his arms over his toned chest. "You ever hear of *The X-Files*?" He nodded to his book. "This is The Idiot Files. I'm documenting all the stupid things Phyllis says and does. If it's comical enough, maybe I'll send it to Hollywood. They're always looking for good material."

I didn't know how to respond to this idea, but a flood of images from Phyllis's exploits rushed to mind. Like the time she coaxed Clive—her name for the tiny, white-bearded man in a constant alcoholic fog on our recent cruise—into a hair contest. Or the time she butchered Ziggy Stoaks's hair, unaware he was an escaped murder convict. And what about the bathroom explosion that singed her cornrows and brows?

While I could see the humor in Max's mission, it seemed wrong to use Phyllis and her disasters as the material to build on. Then again, Phyllis's life could provide ample fodder for a dozen seasons of a sitcom. So who was I to judge?

"I have a better question for you." Max gave one of his shrewd, wise-guy stances. "Why are you walking like you've been horseback riding?" He gaped at me with huge eyes, realization suddenly dawning. "*Valentine!* How many times is that this week? You keep this up, and that stallion you're riding will have to be put out to pasture."

"Stop it." I sat delicately on the wheeled stool, controlling my smile from getting away from me. "There aren't any pastures in Rueland."

He blinked at my rascally comeback, at a loss to say anything.

I looked from Max to Phyllis. "Does she know you're documenting her actions?"

He grinned. "She thinks I'm detailing her training as a geisha."

"You mean this isn't simply another homemade outfit?"

"You got it. She's taking lessons in the Japanese art of entertaining." He snorted and plopped onto the second wheeled stool. "If you can believe it."

What *didn't* I believe when it came to Phyllis? "There's something wrong with this picture. I mean, I don't know much about Japanese traditions, but aren't geishas supposed to be Japanese? And don't they start training as teens?"

Max shrugged. "Tell that to the idiot out there."

More questions flooded me, things I wondered if Phyllis had thought through. "Has she considered she might be exploiting another culture by dressing up as a geisha?"

"Lovey, you know Phyllis as well as I do. She doesn't think. Why not let her take the ride? We both know what the outcome will be. I don't know about you, but I'm due for a good laugh."

I smacked his arm. "You're awful. You could set her straight, and the whole messy outcome would be avoided."

He jerked his head back. "Where would the fun be in that? Anyway, have you ever known Phyllis to take advice? I warned her last week against using chlorine bleach to remove mustard stains from her red pantsuit. Did she listen? No."

"What happened?"

"Let's just say if Phyllis wears that outfit again, she'll resemble Miss Piggy in the raw."

I sighed. I had enough on my mind without worrying about Phyllis's fiascos. I stared at the page again, getting on with the day. "You know who that Carrier car belongs to?"

"What Carrier car?"

"The silver car out back. The sporty one. It says *Carrier* on it."

He slapped his hand on the counter, almost knocking the fancy handset from the French provincial phone onto the floor. "That's Jock's new Porsche, lovey!"

Of course. The other day. Left early to look at a car. If I hadn't had so many distractions this morning, I would've thought of this.

Jock strode into the dispensary. "And it's not Carrier, it's Car-rera. It's a 4S."

"I knew that." Big lie. I knew little about cars except you got in, started the engine, and put it in *D* to go.

I wasn't sure how I felt about Jock's new mode of transportation. But the sleek and seductive look was as mysterious, magnetic, and dangerous as its owner. Plus, we were talking expensive. Jock made a good living at hair, but I suspected his private life as a stunt double was what afforded him finer luxuries. "What happened to the bike?"

He leaned his well-defined butt against the cupboards and spread his palms on the counter behind him. "It needed maintenance."

I bobbed my head thoughtfully. "Next time I need maintenance on my car, I'll buy a Lamborghini."

He curled his toe under the stool legs and wheeled me toward him. "I hope you're this witty tonight on our date."

"Date?" I coughed on saliva that caught in my throat.

"D-a-t-e," he spelled out, peering down into my eyes.

Max's silence screamed he was waiting for the next move.

"You've forgotten," Jock said, his tone even.

How could I remember anything with his erotic leather-citrus aroma stirring my senses? "Not really forgotten." I held my ground. "Just…not remembered."

A smile crept up Jock's face. "Does it ring a bell that I bought tickets a week ago to the ballet?"

Gulp. A bell. A gong. And an alarm. After recently teasing me about being a child ballerina, Jock had offered two front-row seats to the ballet. I didn't want to know how he'd secured them on such late notice, but in a weak moment, I'd agreed. I mean, front-row seats to the ballet! Who'd turn down those?

"I know you dread riding my Harley, so I thought why not go in style."

"A minute ago you said you bought the Porsche because your bike needed maintenance."

He winked. "Killing two birds with one stone."

Butterflies fluttered in my belly from his sexy wink. "Are you saying I'm a bird you're trying to stone?"

"Stone isn't the word I'd use."

A nervous gasp erupted from Max. I knew what he was thinking, and he was right. I was romantically involved with Romero, the hard-muscled cop in my life, the man of my dreams. There was no reason I should be tempted to go out with anyone else. I peeked up at Jock. Even if he *was* the second-hottest man in the world.

I backed up and stood, gathering my wits. "So we're clear: this isn't a date."

Max regained his voice and stood next to me. "Sounds like a date to me."

I cut him a dirty look, then eyed them both. "A promise is a promise. That's all."

"Call it what you want." Jock gave a confident nod. "This ballet is so popular, they've added an extra performance. I'll be at your place by eight tonight." His hot stare traveled down the front of my dress. "I like the mod look, but you might want to get rid of the coffee stains."

With that, he headed to the gorgeous client waiting in his chair. Thank goodness. Every time I thought about going to the ballet with Jock in his sleek car, my heart palpitated harder.

The morning slid by, a steady stream of seductresses filling Jock's chair, a steady stream of traumatized clients leaving Phyllis's. Max kept his eye on his colleague click-clacking around in her wooden flip-flops. Likely taking mental notes for The Idiot Files.

I waxed Mrs. Benedetti's legs and confirmed her daughter's appointment for tomorrow. Mrs. Benedetti left the shop on top of the world, confident Carla would be a changed woman after Jock worked his magic on her.

I wished I felt as confident about my near future as Mrs. Benedetti felt about Carla's. But the end of the day was closing in, and what I felt was indecisive. My legs were still weak after last night's exploits with Romero, and here I was stepping out again…with Jock. Not that I was seeking trouble, but Romero wasn't going to be thrilled with this idea.

The minute Jock roared away for the day in his Porsche, Max pushed me into my office, all ruffled. "What are you telling Mr. Long Arm of the Law when he finds out you're cheating on him with Mr. Argentina?"

Trust Max to make the most of my sticky situation. I elbowed past him with a handful of combs I was taking into the dispensary to wash, my heart palpitations returning. "I'm not cheating on Romero. He knows my relationship with Jock is strictly platonic. I'll be home before midnight."

Max waited at the dispensary doorway and tapped his toes, arms crossed defiantly. "Cinderella thought the same thing. And look what happened to *her*. In rags before she made it through the door, and *without* her sparkly carriage."

Why me? I disinfected the combs and set them on a towel to dry overnight. "Don't you have anything better to do than slow me down? I plan on telling Romero about my night out with Jock. Okay?"

"When?" Max was in my face, eyes narrowed with suspicion. You'd have thought I was cheating on *him*.

"I'll tell him after my outing. Probably tomorrow." Or next year.

I dampened a rag and sponge-cleaned the coffee stains off my boots, not sure why I was stalling. "It's not as though he'll miss me. He's working tonight."

"While the cat's away, Cinderella and the mice will play."

Oh Lord. I smacked the rag on the counter. "You've seen Jock. Is there any part on that man that resembles a mouse?"

He narrowed his eyes more, not impressed with my retort. I couldn't blame him. Panic was building inside me at an alarming rate. What was I getting myself into?

"You heard what Jock said," I squeaked as if *I* were turning into a mouse. "He'll be at my place by eight. That's an hour from now."

I returned the rag under the sink, tripped out of the dispensary, and rushed to lock the front door, acutely aware that Lady Geisha was also gone. "Where's your subject? You can't do much documenting if she isn't around."

"Don't change the topic." Max was on my heels as I turned the deadbolt. "Phyllis left along with Jock. I'm meeting her at the Geisha Gap in an hour."

I was afraid to ask. "Geisha Gap?"

"The *okiya* or geisha house." He gave an impish grin. "Remember when I said she was taking lessons in the Japanese art of entertaining? She's training to sing, dance, play an instrument, and become the perfect hostess."

"What are *you* doing while she's learning all this?"

He shrugged. "Taking notes. Clicking pictures. Whatever feels most amusing."

"And they're allowing you to be present during her training." It was a statement filled with doubt.

He gave a head tilt. "The Okiya Corral is a Japanese restaurant in a seedy area in Cambridge. The Geisha Gap is in the back of the restaurant. There's a sitting area for family to wait." He chuckled. "So you're now looking at Phyllis's long-lost cousin."

I gulped. Hard as I tried, I couldn't find the humor in his words. My relationship with Phyllis was the very secret I'd kept from him all this time. Sustaining a neutral expression, I grabbed my bag, flicked off the lights, and sprinted down the hall to the rear door. "Have fun."

"Don't *you* have too much fun." He snapped the lock in place after we'd exited the building, then pointed his finger in my face. "*You* may have forgotten you've got a hot stallion at your disposal. But *I* haven't."

I slanted into my Bug and gave him a shaky thumbs-up. He had no need to worry. Nothing would ever make me forget I had Romero.

Chapter 2

I live in a Cape Cod bungalow in a neighborhood dominated by Italian-Americans. Hard-working, honest, friendly people, except for the odd crank—namely Mrs. Lombardi whom you'd expect more from since her son was a priest. Clearly, the benevolent gene skipped a generation.

I passed Ray Donoochi's and could smell Nina's fresh-out-of-the-oven bread wafting into the street. Ray worked for the Boston PD and was a good cop regardless of his ample size. That alone would scare the pants off me if I were a crook and saw him coming.

I parked in my driveway and was heading up the porch when Leo Donoochi, their oldest teen, jogged toward me from across the street. "Mom said to give you this bread and veal parmigiana." He handed me a container and a loaf partially wrapped in a paper towel, threadlike steam swirling around it into the air.

I inhaled the yeasty smell. "Mmm. Thanks, Leo." I was often the recipient of Nina's home cooking because I was "a bella donna" living on my own with, admittedly, not much in my fridge. "Your mom," I said with affection, "she didn't have to do this."

Leo was as muscled, handsome, and tough as his younger brother, Jake. They roughhoused with each other and acted macho in public, but their behavior always softened around me. "Aww, she likes doing it."

With Leo's dark looks and cool swagger, he could likely sweet-talk the girls his age into anything. Visions of another sweet-talking, cool-swaggering Italian named Romero came to mind. Probably what he'd been like as a teen.

"Still, tell her to come in for a free manicure sometime, okay?"

Leo gave me a quick smile and nod, then jogged back home, looking over his shoulder once. *"Buon appetito."*

I let myself into the house, dropped my bag by the door, and carted the food onto the kitchen counter. I tore off a piece of loaf and popped it into my mouth. *Mmm.* Sweet, warm, and buttery. I wrapped the rest up, tucked it in the corner of the counter for later, and placed the veal in the fridge. Then I peeled out of my go-go boots and set them by the front door next to my bag.

"Howdy, Yitts." I bent over the black beanbag chair in the living room and kissed the top of my black cat's head. Then I hurried into the bathroom to brush my teeth. "I'll feed you in a minute," I promised.

Yitts hopped onto the pine floor and immediately took her paw and washed the mix of lipstick and butter off the top of her head. Meanwhile, *a promise is a promise*, the five words I'd uttered from the top of my high horse to Jock and Max earlier came to mind. Right.

I coughed and choked on the minty toothpaste at the consequences of those words.

Not bothered that I was gagging or in another predicament, Yitts sauntered over to Ellie, our latest addition to the free-spirited décor, and plunked herself at the wooden elephant's feet.

I cleared my throat. "Thanks for the concern."

I topped her food and tossed her a sprig of catnip that I'd snipped yesterday from Mrs. Calvino's garden. Tobacco was Mrs. Calvino's plant of choice, but she knew Yitts loved catnip and had suggested I help myself to the herb she grew in her flowerbed between our houses. No wonder Yitts liked Mrs. Calvino.

Not bothering with her food, Yitts dove for the sprig and rolled on the ground, rubbing her head and face in the stimulant.

Yowza! Here I was, giving Yitts this feel-good plant when it struck me that Jock was *my* stimulant.

"You're welcome," I said to Yitts, refusing to put any stock into that thought. Maybe my relationship with Jock *was* a tad intoxicating, but that was as far as it went.

I wiggled out of my spotted dress, sprayed it with stain remover, lobbed it over the shower rod, then touched up my makeup. After enhancing my eyes and frosting my lips, I slipped into a sleek pair of black palazzo pants, perfect for the ballet, and a cropped silver ribbed turtleneck that I was saving for a special occasion.

I switched earrings for a sparkly square-hooped platinum pair, then brushed my hair. My heightened mane plus my see-through square heels that I dug out of my closet brought me up to a respectable 5'9", five inches taller than my natural size and more compatible next to Jock.

Who was I kidding? *Jocko* would still be another seven or so inches taller than me. To be well matched to Hercules, I'd need to be built like a Greek Amazon.

I took a final look in the mirror. *Not bad.* The only thing missing from the elegant look was an evening bag. I couldn't go to the ballet with my usual beauty sack slung over my shoulder. How would that look? I wasn't a jet-setting millionaire, but I did have *some* class. Why would I even need my tools? I was going out with the son of Zeus. If he couldn't protect me, nobody could.

I rifled through my box of purses and found my black satin clutch with rhinestones on the snap. Perfect for my phone, keys, lipstick, a few dollars, and tissue—since I wouldn't escape a performance at the ballet without shedding a few tears.

Giving my palazzo pants credit for the extra flourish in my step, I sashayed into the living room with the clutch and knelt in front of my beauty bag. I was rummaging for the things I needed when a loud bike engine rumbled to a stop outside. I twisted toward the window, my ears perked. Probably one of Mrs. Calvino's kids visiting. Didn't one of them have a motorcycle? There was silence, then the sound of footsteps mounting the porch steps, followed by a knock on the door.

I stiffened. Jock had claimed his bike was having maintenance. Hence the Porsche. In which he was taking me to the ballet. Or was that a ruse to get me to agree to the evening? A sneaky move to get me to hold on tight to him? I smacked my evening bag on the floor, lips pressed together, none too thrilled with this turn of events.

I flung open the door, ready to give him a piece of my mind, but something was off about my helmeted visitor. While the tall, muscular frame indicated the individual before me worked out at the gym, a place Jock regularly visited, this person clothed in black leather was not Jock. The tinted face shield didn't make it any easier to distinguish my caller. He snapped off the chinstrap, tugged off the helmet, and shook his wavy dark hair onto his collar.

Romero!

I blinked in shock. "Um. Hello?"

His eyes dilated as they skimmed over my outfit, his full lips twitching into a wicked grin, a look I was getting quite used to. He unzipped his leather jacket, tossed his helmet onto the beanbag chair, and, without as much as a hello back, scooped me into his arms.

Romero was a tough, streetwise detective with skills that went beyond serving and protecting. With or without the badge, he wasn't someone you'd want to go up against. His fingers touched my bare midriff and worked the fabric of my top until he was inside, inching his hands higher, his eyes fixed on my face.

I groaned, wanting more, and he sensed it. He nudged my legs apart with his thigh, pulled me in tighter, and kissed me with urgency. His deft hands roved from my breasts to my sleek-covered butt, my outfit clearly turning him on. I arched into him, my body going up in flames despite the cold buckles and zipper on his jacket pressing into my bare waist.

He pulled us apart and licked his lips, assessing my manhandled outfit more thoroughly. "On your way out?"

His blue eyes scorched through me with longing while he waited for an answer, but I was still reeling from the kiss. When Romero fixed his lips to mine, he teased and conquered. After our recent stretch of lovemaking, I only needed to imagine his mouth on my flesh, and I was a weak mess.

Taking in a lungful of air, I balanced myself and straightened my clothes. "Actually, I *am* going out." I thought of Max's words. The sooner I shared my plans with Romero the better.

He crossed his arms in front and jutted out his unshaved jaw, his swollen lips pursed while he contemplated my response. "Looks like you're going to the opera."

I did a small nod. "Ballet, to be exact."

One eyebrow hiked up. "Let me take a stab at this. You won free tickets, and since you knew I was working tonight, you opted to take your partner in crime, Twix."

Boy, he was good. Twix Bonelli had been my best friend since our childhood days in ballet. Romero had had dealings with Twix, only because yours truly had asked her to spy on him when it seemed he was romantically involved with a former police partner. I winced inside, berating myself again for that overactive thinking. "You're half right."

He tilted his head down at me, his stance widening as if his suspicion meter was on the rise. "Which half?"

I smiled sweetly. "The half about the free tickets…which amazingly is more like *one* free ticket."

He nodded and rolled his tongue over his dazzling white teeth, processing this. "Amazing. And I presume there's a second ticket out there."

Before he had a chance to grill me further, I wrapped my arms around his neck and went in for another kiss, using a technique on his bottom lip that I knew drove him crazy with desire. Didn't hurt to think this would soften the blow when he found out the truth.

He took the bait, jerked me into his hard form, and kissed me with a yearning so deep it took my breath away. He broke loose and looked me in the eye. "So who's taking you?"

Smart aleck.

"Jock." I backed up a foot, giving him space to absorb this. Since Romero and I had become intimate, I'd done my best to push Jock away. But it wasn't easy working daily alongside Superman or being involved with two heroes with extremely high testosterone levels. "There's nothing to worry about. I'll be home before midnight."

A charged silence hung in the air because we both knew bad stuff didn't only happen after midnight.

He studied me, deliberating on this for a long second, the cop in him looking for signs of deceit, the man in him searching for signs of betrayal. "A male ridden with insecurities would ask you not to go."

I chose the smart path, keeping my mouth shut. Romero was secure in who he was, but he also was *not* the type of man who'd be willing to share his girlfriend. Added to that, he'd had his doubts in the past about whether Jock's intentions toward me were strictly platonic.

Considering where Romero and I were in our relationship, he had the advantage over Jock. Sounded ridiculous, yet life experience had revealed that most males tended to keep score on this.

I pretended I hadn't noticed him deliberating and waited with an innocent smile in place.

He nodded. "Okay. Make sure he brings you right to your door after the ballet."

"I will." I glanced down his leather-clad body and back up into his eyes. "Why are you here?"

He reached inside his jacket, his wicked grin returning. "You forgot this last night." He held out my black lacy thong and rubbed this thumb along the delicate fabric as if recalling how he'd removed it.

An instant flash of heat soared through me, and my heartbeat picked up like a horse jumping hurdles. Damn

Max and his *stallion* comment earlier. Truth was, I was surprised I hadn't forgotten my bra, dress, and heels after the night of passion we'd had.

I got myself under control. Jock would be here any minute. Not that I cared if he saw Romero and me together, but I didn't need him teasing me about my underwear. Certain my face was red, I reached for the thong and thanked Romero.

He gave me another quick kiss, told me to enjoy the ballet, and turned to leave.

"Wait!" I held up my thong like a flag. "What's with the bike?"

"It's this case I'm on." And with that, he was gone.

Chapter 3

Jock pulled up in his Porsche mere seconds after the dust settled from Romero's roaring exit. He angled out of the car dressed in a lilac tailored shirt, a pair of black dress pants that clung in all the right places, and shoes that were likely more expensive than my entire wardrobe.

He strode up the front steps of the porch, not bothering with a second glance back at his new wheels. Something inside me warmed at that. I'd dated guys who'd requested I take off my shoes before stepping into their cars.

I dashed from the living room window to the front door and let Jock in after the third rap. "*Bonsoir.*" Didn't want to appear too anxious about our evening out, even though I was nearly bouncing on my tiptoes in anticipation of the ballet.

"*Buenas noches.*" He ducked, stepping over the threshold.

I pushed down a swallow at his clever response, always in tune to mine. My gaze traveled from his chestnut hair, pulled back in a short ponytail, to his caramel-brown eyes, muscled neck, and tanned chest that glistened where his shirt was unbuttoned. He looked and smelled delectable as ever, though the scent of leather was more subtle. New mode of transportation, new aroma was my guess.

I knew by the deep stare and penetrating silence that he was also appraising me. He stalked a foot closer, placed his hands where my palazzo pants edged my midriff, and waited until I peered up into his eyes. "Nice." He paused, his expression curious. "But isn't the thong meant to go on *before* the pants?"

I looked at my hand still clutching the lacy thong. *Doh!* I stepped out of his embrace and whipped my hand behind my back. "Er, I was folding laundry before you showed up."

He nodded appreciatively, his gaze traveling over my shoulder. "Your laundry basket seems to have disappeared."

I hastily pitched the thong at the coffee table. Naturally, because I was in Jock's glorious presence, it landed on my Winnie the Pooh phone by mistake. Sighing inside, I rammed my hands on my hips. "Are we going to talk laundry all night or go to the ballet?"

He grinned, his gaze rolling from Winnie's lace-covered head to me. "I'm starting to think talking laundry might be more fun."

No matter what the guy said, it always sounded provocative. Thankfully, he switched gears and backed toward the door, checking his phone, which I thought was odd. Jock was not tied to techie devices, something we had in common. He went for the doorknob, his neck muscles tight. "Got to run if we're going to make the opening act."

I reached for my evening bag that I'd left on the floor next to my beauty bag. "I have to switch—"

"No time." He peeked at his sleek watch draped on his wrist. "We have to go."

I gave him a strange look but didn't question his manner. Still, I wasn't going to the ballet with a mammoth sack over my back. "I've got to use the bathroom before we leave." I crossed my legs and bent at the knees for emphasis. "I'll meet you at the car."

Too much of a gentleman to argue, he bowed his head and took the porch steps two at a time. I slammed the door behind him, threw everything I needed from my beauty bag into my clutch, and locked up after me.

I descended the steps, proper purse in hand, a smile planted on my face. "Ready."

The ride into Boston in Jock's Porsche was fast, smooth, and exhilarating. By the time we arrived on Washington Street and cruised past the Opera House and its awning lit with a thousand bulbs, I was bubbling with excitement. Jock found a parking spot nearby—natch—and we wasted no time hoofing it inside the grand theater.

Eagerness raced through me as we approached the majestic lobby stairs that would take us to our seats. The enthusiastic crowd bumped me this way and that, but Jock took my hand in his warm, secure grip, making me feel protected. He led me through the hall, which allowed me to gaze distractedly at the gold ceiling, tall pillars, and regal chandeliers.

When his cell phone buzzed, he scanned the readout with a frown, then gave my hand a squeeze. "I have to take this," he said, ushering me to a spot out of the way of traffic.

I tapped my toes, patiently waiting, watching the crowd, when out of the blue, I heard a familiar shrill voice call my name.

I turned and spied Candace Needlemeyer, my adversary since beauty school, pushing toward me like she was leading a herd of elephants.

I glanced left and right, but there was no escaping the battle-ax. She halted a foot from my nose, dressed in an un-Candace-like black frock, buttoned up to her white-collared neck and with a flowing hem that hung well below her calves. No sign of cleavage or thigh anywhere. If I weren't seeing it with my own eyes, I wouldn't believe this was the same blond bombshell who owned Supremo Stylists, my biggest competition, three blocks from Beaumont's, *and* who'd once tried to steal Max and Jock from under me to work in her salon.

Not that I wanted to talk to Candace, cleavage-free or not. But for the sake of appearances, I'd make the best of it. "Evening, Candace."

"What are *you* doing here?" She gave me her typical suspicious scowl.

"Going to a Bruins game. You?" What could I say? My neck hairs spiked like a porcupine when Candace started with the accusatory tone, and my tongue seemed to take on a life of its own.

She tugged down her matronly dress at the hip, sniffing with superiority. "You're such a dunce, Valentine. Everyone knows the Bruins play at Fenway Park."

A man in a polo shirt strolled by, doing a double take at Candace's remark. He whirled his head toward me, mouth open, as if wondering whether he should clarify it was the Red Sox who played at Fenway. I gave him a *why bother?* shrug.

Candace scanned the entrance, then centered on me. "Not that this concerns you, but I'm here because Hoagy and I are broadening our tastes."

Hoagy MacEwen was Candace's latest conquest. A Scotsman with a sturdy build, a surly temper, and a thick brogue only Candace understood.

"Thought a night at the ballet would be a nice change," she spouted, nose in the air.

"From what? Visiting the backseat of his car?" Exactly where I'd once discovered them, not that I'd been hanging onto *that* memory.

"Very funny, Miss Palazzo Pants."

I grinned mischievously. "Where is Mr. MacEwen? Testing for STDs?"

"*Parking*," she sneered. "Don't worry, he'll be here. At least I *have* a date." She pointed her shortened, unpolished fingernail in my face. "Who are *you* here with? The Invisible Man?"

I barely heard her insult because my attention was glued to her unadorned nails. What was up with that? First, the modest attire. Now this? Had Candace been hit on the head? Come to think of it, even her hair looked less fluffy than normal. *Yikes!* Were those dark roots sprouting from her scalp?

I gave her a polite—albeit Cheshire cat-like—smile in answer to her question. "I'm here with Jock." I knew Mr. Argentina would forever be a sore spot with Candace since he'd declined her offer to work in her salon.

She scrunched up her lips, not one bit pleased at this news. "Jock de Marco?"

"You know of any other Jock?" That was a loaded question. Candace had been around the block with so many men, who knew how many "jocks" she'd been with?

"For your information," she said, hands on hips, "now that I'm with Hoagy, other men pale by comparison. In fact, I'm a new woman."

"New to what?"

She opened her mouth, then snapped it shut, a confused look on her face. "New to...to *this*!" She gestured to her dress and shoes that she revealed under her full skirt.

Egad. Candace was wearing round-toed, laced-up black shoes. Tantig, my great-aunt, had an identical pair. I gulped back the astonishment before the drool seeped out. "Are you trying out for a part in a play, Candace? 'Cause this Amish look is baffling. Not to mention, I'm not used to *not* seeing your chest fall out of your top." I slanted my head down at her shoes. "And I don't think I'll ever get used to the granny loafers."

"You'll have to get used to them because you're going to see less heels on me. And a lot less of the twins." She hastily shoved up her boobs, which looked painfully squashed under her dress.

Who could I thank for that?

I felt a warmth at my back and a citrus scent in the air. I knew without spinning around that Jock had returned. The syrupy look on Candace's face confirmed it.

"Candace." Jock gave her a respectful nod.

"Jock..." She licked her lips like a fox eyeing its dinner.

Jock wrapped his arm around my waist and twirled me in the opposite direction. "Sorry to interrupt," he said, "but the ballet is about to start."

With that, we strode into the theater, leaving Candace

twiddling her short-nailed thumbs while she waited for Hoagy.

The ballet, a rendition of *Sleeping Beauty*, was breathtaking. The costumes. The music. The setting. The choreography and the grace of the dancers alone had me in tears off and on during the performance. By the end of the night, I was both elated and emotionally exhausted.

Jock meanwhile had been attentive during the performance but seemed slightly on edge.

"Is everything okay?" I asked on our walk to the car.

He gave a cursory look around the street as we neared his Porsche. "Yeah. It's been a long day. I'm beat."

Jock? Beat? It wasn't the first time tonight I'd noticed his subtle unease. When he'd picked me up, I'd felt a twinge of angst in his manner, especially after he'd checked his phone. Unusual for a superhero always in control. He also hadn't made any moves on me during the ballet, tried anything funny, or made any sexual quips. As much as I appreciated that, something was wrong. I could feel it in my bones.

I thought back to the lobby. Before the performance, Jock had received a phone call. Although his mood had already been off, whomever he'd spoken to seemed to have contributed to the grim atmosphere.

There was no point in pressing him about what was up. Jock was like Romero when it came to answering my questions. Nobody ever wanted me to get hurt, involved, or upset. Darn chivalrous men. In truth, I was already involved, getting more upset by the minute, and *less* likely to get hurt if Jock went ahead and shared what was worrying him.

I'd have to play it safe. Follow his lead. I'd find out what was up sooner or later.

He opened the car door for me. "I need to stop by my place before I take you home. That okay?"

"Sure…" I hesitated, warning bells clanging in my ears. I'd never seen where Jock lived. I had his Cambridge address on file at work and always fought the impulse to look up his place whenever I went into Boston. Given our flirting history, was he planning on making a move in the privacy of his home?

"Thanks again for the ballet," I said in a calm voice that belied the nervousness inside.

He gave me a curt nod, waited until I lowered myself into the Porsche, then gently closed the door.

We drove in silence, the tension mounting, my emotions all over the place. I didn't have a clue what was going on. The ballet had been phenomenal, the evening magical, even with my nervousness about what he might have in store for me. But Jock's mind was somewhere else, somewhere dark, and this fueled my growing concern.

Ten minutes later, we veered off a quiet road into an abandoned factory lot. A single tall streetlight funneled a wide beam over the property. There were no trees. No grass or landscaping. No signs of other life. Merely a huge empty lot with an old brick multi-level factory standing before us, a large rolling garage door in front to the right of dozens of windows dimly glowing from inside.

I gazed from the vintage sign near the top of the warehouse wall that read *Pulp & Paper Co.*, then back to Jock. "Are we going to your place or buying stationery?" No harm in trying to lighten the mood even if it felt like I was traveling down a deep pit.

Jock gave a soft grunt. No comment. No wink. He cranked the wheel to the left, kicking up dust as he skidded into a semicircle in the lot. Then he backed into the shadow on the left side of the building and shut off the ignition.

I peered beyond his troubled face to the warehouse through the driver's side window. Figured Jock would live somewhere out of the ordinary.

He rubbed the side of his jaw, giving the silent lot a subtle once-over, hesitant about something. This didn't get by me. After another quick look around, he invited me in.

What was up with this man? His mysterious past was one thing, but the hollow in my gut and pulsating in my ears was a sign that something was about to happen. Generally, when I got this feeling, I was met with disaster, usually in the form of a dead body. I'd learned enough from those experiences to know that by now I should be running for the hills or, at least, asking Jock to change his plans and take me straight home. So why was I glued to the spot?

Jock had said he needed to drop by his place. His current disposition told me he wouldn't have proposed that if it weren't important. Plus, didn't I always feel safe when I was with him? He'd never let any harm come to me. I glanced down at my clutch. I'd even left my arsenal at home. I gulped back my trepidation and followed him to the garage door.

He lifted his keychain and swiped a fob that resembled a tiny credit card through a barely seen slit in the brick wall. Immediately, the garage door rolled up, the mechanism clunking laboriously as if it hadn't been oiled since the Industrial Revolution.

I blinked in awe. "What's in there? Your chariot?"

No answer.

Shrugging off the sudden vision I had of him in a toga and gladiator shoes, I trailed him into the left side of the garage, jumping at the clanking garage door unrolling back to the ground. We climbed five crumbling concrete steps straight ahead to a four-by-four landing and a door on the left-hand wall. Using the fob again, he opened the door, stepped inside, and turned up the lights.

I stood at the entry, eyes and mouth wide open, gawking from the ancient garage steps behind me to a beautiful, sprawling one-room condo filled with rustic character and modern design. More astonishing were how the rows of windows that I'd seen from outside reflected the warm lights on the inside.

At first glance of Jock's home, I felt like curling up on a comfy sofa. At the same time, I had an urge to run, arms wide, as if I were Maria, singing on a hilltop in *The Sound of Music*.

I stepped forward, my heart beating in awe at the wooden beams arching across the high ceiling, the state-of-the-art white kitchen under the windows, and the dining and spacious living areas, both decked in warm wooden colors. Most of all, the place had a private quality.

On the opposite wall, a winding staircase with black railings, most likely the restored original, led to what appeared to be a gigantic loft. Hmm. What was upstairs? Jock's harem den? A king-sized bed? Ha. More like continental-sized.

Jock tossed his keys beside loose change in a marble bowl sitting on a decorative ladder. "I'll only be a minute. Make yourself comfortable."

He strode purposefully to his desk built into an alcove under the second-floor landing and opened his laptop. I didn't want to pry, so with my evening bag in hand, I clacked my clunky heels on the hardwood floor, getting a feel for his place.

A few striking plants added warmth to the condo, setting off the bare antique-style light bulbs strategically draped from the ceiling, one hanging especially low from a black rope over his dining room table. While a tinge of pulp and paper seeped from the pores of the old factory, the place smelled clean with a hint of Jock's exotic cologne and a trace of ginger and coconut. Spices lingering from tonight's dinner?

An instant picture of Romero's place that hummed of barbequed steak and fried onions flashed to mind, and I warmed at the differences between the two men.

Both had functional kitchens, but where Jock's was stylish, Romero's was home to mismatched salt and pepper shakers, a toaster, coffeemaker, take-out menus, keys, loose change, and, when he wasn't wearing it, his platinum Iron Man watch. What's more, when Romero removed his shoulder holster, it hung over a kitchen chair.

Jock had a marble bowl for his keys and loose change, and if he owned a gun it was hidden. I didn't see much evidence of his past life in the navy except for an exquisite seven-inch-tall glass ship, sitting on a sideboard cupboard in the corner against the brick wall. Next to it, a bit smaller, was a bronze rope-and-anchor sculpture.

I squinted at the carving. Where had I seen that image before? On a painting? Last fall's cruise? Social media?

Tucked behind the ship was a white-gold metal frame with a photo of four men in white uniforms. I assumed Jock was one of the men in the photo, but I wasn't close enough to make out details.

I swung my gaze from the photo to Jock on the other side of the room, clicking away on his laptop. For someone not tied to his techie devices, he seemed absorbed in what he was doing.

I edged closer to the alcove where he was deep in thought and spotted a diamond-shaped symbol flash on the screen. At once, Jock's wide shoulders tensed. He leaned in and typed something short on his phone, then slammed the laptop lid down.

"Come on." He tore out of his chair, stuffing his phone in his trousers pocket. "We've got to go." He grabbed my hand with such force I almost tripped out of my heels.

"Wait a minute." I pulled back from his grasp. "What's going on? Why are you—"

A violent bang outside on the garage door brought us both up straight. Jock whirled around and pointed to a door near the winding stairs. "Go lock yourself in the bathroom and *stay* there. If I'm not back in half an hour, call a cab and take it home. Go. *Now.*" His normally sexy timbre had disappeared, his firm and urgent manner warning me not to argue.

The only other man who could scare me like this by his authoritative and intimidating tone was Romero. The times were few yet well remembered. I peered up into Jock's hooded eyes and saw something I'd never seen before. Fear? Alarm? Uncertainty?

I choked down a hard lump, every muscle in my body quaking. I didn't know what was happening, but I thought it wise not to make him repeat himself.

I ran into the bathroom and did as he instructed, my

insides quivering in the frightful silence, terrified the outcome of the next few minutes wouldn't be good.

Ear pressed to the door, I heard Jock's footsteps fade toward the entrance, followed by muffled sounds of him pounding down the cement stairs. I didn't hear the garage door crank up, but after another moment, I heard thudding sounds, then voices. One belonged to Jock, the other voice, a man's. Deep. Angry. Threatening.

Panic sped through my veins, my throat dry. What if someone was attacking Jock on his doorstep? I'd built Jock up as a man with superhuman powers, a mythical god, one who was virtually untouchable. While some of that may have been true, it wasn't beyond the realm of possibility that someone with extreme force and size or someone with a weapon could overtake him. No matter what I thought of Jock, he was mortal, after all.

My heart hammered in my chest, my surroundings a blur around me. I argued with myself to stay put, to honor Jock's request. But how could I stay locked in this bathroom when he might need me?

I was petite by most standards, and Jock was built like Thor. Nevertheless, if the man was in trouble, there had to be something I could do.

I fingered the rhinestones on my clutch. *Damn!* Left my beauty bag at home because I had to look stylish. *Bloody wonderful.* That wouldn't prevent me from helping a man in need.

I took a steadying breath and told myself I had what it took to rescue Jock. I didn't know what *that* was, but I wasn't staying in here a minute longer. I unlocked the door, tightened my grip on my handbag, and tiptoed out of the bathroom. I was met with darkness, except for a moonbeam filtering through the windows. Did Jock switch off the lights? If so, why? To protect me? So the angry visitor would think Jock was alone?

I gave my eyes a second to adjust, then, back pressed to the wall, I sidestepped to the front until I reached the door.

Stilling my heart, I counted to three, then opened it and peeked down the stairs.

The steps weren't well lit, not that it mattered. The action was outside beyond the huge garage door, the sounds definitely of two men fighting. I hugged the wall for support, my pulse running wild with each descending step. At the bottom, I ducked to the corner and plotted frantically how best to help Jock. If I yelled out, that might distract the assailant, but it also might put Jock in more danger. I didn't want to risk that.

First question was how did I get out of here. The garage door was still closed, so where did Jock exit from? A dark shadow on the opposite wall looked like it might be a door. I raced toward it, shuddering at the punching and grunting noises on the other side of the rolling garage door.

There was a swift blow to the ancient door, and I spun around, biting back a scream. I expected it to cave in, but it remained intact except for a crack at eye level that allowed a thin stream of moonlight in. Momentarily forgetting about the side exit, I scurried over and leaned on my tiptoes, nose to the crack in the horizontal panels, hoping to identify the aggressive visitor.

Jock hadn't become a master-at-arms without seeing his share of violence, but it had never occurred to me that he had enemies. Everyone loved the guy. Even his rivals seemed to admire him, which added to the questions about the scene before me.

The attacker raised a fist to punch Jock in the face, but Jock deflected the guy's arm in one fluid motion and slammed him headfirst into the garage door. *Thunk.*

I sprang back in shock, releasing my bag, shoving my knuckle in my mouth to keep from shrieking. Horrifying me more, the man's face looked like a molten replica of Freddy Krueger's from the old horror flick *A Nightmare on Elm Street.*

Easy, Valentine. It's a man wearing a mask. That's all.

Right. Tell that to someone who wasn't prone to squealing when scared.

The fighting continued, and I paced the garage, flapping my hands in a panic, helpless to do anything useful. I berated myself again for leaving my beauty bag at home. I was such a dope! I kicked the stupid clutch away. Nothing in it but soggy tissues and lipstick.

Suddenly, there was a muted *crack* and a shuffling sound. I leaped back, eyes wide. Was that a gunshot? A car backfiring? Was I hearing things? *Oh Lord, please let Jock be okay.*

My pulse boomed in my ears so loudly I couldn't think straight. I peeked through the slats again but saw nothing in the dim moonlight. No Jock. No assailant. I couldn't even see Jock's car parked at the side. And where was the other guy's vehicle?

An eerie silence loomed. The seconds crept by, causing the hairs on my neck to bristle. Taking shallow breaths, I pressed my forehead closer, angling my head left and right, hoping to spy something through the crack. Anything.

Nothing.

I turned my back, and abruptly a fist wrapped in a leather jacket punched through the crack in the door. Splinters of metal and wood flew everywhere. I caught a blur of motion, then was jerked back against the door, a large hairy arm wrapped around my neck.

I gagged and writhed, attempting to get loose. It was futile. The aggressor tightened his chokehold, his jacket slipping from sight. I thought I noticed a marking on his skin, but between the bad lighting, the hair on his arm, and him wrenching it tighter around my neck, I was sure I was seeing things.

Rattled with fear, I yanked my head to the side, my heavy earring smacking my cheek. The sting brought back this morning's episode with Austin, when by mistake I'd ripped out my hoop. Suddenly, an idea struck.

I tugged the earring from my ear and raked the pointy, solid stem up and down my attacker's arm. Feeling him loosen his hold, I stabbed the thick post into his inner wrist.

He howled and jerked his arm back out through the hole he'd made, my earring skewered to him.

Angry sirens wailed in the distance. Closer, there was a single *clink*, which I figured was my earring landing on the pavement. Then there was the blessed sound of tires burning rubber.

I collapsed on the cement floor, hyperventilating, holding back the tears. What had just happened? Where was Jock? My hands were shaking, and I couldn't seem to get control over my legs.

The sirens neared, closer and closer, then faded into the background. All went quiet, the frightening stillness outside unnerving.

With trembling fingers, I pushed off from the ground and lurched for the side door. I had to go out there and find Jock. What if he was bleeding to death? *Shoot*. Door was locked. Where was the latch on this thing? Couldn't the guy own normal garage doors like everyone else?

The hole in the rolling door was too high to see out of properly or get a glimpse at the ground. I rushed over to it anyway. I pounded the door, tears spilling down my face, my hoarse voice barely recognizable.

"*Jock*. Are you there?" It was a stupid question. The dead didn't speak. And if Jock were there and alive, he'd have made his presence known by now.

I swiped away the tears and got a grip, searching my brain for how Jock had entered the garage when we first arrived. Right! The fob on his keys. I staggered back upstairs, flung on the lights, and darted for the keys in the marble bowl. There had to be an easier way to get out of his place, but until I had it figured out, I'd have these.

I forced back an anxious breath, flew down the stairs again, and tapped the wall by the rolling door until I felt a metal plate with a round indent. I couldn't find a slit to insert the fob like the one on the outside wall, but with all my waving with the fancy card, I must've triggered a sensor. Like magic, the door rolled open, grinding to a halt where the busted portion curved at the ceiling.

I stared up at the stuck door and gave the bottom an upward shove with my hands. It made a whirring sound, then quit. I put muscle behind it and used my shoulder for leverage. More grinding. Fabulous. Abandoning this tactic, I concentrated on getting to Jock.

My mouth felt dry, my throat choked with emotion at what I might find. Grappling for a calm breath, I crawled under the jammed door. Once outside, I uncurled myself, expecting to see Jock lying in a puddle of blood. What I saw was nothing.

No puddle.

No blood.

No Jock.

Chapter 4

I snatched my evening bag off the ground and tripped back into Jock's condo. I paced nervous circles around the kitchen, my head swimming. I had to call for help.

If it had been the middle of the day, I would've phoned my older sister, Detective Holly Dennison, who works in vice. I glanced at the enormous, softly lit clock Jock had hanging on the brick wall. Going on one a.m. I bit my lip. Did I bother Holly in the middle of the night? Chances were she'd be working. If she wasn't, she'd be in bed sleeping, resting for an early-morning start to the next day, which was today. *Grr.*

Besides, I couldn't depend on Holly not blabbing to my mother that Jock was missing and possibly in mortal danger. I loved my family, but I didn't want to encourage a full-blown interrogation on what happened tonight or why I was even out with Jock when I was dating the handsome detective.

As far as I could see, there was no avoiding Romero. He wouldn't be happy that I called at this hour, but that was the least of my worries. I had to inform the police of Jock's disappearance.

Sliding his keys onto the kitchen counter, I dug out my phone, put my thoughts in order, and said a quiet prayer that, as a cop, Romero would be understanding. He answered on the first ring, and my heart swelled at the quiet assurance in his voice. I didn't get too excited. Once he heard my story, his peaceful night would be blown away.

I took a bold breath and proceeded carefully. "Remember when I told you I was going to the ballet with Jock?"

The silence on the other end was deafening.

"Hello?" I shook the phone, worried we'd been cut off. "I'm here...waiting."

"For what?"

"Whatever bad news you're delivering."

I flattened my lips. Why didn't I dial Holly? Or 911? I wouldn't have to put up with this nonsense. "Why do you always assume the worst?"

"Because I know you. Because I'm a cop. And because of a minor thing called deductive reasoning. On top of which, if it were good news, you wouldn't be calling me at this hour."

He paused, and I could hear the bad boy in his voice. "Unless you were hungry for me, but after the week we've had, and the fact that I'm more worn out than I've ever been in my entire life, I don't assume that'd be the reason for the call. Which leaves me to believe you're either *in* trouble, running from trouble, or trying to avoid trouble. How am I doing?"

I swallowed my pride in the face of his sarcasm and did my best to keep it together. "It's about my night out at the ballet."

"I'm listening."

Easing into it was the best way. "Remember when I said I'd be home before midnight?"

"Yes."

"And remember when I said you had nothing to worry about?"

"Yes." There was a touch of growing concern coming through the phone line.

"And remember—"

"Valentine! Remembering won't help anything when you tell me where you are. Now who's dead? And how did you find the victim?"

I gave an indignant huff. "See? Always assuming the worst. For your information, nobody's dead…I don't think." My anxiety level was climbing, and my insides ached. I was worried sick about Jock and his whereabouts, and that meant I had to be honest with Romero. "I'm at Jock's. In Cambridge."

"An-n-nd?"

"And he's gone."

"Gone, as in he stepped out for a minute, or 'Don't Cry for me Argentina' gone?"

I felt tears pooling in my eyes again. "I don't know. The first maybe, or the second."

"Tell me from the beginning what happened."

I relayed it all to him over the phone, except the part about the guy attacking me. One thing at a time, right? I'd explain that part in person, later. Or, hopefully, not at all.

"At first, when we heard the bang outside, I thought Jock was merely reacting to the noise of someone he thought might be trying to break in. But then he ordered me into the bathroom. Warned me to lock the door and stay there. Then he went outside, and I heard arguing and fighting."

Romero exhaled long and slow. "I'm going to be sorry I asked this, but you didn't stay put, did you?"

"What do you think?"

"I think this is where things go south. What happened when you left the bathroom?"

"I crept down the steps to the big garage door," I explained. "Jock lives in a renovated factory with this cryptic rolling door. It's like the Batcave above ground."

"Of course it is."

"The door had a crack in it, allowing me to peek outside."

"Did you see the guy he was fighting with?"

I shuddered at the memory of his gruesome face. "Yes."

"And what Disney villain did he look like? Captain Hook or the Joker?"

"I don't know! I think he was wearing a mask. And for

your information, the Joker isn't a Disney character. Yet, anyway."

He blew out a sigh. "Pardon me. In my spare time, when I'm not catching bad guys, I'll brush up on Disney's acquisitions. You sure he was wearing a mask?"

"I'm not sure of anything. Least of all what happened to Jock." I forced back the fear building at a terrifying rate. "Something awful's happened. I can feel it. He even said he might not be back. I think he's in danger."

He lost the cynicism. "Look, the guy's an enigma, a lone wolf. He probably got tired of the everyday life as a hairstylist and rejoined the navy. Or went back to making movies. Wasn't he some stunt double?"

"Yes." I shook my head left and right, more to myself than anything. "That's not what happened here."

"Why not? Could be you misinterpreted the voices. Maybe an old navy buddy dropped by, and they were horsing around. Or another stunt double stopped over to practice a role."

"It seemed like he knew the guy. But in either case, why wouldn't Jock tell me he was leaving?"

"I presume he didn't have time. The navy waits for no man. And if it was for a movie part, Hollywood can be fickle. If he didn't jump at the role, they could've given it to the next guy wanting work."

Romero was a pro at playing devil's advocate, but he hadn't been here, hadn't experienced what I had. Even the circus would give someone time to pack a bag. More, there was nothing playful or friendly between Jock's interaction with the intruder.

"Apart from gleaning a bit about Jock's past," he went on, "you don't know much about the guy. His friends. Family."

He had a semi-valid point. Jock had never gone into great detail about his past. I'd learned his father was an American ship builder who'd traveled to Argentina and fallen in love with Jock's mother. After they married, his father had traveled back and forth to the States while his mother ran a salon in her homeland. Jock also had a kid sister. That was all I knew in the family department.

As for friends, in the time since Jock had worked in the salon, I'd met the odd pal by chance. Captain Madera from our cruise, or Carlo as Jock had called him, had been stationed at the same naval base. There was also Darryl, the warden at Rivers View Correctional Center, who had stunt-doubled with Jock, and whom I'd met on a previous case. I attempted to bring to mind other acquaintances, like the string of gorgeous female models who frequented the salon, asking myself if I was overreacting, but Romero interrupted my thoughts.

"Jock's a wild card. He could have a deep, dark past. Maybe something bad caught up to him."

As much as I hated to admit it, I'd been thinking the same thing. I wasn't voicing this at the present. Romero was a detective, and a darn good one. But he was also involved with a woman who worked with a gorgeous idol with very large muscles, sexy eyes, and an alluring manner. Jock could pose a romantic threat to any male, let alone one with a macho image and an Italian Stallion reputation.

Deep down, I knew nothing would please Romero more than to know Jock had disappeared from my life. I, on the other hand, needed to know my star employee was all right.

"I'm not sure what to think, but I'm worried." I struggled to keep the hysteria out of my voice. "Jock wouldn't have left unless something terrible took place."

I thought for a second, fiddling with his keys. "He even turned off the lights before he stepped out and made sure I was safely locked inside, with his visitor having no way to get to me. Why would he have done that if he weren't trying to protect me from something in case things went bad?"

Before Romero could answer, I went on. "From the moment he told me to lock myself in the bathroom, he *knew* what he was about to face wasn't going to be friendly."

What I omitted was that the assailant had attacked me last, and that I knew in my heart Jock wouldn't let that happen, then just take off.

He seemed to consider things. "Okay. Sit tight. This is a little out of my jurisdiction, but I'll make a few calls. In the meantime, give me his address. I presume you need a ride home."

His address? *Shoot.* I hadn't watched street signs on our way to Cambridge. Added to that, I had Jock's address on file at the shop, not in my phone.

I was working on a solution for my oversight when Romero cleared his throat. "Forget it. I'm a cop. I'll find it."

That reassured me. But I hung up, another question coming to mind. If Romero could easily find Jock's address, what other snooping had he done into his rival?

I pulled myself together, shut off the lights in Jock's condo, locked up, and closed the rolling door with the magic tag. Once I was outdoors again, I rushed to the side of the building and noticed that Jock's car was indeed gone.

Was that the burning rubber sound I'd heard after the brawl? Or had that come from another vehicle? Wait. I had Jock's keys. How would he have started the car? That was easy. He'd hotwire it. With Jock's know-how and multi-faceted background, that'd be as simple as snapping open an anti-oxidative ampoule.

By the time Romero swerved into the parking lot, I was crouched outside on the gravelly pavement, using the beam from the streetlight to search for my platinum earring. These beauties were irreplaceable, inherited from a favorite aunt. Leaving one behind wasn't an option.

Romero watched me for a second before getting out of his truck, our eyes connecting in the glow from his headlights, his expression grim.

My eyebrows crept up to my hairline, and I put my arms wide. "*What!*"

He swung out of his vehicle, the motorcycle and black-leather gear gone. He was wearing a beige knit sweater and jeans and looked exceptionally cozy. I wanted to bury myself in his warmth and strength, to feel his love draped around me. I wanted to run into his arms so bad it hurt. The look on his face stopped me.

"*What?*" he said louder than necessary. "Only *you'd* get me out of bed at a god-awful hour, have me drive into Boston because you're worried about an AWOL employee the size of the Hulk, and ask me *what*."

My sigh nearly came out as a snort. "Jock's not the size of the Hulk." He's bigger, I wanted to add but knew I wouldn't get a pat on the back for pointing that out. "And technically, you're not in Boston. You're in Cambridge."

"Thanks for the clarification." He rammed his hands on his lean hips and stared down at me from his six-foot-tall frame, a sign saying I was better off keeping my mouth shut.

I pretended to ignore the warning and went back to my search, clutch under my arm.

He stepped a foot closer, his tone softening. "Did Jock say anything else before he disappeared?"

I stilled myself, thinking back. "Only that if he didn't return in half an hour, to call a cab."

Romero raised a palm. "See? I'm sure he's okay."

"*Okay!* What about the fighting and the angry voices? And…and his Porsche is gone."

"Porsche?" He looked around the empty lot. "What happened to the Harley?"

"It needed maintenance." I recalled my earlier banter with Jock on this. Somehow it didn't seem funny now. "But he didn't have his car keys."

Romero tried not to grin. "Sweetheart, if Jock was driving a Porsche, he'd have lots of high-tech keyless options, maybe even a virtual key from his phone."

Okay. I hadn't thought of that.

"His missing car proves my point. He likely left willingly."

I fumed. "*Likely*, huh?"

He sighed as if he didn't want to get into it with me again. "I made a few phone calls. Seems someone contacted the police earlier because of a disturbance in the neighborhood.

Ray Donoochi and his partner Ox were in the area and did a drive-by, sirens wailing. Didn't find a thing."

I brought to mind the sirens from earlier and took a guarded look around the desolate area. Wasn't much of a neighborhood, but the main thing was the cops had scared away the perpetrator.

"And because it looks like Jock left on his own accord, you'll have to wait forty-eight hours to file a missing persons report."

I leaped to my feet, my evening bag hitting the ground with a *thunk*. "Forty-eight hours! What if he's been taken hostage?"

"That means his alleged abductor wants something in exchange. That doesn't fit anything that's happened here."

"And if he's dead?"

His tone leveled. "Then we'll have to deal with that. We're also dealing with the possibility of two vehicles: one belonging to Jock, the other the perp's. So if Jock was abducted, someone had to be extremely clever to make two cars disappear. Hell, maybe the guy's a magician."

He shoved up his sleeves, the hands on his Iron Man watch glowing from where he was standing six feet away. "Did you happen to see what the guy was driving?" He strolled closer, the weight of his question not lost on me. "I mean, was it red? Blue? Or was there even a vehicle besides Jock's?"

Smartass. Even if I'd seen a vehicle, he knew there was no point in asking make or model. Color and size were the most he'd get from this girl.

I swept my handbag off the ground, escaping the heat from his sapphire-eyed stare. "I can't place a vehicle. I heard a motor and tires squeal away." The rest I couldn't evoke. Maybe because I'd been crumpling into a hyperventilating mess on the garage floor.

He scratched his whiskered jaw, his stance telling me he was thinking things through. He might have been acting cavalier about all this, but he was an excellent cop. He wouldn't have shrugged and ignored evidence of a possible crime. My best guess was that he was trying to ease my worries. "Maybe the sirens drowned out the sound of a possible other vehicle that could've left seconds earlier," he said. "Or maybe one car chased the other out of the lot."

He gestured to the ground. "May I ask what you were looking for?"

I followed his gaze. "Uh, my earring."

"Your earring."

"Yes." I snubbed his cocky look and crouched again, surveying the ground. "We can go as soon as we find it."

"We?"

"You *are* just standing there." I was walking a fine line, but did I care?

He nodded slowly and skimmed the ground. "Is there a reason we're looking for your earring in the parking lot?"

I moved away from him and felt along the rough pavement. "*Yes*, there's a reason. It fell."

"Of course. Why didn't I think of that?"

He strode back to where Jock's Porsche had been, bent over, and picked up something glittering in the dim light. "Is this the earring in question?"

I hurried over and stared at the square hoop dangling high from his pinky. "That's it. Thank you." I went to grab it, but he pulled away.

"Not so fast." He took the back of his fingers and swept my hair away from my right ear where my earring was intact. He did the same treatment on my left side. No earring. "When you say your earring fell, you mean from your ear?"

I wrenched away, my hair cascading down my back. "I wouldn't be wearing one earring without the other." Jeepers.

He hauled out his phone and flashed the light on the hoop directly above my nose, revealing a smudge of blood on the metal. "Uh-huh." He tilted his head down at me, the look in his blue eyes sharp enough to pierce glass. "The part you left out."

"Excuse me?"

"On the phone, earlier. You didn't mention your ear had been bleeding."

I knew where he was going with this. "Didn't I?"

"No. And I see no signs of blood. Nor did you tell me exactly what happened to the thug. If I had to add two and two, I can assume he became acquainted with one of your beauty tools."

I bit the inside of my cheek, blinking hopelessly up at my earring dangling in front of me. "Technically, that's not one of my beauty tools. As you can *see*, I don't even have my beauty bag *on me*." For good measure, I waved my clutch in his face. It was a cheeky thing to do, but he wasn't getting the better of me.

He gave me a hot, suggestive appraisal from the tips of my fingers down to my ribbed turtleneck, undoubtedly recalling his earlier roguish feel of my bare breasts. My legs buckled under the weight of his sexy stare, but I remained brave. I lowered my arms and tightened my thighs, refusing to appear ruffled.

Romero didn't buy it. We'd been intimate over and over...and over. He knew every curve of my body and my innermost vulnerabilities, and could read my actions like the clever detective he was. Giving me his *gotcha* look, he slid his phone back in his pocket and leaned heavily on one leg in his menacing cop way. "So the question is how did this earring leave your ear and land on the ground...with blood on it?"

"That's a good question."

"Thank you. Since it's been a long day, and I'm not up to speculating in the wee hours of the morning, maybe you have a good answer."

I groaned. "I simply stabbed the guy with the metal post. Happy?"

"You want to share the part of the anatomy where you stabbed the guy? When it comes to that creative, impulsive head of yours, I can only imagine."

"Sheesh. The inner wrist, okay? If you want to know the whole truth, he punched his arm through the garage door, wrapped it around my neck, and held on tight."

Romero glanced at the jagged gap on the rolling door as if he was getting the full picture, the look on his face shifting to one of concern. Like maybe there was more to this whole thing than just two guys throwing a few punches. I also knew him well enough to realize he wasn't thrilled that Jock had vanished, and I'd been left in potential danger. Served him right for acting like a jerk.

"In defense, I tore out my earring, raked the post down the length of the guy's arm, then stabbed him in the wrist." I cracked my knuckles. "It was nothing more than a couple of scratches, and I didn't see any blood. Of course, it *was* dark," I added as an afterthought.

"I guess you didn't hit an artery." He did an exaggerated fist pump. "Yay you."

Romero wasn't a comedian by nature, but that didn't prevent him from attempting to rile me with his dry wit.

He tipped the earring into a crumpled piece of notepaper he produced from his jeans pocket. "Perhaps our villain wasn't thrilled about keeping the earring as a memento." He brushed a strand of hair from my face. "Probably didn't have the right hair for it."

Rising above his cynicism, I stepped back and gave him a shrewd glare. "Speaking of hair, the guy you're looking for had hairy arms."

He pocketed the evidence bound for the crime lab, then squared his shoulders. "You weren't certain whether the perp was wearing a mask. You didn't notice what type of vehicle he was driving—if one at all, and you couldn't tell whether he was oozing blood from your actions. But you *are* sure he had hairy arms." He gave a head shake. "Anything else you want to add?"

"Only that I won't give up looking for Jock until I find him. Anything *you* want to add?"

He gave a short chuckle, unmistakably masking his exasperation with me. Then he rubbed the back of his neck as if weighing everything we'd talked about. "I'll put out an alert for Jock's car. At this point, that's all I can do."

"Thanks." It was better than nothing.

He paused. "You don't by any chance know his license plate number."

"No." I shrank back, then perked up. "But I do know he drives a Carrera 4S." At least I'd remembered that much. "And it's silver," I added, just to get his goat. "Shiny silver."

Our eyes held, the humor gone from his voice. "I know you care about the guy, and I'll do what I can to find him, but I'm advising you to stay out of it. Got it?"

"Loud and clear."

Chapter 5

I fought sleep, wrestling with the notion that there had to be something I could do to find Jock. At this point, I didn't know what that something was. But I sure as hell wasn't staying out of it as Romero advised.

I'd probably pushed it a bit far tonight, ranting at him, not that *that* had gotten me anywhere. But the more reasons he gave that I was off base, the more determined I was to investigate on my own. If I were any more driven, I would've parked myself at the police station with a picket sign that read *Help Save Jock*.

Comforted that, at a minimum, Romero would be on the lookout for Jock's car, I took deep breaths, lecturing myself to relax. After a good sleep, I'd plot with a clear mind. I'd be no help to Jock at the present.

I finally fell into an erratic slumber, disturbed by nightmares that I was screaming blindly down a dark road, villains chasing after me. I tossed and turned, feeling myself falling into a gravelly ditch, struggling to my feet again and again. The Joker finally caught me, spun me around, and abruptly turned into Freddy Krueger. His frightening face caused me to jolt myself awake.

I sat up in a sweat, my heart thrashing. I took a handful of calming breaths and glanced at my alarm clock. Terrific.

Six a.m. No sense trying to get back to sleep when Saturday's workday started in a few hours.

I rubbed my damp forehead, and a wave of exhaustion swamped me, letting me know my body wasn't yet rested. I yawned and blinked and yawned again, looking back at my comfy pillow. Figured. *Now* I could sleep. I rationalized I could forgo the makeup, stylish hairdo, and chic ensemble, but the idea was to gain customers, not lose them. I had Phyllis in my employ for that. No, the day must go on.

I made a trip to the bathroom and washed away the cobwebs and violent dreams haunting me. After showering and spraying on my signature Musk perfume, I toned my face when a sudden thought occurred. What if Jock had been trying to get in touch with me during the night? Except for showing up at my door, phoning was his best course of action. He'd vanished in the same clothes that he'd worn to the ballet. Who knew whether he had his phone on him?

He would've needed his cell if it had a virtual car key as Romero had suggested. I'd seen him slip his phone in his pocket at his condo after he'd been at his computer, and I assumed he still had it when he joined his attacker, but that could've changed during or after the brawl.

I scooted into the kitchen and glanced around for my cell phone. Where was the dumb thing? I asked Yitts if she'd seen it, but she was stretched out on the floor, groggy from being woken after my restlessness.

I rounded the corner into the living room and spotted my beauty bag by the front door. My clutch was sitting on top. Splendid. In my distressed state last night, I hadn't thought to pluck my phone out of my evening bag, or even look at it. Typical.

I snatched the phone out of my clutch and absently dumped everything else into my beauty bag.

Hmm. Zilch from Jock.

My heart sank. Okay, this wasn't necessarily a bad sign. I wasn't sure *what* it was, but I charged my phone so I'd be ready when he *did* call.

I picked up Yitts under her armpits and held her nose to

nose, inhaling the remnants of my vanilla-scented lipstick on her head from last night's kisses. "Where is Jock?"

Yitts wasn't much for conversation. Nor was she thrilled about her legs dangling in midair. She provided comfort. After that, I was on my own.

I brushed and fed her, tossed my slightly improved, coffee-stained dress into the clothes hamper, then trudged back into the kitchen and ate a slice of Nina's loaf with some homemade strawberry jam my mother had pushed on me.

I dressed for work in a stretchy, fitted, spaghetti-strapped neon-pink dress with matching earrings and hairband, already contemplating what I'd say to Max and Phyllis about my night and, more importantly, Jock's disappearance. If I could find out who the angry attacker was or the reason he was fighting with Jock, maybe that would lead me to my missing employee.

A nervous feeling prickled inside from these unpleasant thoughts, increasing my unease. Now I had to face the bickering duo at work. What if they mucked up my plans to investigate, as often was the case?

Phyllis, for one, never made anything I had to say easy. Of course, in this case, she wouldn't blink an eye at my news. Why would she? Training as a geisha was consuming her and was more than she could handle.

Then there was Max. He'd be all over this, questioning me like he was a cop in one of those detective shows. It'd be worse than dealing with Romero, who, incidentally, was right. There was nothing saying Jock was dead...or even injured. But the fact that he took off, leaving me in his condo, locked and hiding in the bathroom with no car or way to get home, indicated something was up.

After brushing my teeth and swiping on my frosted lipstick, I slid into bright-pink spikes with glittery buckles, chucked my phone into my bag with everything else, then drove to work. I pulled into the parking lot behind Beaumont's, deciding to let nature take its course. Bonus if I could remain calm.

I shut off the ignition and felt a booming vibration that shook from my rib cage up to my hair follicles. I clenched my teeth and gripped the door handle. What was going on? Were construction workers jackhammering down the street? Couldn't be an earthquake, could it? I clamped my bag and dashed into the salon, hoping to escape the noise.

The deafening racket increased. Whatever it was, it was coming from downstairs, making the whole salon reverberate.

I click-clacked down the steps, swung around the railing into the basement, and barreled into the kitchen where Phyllis was banging the life out of a set of drums.

"Phyllis!" I screamed, holding my ears before my head exploded.

She hammered the bass drum and smashed the cymbals, then looked up at me as if I was disturbing her. "How's a person supposed to practice with you hollering and making a racket?"

I gulped back some four-letter words, glaring at her in disbelief. "*You're* the one causing the racket! What are you doing?"

"I already told you. I'm practicing."

"For what? A spot in a heavy metal band?"

"It's part of my training. And don't pretend you don't know what I'm talking about."

I threw my hands up in the air, at my wits' end trying to understand Phyllis. Just then, Max thundered down the stairs. "What was that pounding? I parked the car and thought the ground was about to crack open."

I gave a curt head tilt toward Phyllis in her kimono, holding two drumsticks in the air like Mötley Crüe's Tommy Lee.

Max gaped from Phyllis back to me. "There are no words."

"I have to practice *somewhere*." Phyllis plunked the drumsticks down on the snare drum, swiveled off the stool, and fell flat on her face, forgetting about her tapered kimono.

Max rolled his eyes at me with a sigh, then went over and helped Phyllis to her feet.

She shook him off, shoved back her dangly chopsticks that had migrated to her forehead, and gave me an accusing eye. "Why didn't you come to the Geisha Gap last night like I asked you?"

"I beg your pardon?" My mind was still in turmoil over last night's occurrence, and Phyllis was reprimanding me for Lord-knows-what.

"*You know.* My training as a geisha. I told you about it yesterday."

I slid my gaze from her to Max, not willing to betray his confidence. "Phyllis, I went to the ballet last night, and you never mentioned you were in training to be a geisha."

"Well, I am. It's an art form not many can master. Those nine other little trainees might as well pack their bags and head back to where they came from. With my body type, personality, and endurance level, I've got what it takes."

"Could you take it somewhere else?" Max piped.

"And *then*," she continued, ignoring Max's quip, "I can blow this Popsicle stand. Once I learn how to play the drums, they'll promote me to head geisha."

"You're already a head *case*," Max said. "Does that qualify?"

I waved a discouraging hand to Max behind Phyllis's head. "Ixnay on yllisphay," I murmured to him in Pig Latin. Then I centered on Phyllis. "Learning the drums. That's what this is all about? Shouldn't you be studying something like the flute?"

She huffed out her nose and thrust her hands on her hips. "Everyone learns the flute. This'll catch more attention."

"Maybe it'll catch the attention of a hitman," Max reflected.

"You have to come tonight," Phyllis said to me as if Max hadn't spoken. "You'll be impressed with how much I've learned."

Watching Phyllis train to be a geisha was up there on my list of favorite things to do along with having a root canal and eating slugs. "Sorry. I'm busy."

"With what?" she demanded.

Since they were both standing there, it was now or never. "Jock is missing."

Max's brows reached new heights, and Phyllis stood hands on hips, the rusty wheels creaking slowly.

"What happened, lovey?" Max asked. "Didn't he show up for your date?"

"It wasn't a *date*," I reminded him. "And no, it was after the ballet. We went back to his condo, and then—"

"Time out." Max placed his right palm over the tips of his fingers on his left hand, signaling a *T*. Then he narrowed his eyes at me like he was reading an optometrist's eye chart from ten feet away. "It wasn't a date, yet *after* the ballet you went back to Jock's condo. That spells *date* in my books."

"Your coloring books? Or comic books?"

"Touché."

"*Anyway*," I continued, attempting to keep my cool, "there was an altercation with another man outside. Then Jock was gone."

"Who was it?" Max probed.

I shrugged, the scary face still haunting me. "I wish I knew."

Max snapped into full mystery-solver mode, his hazel eyes shimmering with intrigue. "Maybe it was a lover's boyfriend…or *husband* who found out he was being cheated on! Or maybe an old employer heard of Jock's success in Rueland. He then came here begging Jock to come back, and it turned into a brawl. Or maybe—"

"Are you listening to this pinhead?" Phyllis swiveled her gaze from Max to me, a brash look on her face. "Anyone can dream up stupid ideas about what happened to Jock."

Max shot Phyllis daggers, cheeks red, hands balled into fists. Probably wishing he'd left her on the floor. "What's *your* brilliant theory on what happened to him?"

Phyllis gave a glib wave. "The guy's always disappearing. He'll probably be back by noon."

"The oracle speaketh," Max said.

I bit my lip, pondering Phyllis's words. She was right.

Jock came and went like smoke, but this felt different. From the moment he'd picked me up last night, he'd seemed preoccupied. I'd known something was brewing. But to take off like that, when I was still at his place? No. This was serious.

"I don't think he'll be back by noon, Phyllis. And I need to find out where he went."

She crossed her arms, rolling her eyes at me. "Who do you think you are? Wonder Woman? Just because you've nabbed a killer or two by throwing beauty tools around, you think you're going to get lucky again?"

"If that's what it takes."

Max squinted at Phyllis with contempt. "Valentine is more Wonder Woman than you are a geisha. And not that anyone's counting, but she's caught *more* than a killer or two in the past."

While Phyllis chewed on that, Max turned to me, chest thrust forward with determination. "I want to help find Jock. He's as important to me as he is to you."

I sighed. "This isn't a competition, Max." Plus, if he wanted to help me find Jock, then we'd both be busy with that tonight, which also meant neither one of us would be at the Geisha Gap.

"Hey." Phyllis jabbed her pointer finger at Max, this thought obviously just dawning on her. "If Valentine can't come to my training tonight, then you'll have to."

"I went last night. I don't want to be a hog." Seemed Max already had enough material for The Idiot Files.

"Hog. Shmog. Someone has to take notes. I may be better than those other beginners, and I've got a good handle on the drums, but I don't want to get a swelled head."

"What if I buy you a tube of Preparation H? I hear that brings swelling down."

At the mention of the hemorrhoid cream, Phyllis puckered her lips, eyes narrowed, like she wanted to pound Max into tomorrow.

Max pleaded at me with his eyes.

I didn't have a firm plan for tonight, yet I couldn't be Max's replacement at watching Phyllis make a spectacle of herself. Didn't matter what I wanted. They were both staring at me with expectancy. "Look, if I'm nearby, I'll pop in. Okay? It's the best I can promise. In the meantime, Phyllis, you can't practice here. I have a business to run. You're disturbing the peace."

"I can't practice at my apartment. There are too many old geezers there, and they all go to bed by eight o'clock. The sooner I master the drums and conquer being a geisha, the sooner I'll be out of your hair."

My ears pricked up at the sound of that. Phyllis's goal of becoming a geisha was probably one of the craziest things I'd ever heard. Not that I knew much about this line of work. However, even a simpleton could deduce that it didn't include hard-rock drumming. Another of Phyllis's misguided ideas.

But I wasn't here to rain on anyone's parade. I did a brief calculation in my head at how long it might take for Phyllis to accomplish her task—*if* she accomplished it. Even if it were a few months from now, it'd be worth it to be rid of her. And it'd be her choice to leave, right? How could anyone fault me for that? "All right. You can practice here, but only after hours."

"You got it." She shuffled past Max and me and headed for the stairs. "That's when I do my best work."

The day marched on. First, Phyllis slapped the address to the Geisha Gap on my desk like it was a done deal that I'd make an appearance tonight. Next, I had to explain to Mrs. Benedetti's daughter, Carla, why Jock wasn't able to perform his magic on her.

Carla was my height, roughly my age, and built like a small tank. Her long black hair was pulled into a ponytail, she was dressed in a gray camouflage T-shirt and black cargo pants, and she looked ready for boot camp. "Yo. Where is he?" She scanned the salon, legs spread wide, hands on her hips.

"Um, he had an urgent matter to take care of. But don't worry. You're in good hands. Jock conveyed exactly what he was planning to do for you."

"He did?"

Not even remotely.

"Your mother paid for the works, Carla, and that's what you're going to get."

She ran her gaze from my long lashes down to my vivid pink dress and buckled heels, then cracked her knuckles one by one, making the hairs on my neck stand at attention. "Mom's always going on about you, Valentine. But the beauty gig isn't my thing. Truth is, I can't stand chemical smells, and I don't wear makeup."

Wonderful. That shot several ideas out the window. At first glance, Carla had all the makings to be a glamour queen. She had beautifully symmetrical cheekbones, a straight nose, full lips, and an oval-shaped face. I could still sculpt her unruly eyebrows, treat her to a mustache wax, and add color to her uneven skin tone. "No problem. We'll give you the works without irritating your sense of smell. Deal?"

She gave a confident nod. "Deal."

I started by steaming Carla's face for her facial since her sallow skin needed stimulating. I left her in Ti Amo under the steamer and went to my office to get the new unscented serum I'd taken home to try and that I wanted to use on her skin. Also, I wanted to check my phone again to see if there was a message from Jock. There wasn't much I could do at this point from work, but if he'd been trying to contact me, I wanted to know.

I passed Max giving a consultation to a new client, his arms sweeping in a flourish around the woman's head, his face lit up with the excitement that always captured him when talking beauty. Then I neared Phyllis at the front counter speaking to a girl covered in tattoos.

I had so much on my mind about Jock vanishing and how I was going to find him that I strode into my office and slammed the door behind me without giving Phyllis and the girl a second thought.

I dug my phone out of my bag and swiped the screen, looking for a text or missed call. *Nada* on both counts. I called Jock. Nothing. Voicemail didn't even come up. Was his phone out of service? Out of range? Destroyed?

I tapped my fingers on the desk, telling myself not to get excited. I'd hear from Jock sooner or later. I set the phone on the desk and eyed my beauty bag. Right. The serum. I had the same skin type as Carla, and I'd been impressed with the product's immediate, glowing results.

I rummaged through my sack for the thick two-ounce glass bottle and heard something jingle. I followed the noise to the bottom of my bag and discovered Jock's keys. Of course! I'd deposited them in my clutch last night and must have unwittingly transferred them to my bag at home this morning.

If the cops weren't doing anything about Jock's disappearance, at least I had access to his place. I twirled the keys in my hand. Maybe there was something I might discover at his condo. A missing clue I'd overlooked last night?

Wait a minute. Why not contact Holly? I didn't want to bother my sister last night, but today was a new day, and I was beyond caring whether she'd blab my concerns about Jock to our mother. She'd provided helpful tips in the past on cases I'd solved. Once upon a time, she'd even worked with Romero in vice and still ran into him at the precinct.

Unfortunately, neither of them took me seriously when it came to investigative work. *Cops.* Thought they knew it all. Nonetheless, I could take a bit of teasing if it meant learning if there was news about Jock's disappearance.

I slid the keys back in my bag and seized my phone, checking the time first. Ten minutes left for Carla to steam. This wouldn't take long.

"What now?" Holly asked, papers shuffling in the background.

Hard to believe my sister's name was inspired by the

merriest day of the year. She wasn't, by nature, a bubbly person, nor was she big on pleasantries. This was perfect. I didn't have time for her typical blush-inducing grilling about Romero and what piece of furniture the rugged detective and I had had sex on, how many positions we'd tried, and if it were true he had the stamina of a bull. I only wanted answers on my employee, another man whom I was attached to in more ways than one. "Jock de Marco is missing."

"That Latin lover working in your salon? Damn. I can't believe I still haven't had the pleasure of meeting the guy, especially with all I've heard around town about his sexy manner and hard-muscled body."

"He's a hairstylist, not a porn star. And if you could get your mind out of the gutter, I need you to focus on more than Jock's sex appeal and hard abs."

Papers stopped shuffling at her end. "What could be more important than hard sex?" She gave a throaty laugh. "Like the way I combined those two phrases?"

I groaned. "Yes, you're a literary genius." Even though my sister could make a trucker blush, she was happily married and the mother of two adorable but rascally tots.

She chuckled again. "I need *something* to lift the mood around here. Vice and homicide are teaming up on a nasty case, and it's got every cop in the precinct on edge. I'm the only one who hasn't lost her sense of humor."

"What about Romero?" It was a sincere question.

"Ha. That Italian Stallion's never *had* a sense of humor. But I bet you're giving him lots to laugh about."

"Amusing." I gave her a brief account on my evening with Jock, the story sounding a lot worse today, even with glossing over the attack on me.

"Holy shit!"

"Exactly." My blood pressure surged, having recounted the events again. "And the Italian Stallion said a missing persons report can't be filed for forty-eight hours."

"Yeah. Crappy laws. You sure Jock's missing? Maybe he had to take care of something."

"Did you *hear* my story?"

"I did. But if his car is gone…" Her voice trailed off. "Sounds like he's a big guy capable of looking after himself. He's probably fine." There was a pause. "Wait a minute. What were you doing on a date with Jock when you're shagging Romero?"

"It wasn't a date." How many more times was I going to repeat that?

"Uh-huh. Then what was it? An obligation? Did you have an appointment together after the ballet to do someone's hair?"

"It was simply a friendly offer on Jock's part to take me to the ballet because he knows how much I enjoy it."

"Riiiiight. Everyone knows I enjoy whitewater rafting, but I don't see anyone offering to take *me* for a ride down the rapids."

"Maybe if you chose a sport you didn't need to be insured for, others might see it as fun."

I could see her grinning on the other end. "Romero didn't mind you cheating on him?"

"I wasn't cheating. I'd made a promise to Jock. That's all."

"Hey, as long as our boy in blue is okay with it, who am I to judge?"

"Yes, wouldn't be like you to be judgmental."

She snickered at my sarcasm, but I was already back on track. "Isn't there something you can do at your end regarding Jock?"

"I can keep my ear to the ground."

"You're a tremendous support," I said on an eye roll, then exhaled, thinking of my options. "I'm not sitting back, waiting to see what turns up. Jock may need my help."

The truth in all this was that this mystery was unlike any case I'd ever been involved in. Jock wasn't a stranger or even a client. He was a man I had complicated feelings for. Solving his disappearance wasn't only about my curiosity or stubbornness, or even pride. I was emotionally tied to a man I worked with every day and, okay, to whom I was strongly attracted. This made things a lot more urgent.

"I wouldn't get involved if I were you, Miss Sleuthy Pants." Her warning came out sing-songy.

I tugged the serum bottle out of my bag and whacked it on the desk. "I'm already involved. And for a brilliant wordsmith, that was a two on the comeback scale."

"I'll do better next time." She lowered her voice. "Look, I don't know what's happened to Jock, but seriously, there've been rumblings around the station today."

"Rumblings about what?"

"Hold on." She muffled the phone and with her professional voice gave another cop in the background orders. "I gotta go," she said, coming back on the line. "Things are heating up around here. Just so you know, Romero left an hour ago on what looks like another homicide."

From her tone, I could see the worry on her face, her brows furrowed. That look always meant there was more to the story than she was letting on, and it triggered an anxious sigh out of me. "If you hear or learn anything about Jock, please call me, okay?"

A natural instinct to worry about Romero surfaced before I had a chance to stuff it down. "And you *better* let me know if Romero's in any danger. Got it?" Maybe I was torn between two men, but I couldn't ignore the fact that either might be in serious jeopardy.

"Roger that." Her voice became protective, the big sister pulling rank. "Stay safe, cutesy, and for once, leave this to the police. We really do know what we're doing."

Then she disconnected.

Chapter 6

I stood there, mouth open, not feeling at all reassured by Holly's words. One minute, she professed Jock was probably fine, and the next, she confessed things were heating up at the station. Was that a hint Jock's disappearance was somehow connected? That Jock was at the center of something?

I couldn't control what the police did, but I had no intention of waiting forty-eight hours to file any report. A lot could happen in forty-eight hours. I fiddled with a piece of paper from my desk, gazed down at it, and spotted the address Phyllis had written for the Geisha Gap. Right. The Academy Awards for Geisha Training was on tonight.

I flung the paper back on my desk and rewound last night in my mind to when Jock and I arrived at his place. Though he'd been distracted at the ballet and in the car, his mood had worsened after he looked at his laptop. *Whoa.* That was it. His laptop. He'd obviously read something unsettling, evident by the way he'd slammed the lid down and hustled us to the door.

This gave me new purpose for snooping in Jock's condo, which I'd have to do soon, before the cops decided to take me seriously. But suppose I went there, opened his laptop, and was faced with a locked screen? Then what? Breaking into someone's computer looked easy in the movies, but I had about as much technical skill as Phyllis had fashion sense.

Furthermore, Jock was a multifaceted individual. Without a doubt, his password would be complex. No. I needed help in that department, and since it clearly wasn't going to be in the form of a police computer specialist, I needed a plan.

Who did I know who'd assist me? It had to be someone who worked with computers. Someone who knew them inside and out. Someone with a passion for technology. Instantly, it came to me. Gibson, Mrs. Shales's grandson!

Mrs. Shales lived next to my parents in Burlington, Rueland's twin town. She'd also lived next door to us in Rueland in the house where I grew up. When my parents moved to Burlington after I flew the coop, Mrs. Shales picked up and moved beside them. Who knew living near my parents could be so much fun?

Through the years, Gibson had visited his grandma, and I'd interacted with him on more than one occasion. I worked hard at liking Gippy—as my father called him—but none of our interactions were delightful. As a kid, Gibson was either trying to run me over with his tricycle or cover me in dirt. But he had matured and had become somewhat of a computer geek. Since he wasn't the type to ask questions as to why I was searching through someone else's laptop, he was my best chance at finding out what happened to Jock.

Fresh hope flowed through me as a plan formulated in my mind. I eyed my bag, remembering I'd once crammed Gibson's business card from the computer store inside the tiny zipped pouch. I'd kept odd cards there with phone numbers I wasn't inclined to add to my contacts. Question was, had I kept Gibson's card?

I unzipped the pouch, rummaged through a dozen cards, and came up empty. Great. Must have chucked it. Of course I chucked it. When did I ever fathom a time I'd call Gibson for anything, let alone use him to break into a friend's laptop? *Crap.*

I looked up at the ceiling, envisioning God's searing, all-knowing gaze on me. "I see what You're doing. This is punishment for not dating Gibson like my mother wanted."

I received no response but felt Someone was having a good laugh.

I couldn't bring to mind the name of the computer store where Gibson worked, and I was getting no hints from above. Added to that, there had to be a hundred computer joints in the area. As much as I dreaded asking my mother for help, I had to do it. She had Gibson's number. I'd seen her tuck his business card in their kitchen drawer the time he'd given it to her.

I wasn't sure how I'd make light of the situation, but she'd been after me to let Gibson update my computer. Maybe this was a golden opportunity, a blessing in disguise. I could stick to the computer issue and request Gibson's number without bringing Jock into it, couldn't I?

On the other hand, I could go straight to Mrs. Shales. Only trouble with that, she might tell Gibson I was asking about him, which might be misconstrued. I didn't have to worry about that with my mother. She might hound *me* about calling the guy till she needed a new lung, but I couldn't see her going the extra mile to personally bother Gibson.

I glanced at the time again. *Drat.* Carla's steaming session was almost up. My plan would have to wait. I nicked the serum off the desk and stomped out of the office into the salon. I bumped into Phyllis lingering by the counter, her powder-white face screwed up in a scowl.

"What's the problem, Phyllis?"

She crossed her arms over her kimono and shook her head, the dangly bits from her chopsticks bonking her in the face. "That girl wanted her belly button pierced."

I crooked my neck around the counter to the front door for the missing girl, my jaw muscles tight. "And?" We offered the service, so what was Phyllis's problem?

"I told her I don't do nasty body piercings."

I tried to keep the annoyance out of my voice, but it was

slipping in at a fierce rate. "Then you could've let one of us handle it."

Max's client headed down the hall to the bathroom, and Max joined us at the front. "*And* she told the girl to go home and wash off her tattoos while she was at it. The only female with her own set of teeth to ever cross Phyllis's path, and she frightens the pretty thing away."

I traipsed past the sales counter full of trendy products to the front window and looked right and left for a sign of the customer. "What are the chances of her coming back?"

"About the same as Phyllis turning into a good stylist by afternoon."

Phyllis grunted. "Look, I'm not comfortable giving body piercings to someone with all those tattoos."

"I'm sure she wasn't gung-ho about having someone dressed for Halloween drill her with holes, either." Max tapped his foot, palms in the air. "What do tattoos have to do with anything, anyway? You're just jealous because she wanted a belly button piercing, and it's been years since you've seen *your* belly button."

I drummed my fingers on the serum bottle, listening with half an ear. Something about the girl and her tattoos nagged at me.

"Who cares?" Phyllis argued. "I've got more important things to worry about than some chick who wants to poke holes in her body." She scuffed the floor in her wooden flip-flops on her way to her station, butt swinging side to side.

I squeezed the glass bottle in my hand, a surge of frustration hitting me between the eyes at Phyllis worsening the tint stains on the ceramic tile. I bit back my anger and plodded down the hall. The floor could be cleaned. Losing a potential client was another story. Likewise, if I left Carla for another minute, her face would peel like a banana from too much ozone.

I finished Carla's facial with a massage and a mask. After that, I freshened the look around her eyebrows, opening the eye area considerably. Then I performed my own magic by giving her a cute, bouncy cut that she could still pull back into a no-nonsense ponytail.

"Yow! I look *hot*!" Carla was beaming more triumphantly than if she'd won Miss Rueland. She turned her head this way and that in the mirror. "Who knew I could look this great?" She gave me a firm nod, her face glowing with radiance. "I had my doubts about you, Valentine, but you lived up to your reputation. Thank you."

I warmed at her gratitude. "Glad to help. I'd recommend coming back next week for an upper-lip wax. After exfoliating your skin today and applying a camphor mask, your face has had all the pampering it can take."

"Gotcha. Let's book it now."

We strolled into the dispensary, and I reserved Carla a spot on Thursday between a haircut and a pedicure. She took the card I offered with the time and date confirmed, gave me a massive tip, and added a feminine swagger as she sauntered out the door.

I guided my finger down the appointment book, checking to see how long before I could wrap things up here and trek to my parents', when the French provincial phone rang next to me.

My best friend, Twix, started in before I got out my usual greeting. "You're not going to believe what those little monsters did this time."

Since Twix ran a daycare, I had no idea what little monsters she was referring to. *Her* little monsters, Junie and Joey, were busy toddlers and, from what I'd seen, a handful.

I mouthed *Twix* to Max who was at his station, lightly applying makeup on a flower girl for a wedding. Then I plunked myself on the rolling stool, trying to control my worry about Jock. It wouldn't matter if I'd found out he'd fled to Argentina. I'd never escape Twix's tirade until I heard every last detail.

"Last night," she began, "after the last tot was picked up, I thought the kids were playing in Joey's room. But things got awfully quiet." She groaned, and I could visualize her shaking her head. "Rule number one. If you ever have kids, don't assume everything's fine when they're not screaming. In reality, *that's* when they're up to the most mischief."

Twix didn't fool me. Her kids meant the world to her.

I attempted to put my concerns about Jock aside, giving her my full attention. "What happened?"

"Those little rotters got into my nail polish drawer and painted every nail on Peaches black."

At her bellowing about what her kids did to their pot-bellied pig, I sprang off the stool, pulling the curlicue phone cord with me, and closed the pocket door halfway. "Maybe they're getting back at you for naming a male pig Peaches."

"Hey, *I* didn't give him that name. That was the kids' idea. Who was I to argue? Next week, they'll be calling him Little Lord Fauntleroy or Guinevere. Anyway, not only did they give him a manicure, but they also smeared on a beard and mustache and dressed him up in Joey's tiny black leather jacket and a black police hat they found in the toy bin. Peaches looked like that leather-clad singer from the Village People."

I sank onto the stool again, glad Twix could momentarily make me smile. "So what's the problem? I take it you're not calling to share your kids' latest endeavor."

"I'm calling because I don't know if it's safe to use acetone to remove nail polish off a pig."

"Who do you think I am, a vet?"

"You're the beauty professional! I thought you could tell me *something*! I'm about to tear out my hair here. Tony had to work this morning, and Peaches is covered in black nail polish. Feet. Head. Nose." She heaved a sigh. "You should've seen the little tub. He was so helpless, waddling and squealing in his Village People costume. I managed to pull off the outfit without scraping him with all those tiny buckles, but what about the black *nail polish*?"

"*Okay* already. Try using non-acetone nail polish remover. It should be gentle enough to use on Peaches's skin. For good measure, give him a soapy bath after and hydrate him with an aloe-based lotion."

"Whew. Thank you. Can you suggest a lotion?"

I had a popular line of intensely effective aloe products. "I've got one here you can use."

"You're a lifesaver. Can I come for it after you're done at work? Tony will be home by then. I can pop out while he watches the kids."

I meditated on this for a second, coming back to the reality of my day. First there was a trip to my parents' to get Gibson's number. Then, if all went well, I'd meet Gibson at Jock's. "That timing won't work."

"Why not?"

"It just won't!" The tone of my voice made Max and Phyllis pop their heads up from their customers and shoot me a questioning stare around the half-opened door.

I rolled the stool toward the pocket door, raised my pink heel, and used it to slide the door all the way shut. "Sorry, Twix. It's been a hard day here."

I expected her to make a wiseass retort, but her voice softened, her own problems forgotten. "What do you mean, hard? Tell me everything."

I rolled back to the counter and relayed a condensed version of what had taken place last night.

"Okay," Twix said. "This is what we're going to do. After you're done at work, we're driving to Jock's place, seeing what we can unearth." Mother and multitasker to the rescue.

"You've got feet and skin to clean on Peaches, remember?"

"Tony can handle Peaches. He's a podiatrist, isn't he?"

I scratched my head, struggling to see the similarity. "Tony works on ballplayers, not pigs."

"If he's good enough for the Red Sox, he's good enough for Peaches."

I ruminated on her offer. "I think I should go alone." Except for Gibson. Plus, Max would be out of sorts since I'd already discouraged his help.

"Go *alone*! I care about Jock, too. Did you forget he and I were in *Caribbean Gold* together? We were practically joined at the hip."

This was a slight exaggeration. Jock was the lead stunt double in last fall's pirate movie filmed in Boston while Twix was hired as an extra to scream at the top of her lungs. She outperformed the top-billed star in that regard.

"Jock's like a brother," she said. "Of *course* I'm going."

"Terrific." *I think.* "Thanks."

"You can thank me later…when you bring that lotion for Peaches."

Chapter 7

I hung up from talking to Twix and slid open the door, catching the tail end of a somewhat heated discussion between Max and Phyllis over their clients' heads. I wasn't up to playing referee or learning what the debate was about, so I busied myself, tidying a color cupboard while I waited for my next client to arrive.

I adjusted the order of ash blond colors, followed by golden blond, then reddish blond. Out of the corner of my eye, I saw Max go to the front with the sweetly made-up flower girl and her mother. After they paid and left, Max trooped into the dispensary to wash makeup brushes. "Everything okay with Twix?"

"Yes. Sorry if I was loud. Twix brings that out in me." I gave a half-hearted laugh.

Max sanitized the brushes and set them on a towel by the sink. "You weren't loud. In fact, I didn't hear a thing over Phyllis's phone call."

"What call?"

"Someone from Phyllis's geisha training phoned her cell." He spun around and leaned his backside against the counter. "I can't go with you tonight, after all. I need to help the canary out there take that drum set from downstairs to the Geisha Gap."

"Why?"

"You really want to know? The guy who usually lets them use his equipment there has a gig tonight. The deal is, when he needs his gear, the geishas have to bring in their own instruments."

"Oh."

"Yeah. Not so bad when you play a flute or clarinet." He shook his head in Phyllis's direction, watching her in disbelief as she blew on her client's hair. "Figures Phyllis would be the only one without a dainty instrument."

I gave a small grin. "Max, that's sweet of you to help."

He grinned back as if thinking about what the night would hold. "I know this fiasco will be good. Why don't you come? You'll never get free entertainment like this anywhere else."

My gaze slid to the floor, the tightness in my chest that I'd suppressed all morning resurfacing. "I would if this weren't so important."

He sobered, his smile fading. "I know." He paused with concern and waited until our eyes met. "If something happens and you need my help, call, okay? The Idiot Files can wait for one night."

It was four o'clock, two hours past our Saturday quitting time, and I was never so glad to see a day end. Among the three of us, we'd filled in for Jock and fielded phone calls when newcomers wanted a booking with him.

I promised Phyllis for the tenth time that I'd *try* to make it to the Geisha Gap tonight. Truth was, I did need a good distraction, but jocularity would have to wait until Jock was found.

I packed the tube of lotion I'd promised Twix in my bag and left Max and Phyllis to lock up. Then I drove straight to my parents', retrieving Gibson's number foremost in my mind.

I parked in the driveway of their ranch-style house and, after catching a whiff of cigar smoke in the garage—a sign that my father was outside tinkering around—I strutted inside.

My mother sat beside my father's aunt, Tantig, at the kitchen table. The sink was empty of dishes, and the kitchen smelled of Armenian stuffed peppers that were likely warming in the oven. Now that Tantig was living with my parents, traditional dishes and aromas graced the house more frequently.

The two women acknowledged me as I slid off my heels but seemed more focused on the eight pill bottles and as many pills of every size, shape, and color spread in front of them.

Remember, Valentine, casual. "What are you two doing?"

My mother gave me a thin smile, her strained voice telling me she was at her limit. "We're going over Tantig's meds. After her heart scare last week, Dr. Stucker made a few adjustments."

One morning a week ago, when Tantig didn't rise and shine the minute my mother called her, Mom worried that she'd had a heart attack. My great-aunt admitted to feeling a bit off, and my parents rushed her to the hospital.

Tantig turned her rumpled white-haired head to my mother and gave her a bland look, her thick Armenian accent, flat. "My pacemake-air is broken. That is all." Knowing my great-aunt, she was at her limit as well.

"Your pacemaker is not broken," my mother said. "You needed a few changes in your meds."

Tantig raised her chin and clicked her tongue, signaling she was not impressed with this decision. She shifted her stare back to the table and placed a finger on a blue pill. "This pill, I take." She slid the blue pill to one side.

"That's right," my mother said. "Twice a day."

Tantig concentrated on a red pill next. "This pill, *maybe* I take."

My mother shook her head. "No maybes about it. That's your heart pill. You need to take that every morning." Without ceremony, she slid the red pill beside the blue pill.

Letting that go, Tantig fingered a white capsule, a frown in place. "This pill, I *no* take."

"*What?*" I could've sworn I heard a *ping* go off in my mother's head. "That's your blood pressure pill. You *have* to take that."

"I no like." Tantig was adamant.

"Pretend it's one of your Tic Tacs. Dr. Stucker wants you to start taking that at bedtime." My mother slid a green-and-white tablet in front of Tantig next. "At least *this* pill is only temporary."

"I'm going to fire Stuck-air." This was a common theme with Tantig. "He's making me walk and take pills I don't like."

My mother patted her hand. "He's doing it because he wants the best for you."

"Who-hk cares?" Tantig rolled her eyes in slow motion. "He needs to return my Tupp-air-ware. I made him paklava months ago. I still wait for my contain-air."

"We'll get it next time we visit him," my mother promised, dumping the various pills back in their bottles. She looked up at me, controlling a sigh. "You staying for supper?"

I made a beeline for the kitchen drawer. "No. I'm looking for the number of that computer store where Gibson works."

My mother's eyebrows shot up. "Computer store? Why are you interested in where Gibson works?"

"I, uh, thought I'd get Gibson to update my computer... like you wanted. Remember?"

She narrowed her gaze on me, smelling a rat.

I pretended not to notice and dug around in the drawer. "Aha. Here it is." I snapped up the card. "The Computer Store." Naturally. Why did I think the place would have a creative name like Byts and Bots?

"Are you calling him now?" my mother asked.

"Soon." Like the minute I leave.

"Does this have something to do with Jock?"

I twirled around faster than I'd intended. "Why would Jock have anything to do with me getting in touch with Gibson?"

"Only because he was suspiciously absent from work today."

My mother amazed me. She had the ability to hear news before it was even made. "Who told you that?" *Holly*. As if I didn't know.

"Mary Ann Ganolli. After Phyllis set her hair this morning, she called me asking if I knew what happened to Jock."

"And? What did you tell her?"

She gave me a hard blink. "What *could* I tell her? I'm always the last to know anything around here. If you hadn't canceled *our* appointments, I would've had a clue what she was talking about."

Shoot. I forgot I'd given Mom and Tantig's hair slots to two other clients due to the flood of customers. Promising to do their hair at home ended any further complaints.

She waited a beat. "Well? You going to enlighten me?"

I didn't want to get into it with my mother, but I also knew I wouldn't escape without sharing something. "It seems Jock's disappeared."

"*Disappeared.* How does a man the size of a mountain disappear?"

"I don't know. But he did."

"He didn't call or let you know?"

"Generally, when someone disappears, they don't leave a forwarding address."

Her gaze panned to my hand. "What are you doing with Gibson's card?"

"I told you. I want to update my computer. Think I'll pop in at his shop." I glanced at the wall clock. "And if I don't hop to it, it'll be closed before I get there."

"What about our hair?"

I looked from my mother's soft brown bob, graying by the minute, to Tantig's disheveled white hair. "Tomorrow afternoon. I promise."

I came around the table and kissed Tantig on both cheeks, then I aimed for the door and slid on my shoes.

"Wait." My mother was at the oven, hauling out the huge roasting pan. "Take some dolma with you." She filled a glass container with two stuffed red peppers and snapped on the lid. "Do you have yogurt at home?"

"Yes." Yogurt was one of Yitts's favorite treats, and I liked to keep it on hand. This time, I'd have a spoonful myself.

The Computer Store sat in a strip mall on the borderline between Rueland and Burlington. I pulled into a parking spot and turned off the gas when my phone rang. I combed through my bag, found the sucker, and scanned the readout. Romero. Maybe he had an update on Jock.

"Everything okay?" His voice was quieter than usual, as if he had his back to a crowd, hoping for privacy.

"Yes-s-s." I drew out the words cautiously.

"All right. Making sure."

I skimmed the parking lot, wondering if this was a joke and Romero had been following me. "Where are you?"

"I'm on a case."

Good grief, he could be vague. I squinted, not giving up my search for his vehicle. "You sound awfully close. You wouldn't happen to be following me, would you?"

There was a short pause. "Should I be?"

"No, no," I rushed out. *Dang.* Now I'd opened a can of worms. Next, he'd be inquiring where *I* was, and I had no intention of telling him I was about to ask Gibson for help in accessing Jock's computer. Before the fact, anyway. "I'm heading home from my parents' with some stuffed peppers." It wasn't an outright lie.

"Good. Gotta go. Just checking in." And he hung up.

That was weird. A phone call out of nowhere. The reason: checking in. *Don't knock it, sweetheart. It's how a tough cop who's juggling a dozen cases shows he cares.* I guess, I argued. I shoved the phone back in my bag, reflecting on Romero's gesture, when there was a sharp *rap rap rap* on the driver's side window.

I clapped my hand to my heart and nearly flew out my sunroof. Grinding my teeth, I reeled around and glared out the window. *Candace*, standing there like the neighborhood watch.

I caught my breath, charged out of my car, and slammed the door shut. "What are you trying to do, scare the daylights out of me?" Anyone else, I might've shown mercy.

Even with Candace's looming presence, she was barely recognizable. She was dressed in another Amish-type frock, her face was free of makeup, and her blond hair was pulled back in a tight bun. The last time I'd seen Candace with her hair in a bun, she'd been playing cops and robbers, skimpily dressed as the local sheriff. If she hadn't presently been standing beside her red Corvette, I would've thought she was waiting for a horse and plow to till a field.

"If anyone had the daylights scared out of her, it was *me*!" She jabbed her bare finger onto her compressed boobs.

"Candace, I don't speak baboon. How about you explain yourself before I get back in my Bug and zoom away."

"That's just it," she said, tight-mouthed. "The kook zoomed away and almost nicked my Corvette."

"What kook?" And why was I having this conversation with the queen of kooks?

She balled her hands into fists, obviously still angry from her ordeal. "I pulled onto Jacinth Avenue and thought I spotted your yellow kiddie car half a mile ahead."

I interrupted her. "Candace, if you were on Jacinth Avenue with all its twists and turns, you'd be lucky to see the car in front of you, let alone my yellow Bug from half a mile ahead."

She leaned in with her chest, flat as it was, and rolled back her lips. "I told you I *saw* it. Not only that, but this kook almost took the rear end off my 'Vette, speeding past me to catch up to *you*."

Now she had my attention. A wisp of unease slithered

up my spine, her words ringing in my ears. "Are you sure, Candace?"

"What do I look like? I fell off a turnip truck?"

A better picture couldn't have been painted, but I wasn't going to waste time exchanging insults. What's more, the unease creeping up my spine was branching out to all parts of my body. "What was this kook driving?"

"Some kind of motorcycle. It had a throaty growl and low whine." She threw her hands on her hips and surveyed the parking lot. "I thought I followed the bike into the strip mall, but I don't see it anywhere."

I, too, glanced around the lot, wondering where the biker had picked up my trail. "What do you mean, you *thought*? Did you follow it here or not?"

"There were other vehicles in the way, *you know*. I couldn't zip around everyone to catch up. But I was certain the bike pulled in here." She scowled, her nostrils flared. Candace in hunt mode. "Didn't you notice someone trailing you?"

"No, I didn't."

Something about Candace's description of the bike triggered memories of last night. I remembered the sounds of an engine and tires burning rubber from Jock's lot. Maybe the noise from a vehicle had been drowned out by police sirens, as Romero had suggested, and maybe that vehicle belonged to Jock. But now that I thought about it, the engine noise that had alarmed me wasn't that of a car. It was a motorcycle that had made that distinctive growl and whine. Was it the same bike? The same driver?

Could today's driver be Jock? His bike had been having maintenance. Maybe he had it back. And what about Romero? Last time he'd visited, he'd been riding a motorcycle. Plus, right now his whereabouts were unknown.

A shiver rocked my body because deep down I feared the driver was neither of these men. I looked for signs around the strip mall of the horrifying masked man I'd stabbed with my earring. Was he tracking me? He'd already fought with Jock and attacked me once. Was he looking to do more?

"Why would someone be following you, anyway?" Candace pumped, bringing me back to the present.

I gave myself a moment to calm my nerves, then looked her straight in the eye. "If you want to know, Candace, Jock was attacked last night after the ballet, and he's missing." Not that I wanted to share anything with this floozy, but at this point, if anyone could provide information on Jock's whereabouts, I'd take it.

"*What?*" The color on her makeup-free face drained, and she looked so bereft I thought her bottom lip might start quivering. "We were a perfect item, and now he's *gone?*"

I nearly choked on my spit. "You were never an item, Candace."

She stuck out her chest and flung her head back as if she had a long, flowing mane getting in her way. "You're jealous because he secretly adored me. And now you probably chased him away."

Was she not hearing me? "Candace, Jock was assaulted. We went back to his place after the ballet, and someone came to his condo and attacked him."

Wait a second. If the assailant had been on a bike, and he'd abducted Jock, who was likely injured from the brawl, then who drove Jock's car away? Was there a second perpetrator? Someone who'd arrived with the assailant, then waited in the shadows until Jock had been beaten?

If Jock *had* been injured, had he passed out? Been strapped down to the bike? Drugged? Or had he been thrown in the trunk of the car? This made more sense if there had been two assailants—one to drive the Porsche, the other, the bike.

Or…

What if it was the other way around? Suppose Jock took off on the bike and left the offender or offenders behind? I presumed even naïve criminals would've figured out a way to start his car. No. Jock never would have left me in danger like that.

Did they all leave happily together? Beat each other senseless and then start their engines and go for a joyride? Right. Not even a small chance.

I couldn't come up with a scenario that made sense or a theory that wasn't full of holes, but I was suddenly overwhelmed with the thought that maybe I'd been wrong about Jock all along. Maybe he didn't care about me. I *was* merely his employer. I'd made *that* clear numerous times.

It took me a second to swallow that notion and the implications it produced. Putting feelings aside, I had to plunge on. There was still the mystery of the bike and whatever happened to a man who was important to me. And nothing would stop me from finding out the truth.

Chapter 8

M y interaction with Candace was, as usual, something I wished I could forget. But today she had me thinking. She bustled back to her car, thrust herself into the driver's seat, and screeched out of the parking lot. Marvelous. She couldn't catch the kook trailing me, but she could go from zero to sixty in three seconds.

I took another wary look around and told myself that even if someone were lurking, no one would attack me in broad daylight. I didn't know if I was being stupid or optimistic, but I took it as a win that I didn't spot anyone suspicious on my radar.

Since Gibson would be closing soon, I set my shoulders back, put on a brave face, and marched through the door of his shop.

The Computer Store was not the type of place I'd normally frequent. There was no sparkle, no fragrant smells, and no attractive displays. Aisles of computer hardware filled the store, the air reeked of plastic wrap and computer ink, and the only display was a tall, lanky employee at the front desk who had his head buried in a computer manual.

The worker looked up when the bell tinkled above the door, announcing my arrival. "Can I help you?"

I meandered to the desk, bag over my shoulder. "Is Gibson working today?"

"Yeah." He looked me up and down in my hot pink dress, making it two of us who noted this wasn't the type of shop I'd usually frequent. "Gibson's in the other room. Go through that archway. I'll tell him someone's coming." He fingered a wire hanging by his chest, said a few words into the headset around his ears, and gave me a nod.

I thanked him and wandered into the next room. Dozens of laptops and other devices were piled on a table and the floor, work orders taped to them. In the middle of the room, Gibson sat at a desk behind a computer, eyes glued to the screen. His wavy brown hair was parted down the middle as always, his horn-rimmed glasses framing his plump face.

"Hi, Valentine," he said without enthusiasm, barely looking away from his screen.

"How's it going?" Not that I needed fanfare when I entered a room, but a bit of eye contact would've been nice.

He took his finger and slid his glasses up to his bushy eyebrows. "Fine." A second later, his glasses slid back down, the nose pads settling once again in their indented spots.

Gibson was far from making the cover of *GQ*, but with an eyebrow wax, a new haircut, and contact lenses, he could draw some attention. Unfortunately, that would all have to wait for another time. I pressed on and asked what he was doing tonight.

He peered over his glasses at me, a bead of sweat popping up on his brow as if I'd invited him to an orgy. He shifted his weight to my left and glanced past my shoulder. "Did Riley put you up to this?"

I looked behind me. "Riley?"

"Yeah. You spoke to him at the front desk."

"No. Riley has nothing to do with this. I need your help with something."

He centered back in his seat, fingers clicking the keyboard. "I'm busy tonight."

"With what? You close in an hour, right?"

"Yeah. I have stuff to do."

"More important stuff than making a quick fifty bucks?"

I didn't know where that came from, but I needed Gibson's help. If worse came to worse, I'd double that.

He stopped typing and raised his head, the thought of making extra cash a clear motivator. "What do you need?"

"I don't have time to explain it here." Especially when he'd have the opportunity to say no. I scribbled Jock's address—now inscribed in my brain—on a piece of paper by the desk and handed it to him. "Meet me at this address at seven-thirty. I'll fill you in then."

I walked into my house, set the still-warm dolma my mother had given me on the kitchen counter, and opened the fridge door. Wow. Things were looking up. Veal parmigiana *and* stuffed peppers. Being young and unmarried had its perks.

I took out the yogurt and cracked open the lid. "I have a surprise for you," I sang to Yitts.

There was a slight rustling of kitty litter in the other room, then silence. The rustling picked up, then ceased again. Yitts deciding on the exact spot to do her business.

I dished out a stuffed pepper for myself, dug out a small portion of meat for her, and placed it in a tiny saucer with a dollop of yogurt on top.

I wolfed down my pepper, it suddenly occurring to me I hadn't eaten lunch today. No kidding. Filling in for Jock was no easy task, plus, it had been too busy a day to think about food.

Yitts galloped into the kitchen, reached up, and balanced one paw on my knee, the other on the cupboard door, anxious to see what I had for her. I knelt beside her and put the saucer on the kitchen floor. She purred out a meow I took for thanks and gobbled up the dolma.

I patted her head, then hustled into the bedroom to change out of my neon pink dress for tonight's mission. There was no need to stand out like a flashing sign or raise suspicion if I ran into anyone in Jock's neighborhood.

Dressing in full camo gear or head-to-toe black wasn't necessary either. Casual and comfortable was my best bet.

I searched through my drawers, fingering the black boat-neck top I'd worn during a past case. After Jock had seen me in my slinky black outfit, he'd dubbed me Catwoman. Wiseass.

I stuffed down the memory, determined to focus on tonight's goal. I pulled the hairband from my hair and opted for casual jeans and a brown top. Then I called Twix to make sure she'd be ready at seven.

"I'm having problems deciding what to wear." Twix sighed into the phone, signaling this was serious business.

"You're not going to the symphony," I said.

"Duh. I know that. How often do you think I go out, except for play dates in the park or to the doctor's office to pull a pea out of a kid's nose?"

I understood. At one time, Twix wouldn't have been caught dead in polyester pants and baggy T-shirts. Having kids changed all that.

"What are *you* wearing?" she asked as if we were going on double dates.

"A brown top."

"A brown top. Since when did you ever wear a plain brown top?"

"The cap sleeves are satin, and there's a brown satin bow at the front. Does that suffice?"

"Sounds more like you, but I still don't know what to dig out of the closet."

"Find something. I'll be there in half an hour. Be ready."

"Ten-four." And she hung up.

"Slight change of plans." Twix paraded down her driveway in a black Aerosmith T-shirt, a black leather vest, tights, and spiked black boots that stretched over the knees. Plus, she had something that looked like a tire chain around her neck. Her brown hair was teased out like a rock star, she was wearing black gloves with the fingers cut out, and she was carrying an unidentified tot under her arm and a diaper bag over her shoulder.

I didn't know what to comment on first: the fact she was dressed as if she were on her way to a biker bar or that she had an infant dangling from her hip. I opted for the latter. Less confrontational.

"Um, do you know that the kid you're holding isn't Joey...or Junie?" I leaned against my Bug, right ankle crossed over my left foot, arms folded in front.

"Aren't you the funny one! *Yes*, I know this one doesn't belong to me. This is Lambert. His mom had an emergency dental appointment, and I offered to look after the little beast till she was done."

"And?"

She slid open the backseat door to their family van. "And what? I didn't mention him earlier because it's not interfering with our plans. We'll drop him off on the way to Jock's." She stuck her head in the backseat, chucked the diaper bag on the floor, and buckled Lambert in one of the kids' car seats. Then she slid the door shut and dusted off her gloved hands as if she'd handled a sack of potatoes. "Well?" She opened the driver's side door. "What are you waiting for?"

I tossed her the lotion meant for Peaches. "For you to tell me this is a joke. And what have you done with my friend Twix?"

"Ha. Ha." She thanked me for the lotion, threw it inside, and slid behind the wheel. "Get in. Lambert lives around the corner."

"Whoa. I'll take my own car, thank you very much."

She pivoted around on her seat to face me, her left heel poised on the step panel. "How's that going to look? You need to navigate. And I can't take Lambert home in this outfit. His mother will think I've been dipping into the sauce."

I glanced from the *Baby on Board* sign on the back window to Twix in her spiked boots and questionable jewelry. "Have you?"

"Look, I need a night out. Excuse me if I overdressed. When we get to Lambert's, all you need to do is deposit him at the front door."

"Sounds like he's a parcel, and we're UPS. Won't his mother be concerned that a stranger is handing over her baby?"

"Sally will be so high from her procedure, she won't care if you were the Wicked Witch of the West."

I stared at several other baby-type stickers on the back window. "We can't go to Jock's in your babymobile."

She huffed, nearing her limit. "You want to draw attention in your yellow Bug?"

She had a point.

"No one will suspect a thing with a family van pulling into his driveway. Now let's go."

Jock's *driveway* was more a parking lot, but Twix would learn that for herself soon enough. She started the engine, and immediately "The Wheels on the Bus" blared through the speakers. She smacked the volume down. "Junie crammed a CD into the player, forgetting there was already one in there. Jammed the whole system. Now we listen to 'The Wheels on the Bus' wherever we go, over and over again."

"Sounds delightful." Why was I already regretting this night?

Ten minutes later, Twix rolled to a safe stop in front of Lambert's house.

I gawked at her carefully putting the van into park. "You didn't tell me this thing doesn't go any faster than a baby stroller."

She looked taken aback. "You didn't expect me to drive at breakneck speed with a baby on board, did you?"

"No. But I didn't expect my hair to grow half an inch in the time it took to drive around the corner. And I *would* like to get to Jock's before Thanksgiving."

"Don't worry. I've got it covered."

I gave her a peeved glare, asking myself how I allowed her to talk me into this foolish scheme. Then I unfastened my seatbelt, let it fling back in place with a loud *snap*, and hooked the diaper bag over my shoulder. Huh. It was as heavy as my beauty bag. While interesting in and of itself, I didn't waste time oohing and ahhing over similarities in bags.

I unbuckled Lambert from his car seat, cooed a few words in baby talk, thinking he'd understand my attempt at being friendly, and hoisted him into my arms. He gave me an unsure look and spit up on my chest. Wonderful. Didn't even thank me for the ride.

I glanced back at Twix, trying to control my impatience.

"Go on," she called out the window at me, tapping something on her phone. "They're expecting you."

I made the dropoff without further incident and buckled back into my seat. Then I tugged a baby wipe from a container by the console and rubbed the throw-up from my chest. "Remind me never to have kids."

"*Pff.* That's nothing. You should see what comes out the other end." She put the van in gear and crawled away from the curb, busy obeying signs and speed limits.

I cut her a miffed look. "If it takes us an hour to get to Cambridge, I'm going to kill myself."

"We'll get there. Don't you worry."

By the time we got to Jock's, it was seven-twenty. Gibson was nowhere in sight. Fine. I wanted to search the outside again anyway for Jock's phone or anything else that might be a clue as to where he'd gone.

Twix pulled into the middle of the lot, her head stretched forward over the steering wheel, her eyes focused on the ancient pulp and paper plant in front of us. "Ooh, isn't it romantic? An old brick factory, remnants of the company name still etched on the wall. And look at all those windows!" She was like a kid at Disneyland. "I knew Jock would live in something unconventional. I mean, he's not the kind of guy to live in an ordinary apartment building… or a house." She sighed dreamily. "It's so perfect…and so Jock."

I didn't have time to wait until she came back to earth.

"Are you done gushing? Or should I go on without you?"

She overlooked my sarcasm and blinked at the lot. "Where's his bike?"

"At the garage." *I think.* "He's driving a Porsche."

She swiveled toward me so fast, her tire chain clanked on the steering wheel. "You didn't tell me Jock had a Porsche."

I unbuckled my seatbelt, remembering my luxurious ride in his car. "I just did. And it goes a hell of a lot faster than this nursery on wheels."

She eyed me stonily. "Are you always this testy, or is there something else going on I should know about?" She tapped her fingers on the console, demanding an answer. "Is everything okay with that hot-blooded Lord of Italians?"

I shifted in my seat at her reference to Romero, my mind drifting back to our recent acrobatic lovemaking. "Yes, everything is okay with the hot-blooded Lord of Italians."

"Whew. For a minute, I thought you were going to say you had a fight."

We both knew that wouldn't be a first. "I'm sorry, Twix. Jock's disappearance is getting to me. The truth is, his bike needed maintenance. That's why he's driving a Porsche."

"Must be nice." She looked around the inside of her van littered with baby toys, crayon marks on the seats, and a package of extra diapers. "You're right. This van is a nursery on wheels. And it smells of apple juice. Does it smell of apple juice to you? Hey, you think Jock would consider swapping vehicles?"

"*Twix.*" If I didn't get her back on track, I'd never get this night over with. "Jock's Porsche is gone. Jock's gone. He was attacked last night, and he's disappeared."

"Right. Sorry. I got carried away with the lifestyles of the rich and famous."

I gave a long sigh and squinted at the building. "I've racked my brain with different scenarios, hoping something would shed light on what could've happened to him. The stress of not knowing is making me jumpy."

She patted my arm. "We'll find him." She shoved her van keys in her vest pocket and hopped outside. "What are we looking for first?"

I slammed the van door behind me, bag in hand, and surveyed the ground as we neared the factory. "Jock's phone. I can't get in touch with him, and I figured there's a possibility he might have lost it last night during the scuffle."

"So? What if we find it?"

"I want to know who called him at the ballet. Whoever it was has something to do with his disappearance. I can feel it."

"Good thinking. If I could find Junie's Polly Pocket shoe in a crack between our neighbor's flagstones, I can find anything." Without batting an eye, she hunched forward, her neck chain hanging a foot from the ground, and combed the earth like she was searching for a buried landmine.

We scoured the entire parking lot and the sides of the building, hunting for anything else that might seem significant. We met up in front, empty-handed.

We were about to head inside when a dark car pulled into the lot. "That's Gibson," I said to Twix.

She wrinkled up her nose. "Not that awkward, pain-in-the-ass kid who used to fart in his grandma's pool and pelt iced snowballs at you."

"The very same."

"What's he doing here?"

I explained as Gibson parked beside her van, remembering I needed to fill in Gibson, too.

"Thank heavens." Twix rolled her eyes. "I was afraid you were going to tell me this was a date."

"He's changed." I watched Gibson exit his car, shut the door on his seatbelt buckle, reopen the door, and shut it again. Then he hoisted up his pants, scratched his head, and plodded toward us as if he were on his way to the guillotine. "For the most part," I added under my breath.

Twix ambled to the rolling door where I told her to wait. I pulled Jock's keys from my bag, walked over to Gibson, and explained why he was here.

"Hold your horses." Gibson planted his hands on his wide hips, his voice unbelieving. "You want me to break into another person's home, hack into his computer, and give you the password?"

"No!" Feigned indignation was my specialty. "We're not breaking in. I have access." I dangled Jock's keys high in front of us. "And you wouldn't be hacking his laptop."

"What do you call it?"

"I don't know. I'm not the computer expert—which is why I need your help. But I don't want to ruin anything on Jock's laptop. I only want you to find a way for me to check his emails and stuff."

"And stuff." Gibson sounded disgusted.

Before he had a chance to comment further, I produced the fifty bucks out of my bag, tucked it in his shirt pocket, and gave his chest a pat. "As promised."

He slid me a miserable, cynical look. "I'd rather go to jail."

"Gibson…" I purred, weaving my arm through his, leading him toward the condo. "No one is going to jail. The cops won't even know we're here. And you might end up saving a life. We don't know what happened to Jock. If he's in danger, something I unearth on his laptop may lead to finding him and catching a felon."

"I don't know." He bit his lip, stopping cold, eyes on the condo. "Who's that?"

I glanced from Gibson to the woman trampoline-bouncing at the factory wall, trying to see in the windows. "My friend, Twix."

"Like the chocolate bar?"

"Yes."

Gibson looked from Twix back to me. "Why is she dressed like Hells Angels?"

"She, uh, just came off a shift. She works at a motorcycle plant."

"What plant? What parts do they make?"

"Some plant near Springfield. They make bike parts. You know. Fenders. Wheels. Bells."

"Bicycle bells?" He scrunched up his nose as if thinking of his next question. Couldn't blame him since *I* would've asked for elaboration on the dumb answers I was giving.

"Come on, Gibson." I dragged him along. "We don't have time for questions. Jock's life could be hanging in the balance."

"I...I..." He faltered and came to another halt.

"Look, do you want Jock's death on your hands?" It was a cruel thing to say, but I was running out of reasons why I needed his help, and my patience was wearing thin.

"No," he mumbled, letting out a sigh. "Just a minute. I need my laptop." Reluctantly, he shuffled back to his car, pulled out a briefcase, then followed me to the condo.

I made the introductions brief, then stepped over to the slit in the brick wall where Jock had swiped the fob last night. Now that I was closer to the mechanism, I noticed a keypad with numbers and letters. Probably for entry using a fancy code that Jock had rigged up. I squeezed the keys in my palm. Hallelujah! I had the fob.

I slipped the rectangular tag through the slit, and immediately the garage door rolled up, clanking and clunking.

"Why is there a hole in the door?" Gibson shouted over the noise.

"Uh, I think Jock is remodeling the garage." Why get him more perturbed?

As before, the door stopped rolling up where the hole seemed to damage the track. We crawled under it and climbed the cement stairs where I used the fob again to unlock the door to Jock's condo.

Twix made herself at home, flicking on lights, touching furniture, opening and closing drawers, while Gibson hooked his device up to Jock's laptop.

"How cool is this!" Twix stood on the dining room table, hands clenched around the long black rope hanging from the ceiling with the single light bulb attached at the bottom. She wrapped her long boot-clad legs around the cord like a pole dancer and swung back and forth, causing the light to fluctuate around the room.

Gibson's jaw plummeted to his double chin. "Is she always this excitable?"

"Yes." I dropped my bag by the desk and shook my head at Twix. "You're going to break that light fixture."

She peered up to where it was fixed at the wooden beams. "Not a chance." She was making circles in the air, clinging to the rope with her left hand, swinging her tire chain around her neck with her right like a first-rate striptease.

Why me?

She landed on the table, hopped to the floor, and waltzed around the vast empty space, spinning in sweeping circles like Cinderella at the ball.

Gibson looked as if he'd swallowed his tongue. He spun around to his computer and tapped the keyboard like he wanted to do his job and get the hell out of here. Meanwhile, I did a brief search for Jock's phone, having a sneaking suspicion I wouldn't find it anywhere.

I stood at the bottom of the curved staircase, looking up, tempted to climb the next level and peek in Jock's bedroom. I felt a bit dizzy at the prospect of what I might find.

No. Snooping in the man's bedroom didn't feel right. I already knew Jock, didn't I? True, he was sexy, alluring, and persuasive, and could without a doubt talk the skirt off any female. Yet I couldn't bring myself to go there, physically or mentally. I could barely keep up to the exhilarating sex I'd been having with Romero. Who knew what sexual escapades a man like Jock entertained?

I swallowed down a lump and restrained my nose from twitching. Realistically, I knew I might need to search upstairs even if I didn't want to. But first, I'd see what turned up on this floor. Surely the information I needed would be on Jock's laptop.

I turned my back on the staircase and traipsed once again to the alcove under the second-floor landing where Gibson was hunched over the desk, muttering to himself.

"What's the problem?" I asked. "I thought you'd have cracked the code by now."

He took his finger and slid his glasses up his nose, granting me a disgruntled look. "This isn't splitting open a bicycle lock, you know. If he'd used his name or a birthdate, we'd have broken in long ago. But it takes time to figure these things out."

Boy, grumpy or what. "Could you figure it out faster, please? I haven't got all night."

Gibson clicked away, head down. "You got some hot date waiting, or what?"

"Yeah." With Phyllis at the Geisha Gap. How did I get myself in these messes? Of course, if Gibson didn't have any luck soon, I wouldn't make that date either.

The clock ticked by. I could tell Gibson was close to gaining entry past Jock's locked screen.

Suddenly, there was a *smash* on the other side of the room followed by another *smash*.

Chapter 9

Twix! I whipped around from leaning over Gibson. "What happened?"

"Oops." She gawked down at the mess she'd made.

I stomped across the living room to where she was standing in front of the sideboard cupboard in the corner. There was glass all over the floor.

"Tell me you didn't break Jock's glass ship."

"Well?" she croaked. "Why'd he have it sitting so close to the edge?"

"Gee, I don't know! Maybe because he figured no one with slippery gloved fingers would touch his personal things." I almost didn't recognize my shrill voice. "And what's that?"

"What?" She looked down to where I was pointing.

"A broken picture frame?"

"Oops."

"Again with the *oops*."

"It's just, I was reaching for the picture, and I guess I knocked over the ship. Then, startled that I dropped the ship, I accidentally dropped the picture."

I knelt and picked up the bent white-gold metal frame. It was the picture I'd seen last night after the ballet. Four men in white uniforms, naval uniforms as I now noticed. Of course, that was all I could tell. "Look at it. It's cracked beyond repair. You can't even make out who's who."

"We'll fix it, and we'll clean up the mess." Twix took a step back from the shattered glass on the floor in an attempt not to crunch any more bits under her boots.

"Eureka!" Gibson shouted from across the room. "I got you in, and now I'm leaving." He gathered his stuff, scraped the chair back, and headed for the door. "Goodbye."

"Wait!" I hurried over to him, his feet already clumping down the garage stairs. "What was the password?"

He twisted around and looked up at me standing in the doorway. "Basically just a random combination of letters, numbers, and symbols."

My shoulders relaxed, and I gave him an encouraging smile. "See? You were a big help."

He grunted. "You're welcome." He ducked under the garage door and disappeared, and I trotted back into the condo, not sure what to do with the broken picture frame in my hand.

"Where's Jock's dustpan?" Twix asked, slamming kitchen cupboard doors.

"Gosh, I don't know. Hanging by the lights you were swinging on a while ago?"

She opened another door and eyed me from across the room. "It was only one light I swung from, and I don't see a dustpan anywhere."

"Keep looking. Meantime, I have access to Jock's computer. Give me a few minutes to see what I can find."

I nestled into the cozy alcove, plunked the frame on the desk, and clicked on the screen. I opened a couple of folders and found nothing I deemed important. There were movie files. Numerous printable stuntman badges he'd earned. Master-at-arms certificates. Motorcycle documents. Computer virus protectors. Nothing secretive or private.

I scrolled through his emails, pushing down the guilt that was niggling me about reading his personal stuff. If he'd been a stranger, it would've been different. But Jock was a co-worker and a close friend, someone who should be able to trust me. Somehow, that made this more taboo.

I tapped my fingers on the mouse, debating about

continuing. I wasn't doing this for personal gain. I was prying because a man's life was at stake. And that man was Jock de Marco. Far as I could see, there wasn't a moment to waste.

I clicked the mouse with determination and found recent contacts with the Porsche dealership, the Harley-Davidson dealer, and a few with his family in Argentina, especially his sister who plainly liked keeping Jock up to date with the health and well-being of his parents. *Drat.* Nothing that spelled danger. Whoever contacted Jock last night at the ballet must've texted back later—if it was the same person—because Jock certainly had communication with someone.

My gaze shifted to the trash folder. I didn't think for one moment there'd be anything to see there. I clicked it anyway.

Wait. A. Minute. What was this?

I opened the email from a no-reply address. The same diamond-shaped symbol stared up at me that I'd seen last night before Jock slammed the laptop lid down. Jackpot! But this wasn't any diamond-shaped symbol. This was a kite. A *kite.* What did that have to do with anything? Jock sprang into action after seeing it, but what was its significance?

I took a closer look at the colorful image and let my gaze slide down to the bottom of the email. It said, *It's Tork.* Underneath that, it read, *823 Hock,* and it was signed *Vick.* None of this made sense. Who were Tork and Vick?

Hold on. Jock typed something short before he tore himself away from the computer. I visualized that moment in my mind. *Darn.* He'd tapped that something on his phone, not the computer. His urgent response must've been via text. Had he responded to the person who'd texted *him*? Was it the same person who'd sent the kite email? Another reason why I needed to find his phone. Knowing what his text said or who he sent it to might explain what happened to him.

I raised my eyes to the second-floor landing above me. I'd looked everywhere on this level for his phone. Was it possible it was upstairs? No. He'd had it on him, and then he went straight outside to face his attacker. If it wasn't on this floor, then it was gone. I had to move on and accept that the phone was a dead end.

I fiddled on the laptop for another moment. I clicked on some other folders but didn't learn anything else worth noting. I had Jock's keys. That was most important. I could come back if I chose.

My gaze wandered to the cracked frame beside me. I leaned in and examined it again. The metal was already ruined. Would it matter if I took it apart? If I didn't, I wouldn't see who these men were in the picture.

I exhaled a deep breath. If I was going to finish it off, I might as well make quick work of it. I pried the cold metal casing apart, slid out the four-by-six photo, and blew off the tiny remaining glass shavings from the surface into a wastepaper basket under the desk.

Feeling like an undercover spy, I studied the picture in the shadows of my little nook under the stairs, deciphering as many details as possible. Dressed in white naval uniforms were four men, arm in arm, laughing faces, a ship and harbor in the background. Jock was on the left and easily recognizable. He was leaner, his jawline more angular, his hair buzzed short like the other men in the photo.

Next to Jock was another sturdy sailor his size. Friendly face with carved lines around his eyes and mouth. He looked like a thinker. Next to this man was the smallest of the four. He appeared younger than the others with a touch of innocence in his fresh face. Closing the right end was the burliest of the four. His hair was dark, and he had a similar smile and features as the smaller man. I didn't recognize any of them, but they seemed like the best of friends.

I was about to flip the photo over, hoping there'd be names on the back to go with the faces, when suddenly I heard a noise. I stiffened in my seat, an eerie silence surrounding me. I jerked my head over my right shoulder and looked past the living room to the far corner. Nothing moved or had been disturbed. I slid my gaze back toward the kitchen where I'd left Twix looking for a dustpan. No Twix.

No Twix!

My heart thrashed in my chest as visions of last night's attack came back to haunt me. I fought to ignore it and glanced at the door. No one had come in or out. That much I was sure of. Yet where could Twix have gone in the span of ten minutes?

I dumped the photo and frame into my bag on the floor, shot out of my chair, and whirled into the middle of the condo.

"Twix?" I ventured softly, my voice cracking.

"Yes," she sang.

"Where are you?"

"Up here, darling." Her calm voice came from the top of the stairs.

I exhaled with relief that she was okay, then a new fear took hold. She couldn't have! She wouldn't dare! I took the steps two at a time and found Twix in a room to the right at the top of the landing, sprawled out on Jock's extra-long, king-sized bed.

"What are you doing?" I shrieked, partly from shock at Twix's audacity, partly from worry at being found out that we'd entered Jock's boudoir uninvited. Honestly, I might have marched back into his home without his knowledge, and I might have cracked into his computer, but invading his private bedroom seemed like breaking into a shrine.

"What does it look like I'm doing?" The stylish soft lights in the ceiling beamed down on her as she flapped her arms up and down on the charcoal duvet as if she were making angels in the snow. Yitts made a similar move when she rolled and scratched her back on the porch, meowing with pleasure.

My gaze roamed from Twix to Jock's dimly lit bedroom, a high peep escaping from inside my throat. This was everything I'd imagined and more. Tasteful bedding with white accents. Man-sized pillows. Brick walls. Wood paneling. Skylight.

A dark gray, walk-in closet with two levels of coat racks, built-in shelves, and a floor-to-ceiling sliding door that was open, provided more chic lighting. My gaze fell to the corner of the closet where I recognized the suitcase that Jock had brought on our cruise.

Instantly, a hot rush tore from my toes to my face as memories flooded me of our night together in his luxurious suite. A night that might've turned into much more under different circumstances.

My heart kicked in my chest, my legs shaky. Here I was in another of Jock's bedrooms where he…he…I couldn't even say the words. *Okay.* Where Jock made hard, passionate love! I felt like I was cheating on Romero simply by standing here.

"Feel these sheets," Twix purred. "They've got to be Egyptian cotton."

I forgot about my reticence and snuck over to the massive bed. I ran my fingers along the luxurious fabric. Twix was right. Sheets like this would literally slide right off your body. I mean, if you happened to find yourself wrapped up in one.

I pulled away, coming to my senses. "Come on, Twix. We need to go."

My partner in crime evidently didn't have similar feelings of betrayal. "Do we have to?" She squirmed this way and that, her head smothered in the duvet.

"Yes, we have to." I leaned over the bed, grabbed her by the arm, and tugged.

She jerked to the side, getting up, and a second later we heard *riiiip*. "Oh no!"

I unhanded her and squeezed my eyes tight. "Don't tell me. I don't want to know."

"It's my chain. It snagged on the duvet."

I opened one eye, expecting the worst. It was worse than the worst. Twix's neck chain had produced a gaping hole in the luxurious material. "Why are you wearing something so gaudy in the first place?" I hopped on the bed and worked the hefty chain back and forth to free it.

"I was getting into character for tonight's mission."

"As what? A henchman? Even Gibson wondered why you were dressed like Hells Angels."

"Who cares what Gibson thinks?"

"Apparently not you!" I gave one final yank and freed Twix's chain from the duvet. "How am I explaining this to Jock?" If Twix hadn't been my friend, I would've choked her.

"I don't know!" she vented. "Maybe he'll think mice got into his place. Or that someone broke in, like his attacker, and had a party in his condo."

"Or maybe he'll think his noodle-head boss came back snooping. He'll kill me when he finds out the truth!"

"Jock would never lay a hand on you. He loves you."

I rolled off the bed, instantly overcome by emotion. "Jock doesn't love me."

"Yes, Valentine, he does." It was the first time all night she sounded solemn.

Without meaning for it to happen, a fresh tear ran down my cheek, and I realized with a sudden stabbing pang that I missed Jock terribly.

Twix leaped off the bed and waved a hand in front of my face. "You okay?"

I let out a shuddery breath, the weight of the worry crashing down on me. "It's all happening so fast. Last night. The ballet. The fight. Jock's disappearance. I have to find him, Twix."

"We will." She looked back at the bed, twitching her lips with regret. "We'll make the bed up nice and pretty, and we'll flip over the duvet. He'll never know the difference."

"Right." I swiped away the tear. "Until he tosses the duvet back over."

She shrugged. "Why worry about that until it happens?"

This was what having a best friend was all about? Cripes.

We fixed the bed, hurried downstairs, and stopped short by the alcove.

"What?" Twix looked at me expectantly.

The sun had set a while ago, which meant it had to be

after nine. I should've been happy I'd discovered the email on Jock's laptop. I'd even bagged the photograph, which may or may not have been important. But I needed to see if there were any other pictures lying around. The more photos I had, the more chances I'd have of piecing together Jock's past and perhaps coming up with a link to his disappearance.

Without answering her, I retrieved my bag from where I'd parked it at the desk and paraded over to the sideboard cupboard. Skirting the mess of glass, I ferreted through the drawers.

Twix was on my heels. "What are you looking for now?"

"More pictures." I opened the third and final drawer and discovered a small stack of photos. Pictures of Jock and various people, some in uniform, others casual. I stuffed the pictures in my bag, turned, and bumped into Twix, standing behind me.

"Aren't you getting carried away?"

"What do you mean?"

She gestured to the cupboard. "You just cleaned out that drawer."

"Oh." I shoved my hands on my hips. "It's okay that you broke Jock's ship, swung from his lights, and"—I pointed to the stairs—"ripped his duvet. But I snatch a few pictures in order to find my missing employee, and suddenly *I'm* getting carried away."

She tightened her lips. "You don't have to get crabby about it."

I let out a heavy sigh, then focused on the broken ship at our feet. "Help me with this."

We swept the broken glass into a pile.

"Now what?" Twix asked.

"Well, we can't leave it here." I looked around for something to put the glass chunks into.

"What do you mean? What are you going to do with it?"

"Try to repair it. If Jock comes home and sees his prized ship broken to pieces, he *will* kill me. Trust me, the guy may not have a lot of toys, but he looks after what he does have."

She stared me up and down, then looked down at herself. "If it's between the two of us, you're the one with a bag. I suggest we dump the glass in that."

"What? I'm not dumping shards of glass in there. Hang on." I hunted through my bag and found my black hair cape. "Here. We'll sweep the glass inside this. I've got some Super Glue at the shop. I'll fix it there."

We made short work of tidying up, then shut off the lights, and crept back down the worn garage stairs like the horrible snoops we were.

"I can't see where I'm going." Twix tripped in her stripper boots and grabbed my arm.

I held onto her and was about to duck under the garage door when a motorcycle rumbled into the parking lot.

My heart leaped at the noise. Jock! He was okay? *Had* his bike been fixed? I waited a second, listening to the noise before moving another step. Hold on. That wasn't the sound of Jock's bike. Harleys had a rumble all their own. This one had a low whine and throaty growl…like the bike Candace had said was following me.

Goose bumps prickled my arms, and my forehead broke out in a sweat for fear it was the same person coming after me. Wait. Candace could've been mistaken about someone on my tail. Or maybe the biker thought it was someone else driving a yellow Bug. After all, I didn't have my car at Jock's last night, and I didn't have it tonight either. So who knew I drove one?

Jock's keys were somewhere deep in my bag. No time to dig for them to close the garage door. Plus, I didn't want to alert the intruder that we were here. I pushed Twix into the corner of the garage, shushing her complaints.

"What will we hide under?" she whispered, her voice hoarse.

Thank goodness the garage was dark. But other than a few garbage cans, a ladder, a couple of sawhorses, and other gadgets possibly from Jock's stunt-doubling or master-at-arms days, there wasn't a whole lot to cover us in an emergency.

I peeked down at the black cape I still had bundled in my hands. I had no choice but to use it for cover. Mutely, I tipped the glass fragments in the corner by the garbage cans and dragged a sawhorse beside the cans. I heaved Twix close to me, and we squatted behind the sawhorse. Hoping my idea would make us invisible, I tossed the black cape over the horse's spine and covered us both.

Oh no. Twix's van was out in the middle of the parking lot. *Crap.* Now what? If someone *was* after me, in all probability that person knew what I drove. Right? No Bug. No Valentine. But if that person saw the babymobile, then what?

Anyone would think it was a random person parked in an empty lot. Maybe a stressed parent taking advantage of another location to park and take a baby for a night stroll. Hadn't Holly done that with her kids when they were newborns? Surely the car seats would indicate this notion. Or perhaps someone was using the lot for carpooling. If we were quiet, the biker might keep on motoring.

Unfortunately, the roar of the motorcycle came to a halt on the other side of the garage door. A few seconds went by where the only sound was the scuffle of footsteps outside.

I held my breath and kept as motionless as humanly possible, crouched beneath the hair cape. Twix was so still I thought she'd passed out from fear. All the better. Last thing I needed was her going off on one of her screaming tangents. It may have gotten her a role in a movie, but this wasn't the time or place to exercise her vocal cords.

There was no more movement or noise outside. Maybe the biker was rethinking his decision to stop. Maybe it had nothing to do with Jock. Or suppose he'd found the keypad and was fiddling with it?

I kept my arms firmly wrapped around Twix and dared to take a shallow breath, my heart hammering viciously inside the walls of my chest. *Please, God, keep us safe.*

A second later, there was the sound of someone scraping by underneath the partially opened rolling door. A moment of silence echoed in the garage, a silence that chilled me to the bone. Then the thud of heavy footsteps on the concrete floor came our way.

Chapter 10

Twix moved slightly, a sign she was indeed awake. I held onto her tight and felt her trembling. Or was that me?

The prowler mounted the craggy steps and jiggled the doorknob that led into Jock's condo. Thank heavens I locked the door when we left. I hadn't been *that* careless.

"Maybe it's Jock," Twix whispered in my ear as soft as she could.

I squeezed her shoulder to signal her to be quiet. I knew it wasn't Jock. If it had been, I would've detected his enticing aroma—even from under the cape. Plus, keys or not, he would've, without question, been able to enter his condo, whether by a hidden keypad or busting through the door.

The intruder gave a heavy-fisted pound on the door that made us both jump. "Anybody home?" he shouted, kicking the door with all the grace of the big bad wolf.

I forced down a gulp, thinking of everything that had happened in the past twenty-four hours. Was this the person who'd been in contact with Jock last night? The one who'd set him on edge? Or was this the thug who'd attacked us? What if he was one and the same? In the darkness, I didn't know what was happening, but I could tell the intruder descended the steps and stopped abruptly on the cement floor.

My temples were throbbing, and my heart was thumping so loud I was sure he'd hear it.

He grunted, the venom in his voice unescapable. "What's that?" He barked out a laugh, and I was thinking this guy wasn't mentally all there.

I slid my arm down from Twix's shoulder and felt the ground for one of the sharp chunks of glass I'd set aside moments earlier. I had no desire to play hero, but if I didn't do something, Twix and I could end up dead.

"I believe somebody *is* home," he said in answer to himself.

Swiftly, he swept the cape off Twix and me. The smell of smoky leather rushed at us as he reached down and jerked me to my feet.

Twix went into screaming mode, which was more than I could do since the goon was squeezing my throat, shaking my body like an old rag. I gagged and coughed, holding tight to the piece of glass in my hand.

I hurled my arm up to his neck, but his broad chest and long muscled arms made it impossible to reach his bare skin. Instead, I sliced his leather jacket covering his shoulder, and the glass chunk clattered to the ground.

The thug threw me against the wall, loosening the ladder from its roost. The metal contraption fell on top of me, its weight nearly crushing me. I blinked in the darkness, trying to focus, but my head hurt, and my body was aching from the blow.

Before I could squirm away, my attacker heaved the ladder from me, pitched it against the wall, and hauled me to my feet for a second time. He backhanded me across the face followed by a left hook in the gut.

My teeth cut into my lip, and I doubled over to my knees, sure I was going to pass out. Without giving me time to catch my breath, he took his huge hand and yanked me back by the hair. "Let this go," he shouted in a raspy voice. "Or you'll regret it even more."

Twix sprang into action and tossed a handful of glass at us to disarm him. When that didn't work, she vaulted onto his back, riding him like a cowgirl, flogging his head with her fists, digging her spikes into his legs.

The guy staggered around on his feet, trying to beat me to a pulp and knock off Twix at the same time. Twix wouldn't let go. She continued to kick the back of his knees, missing her target a time or two, booting me instead.

"Twix!" I yelled, wheezing for air. "The ch-chain!"

"What chain?" she cried.

"Your neck—lace!"

I heard her boots clack onto the floor, and a second later I caught a glimpse of her winding up her arm like David readying to slay Goliath. She whacked the culprit square on the temple with her tire chain, and without another word, he crumbled to the ground, a faint tinkling sound accompanying him. I collapsed next to him on the bed of broken glass, massaging my throat, inhaling big time.

Twix groped for me, huffing and puffing. "You okay?"

"Yes." I spit out blood, then scrambled to my feet. "Let's get out of here and call the police before he comes to."

"I want to see him." Twix snagged my phone from my bag and beamed the flashlight on the perp. "*Aaaaah!*" She dropped the phone and sprang back. "He's a *monster*."

I scooped up my phone, peering in the shadows at the man who'd tried to kill us. "That's him." I rocked on my feet, my stomach lurching from the pain of being punched.

"Who, him? And what's he doing here?"

"The guy who assaulted Jock and me last night." The smoky campfire smell of his jacket was new though. "And I don't know why he's here. Looking for Jock?"

Pinpricks skittered down my arms, but, like Twix, I had to get a better look. I leaned closer to his disfigured face, the realization of what I was seeing hitting me with such force I felt the blood drain to my toes.

This guy wasn't wearing a mask after all. This was the face of someone who'd been in a fire or explosion and who'd been badly scarred for life. The crepey skin. Layers of folds.

I'd once seen the same irreparable damage on a firefighter who'd worked with my father and who'd been caught in a blazing house inferno. The empathy I'd felt for that firefighter resurfaced. But our assailant wasn't that man, and whatever tragedy had struck him in the past, he was dangerous *now*. No time for sympathy. We had to get to safety and call the cops.

I swiped my bag from Twix and swept my cape off the floor. *Shoot.* The glass chunks from the ship. I didn't want to leave them behind. I quickly shoveled them back into the cape, bundled up the material, and heaped everything into my bag.

I dumped the ladder on top of our aggressor and stumbled to the rolling door. "Come on," I urged Twix, praying my legs wouldn't give out. "Before he comes to."

Twix peeled out of the parking lot before I even had the van door shut. So much for the nursery on wheels. We were both shuddering from what had happened, neither one of us could verbalize anything. "The Wheels on the Bus" went 'round and 'round inside the phantom CD player despite Twix cranking the volume down earlier. Our minds were elsewhere, like on being alive.

"Stop!" I cried.

Twix almost jumped out of her skin. She careened into an empty strip mall and screeched on the brakes. "*What!*" She panted for air with a white-knuckled grip on the steering wheel.

"We can't just take off. What if he comes to?"

"What if he does?"

"Then we follow him. If he *was* looking for Jock, his actions still might lead us to him."

"Huh? Did you lose a few screws back there?" She killed the engine and the song. "I'm not going anywhere near that goon again." She slanted over and snapped open the glove compartment. "I need a drink."

"No time for that." I caught an empty juice box that tumbled out of the glove compartment, pitched it back inside, and slammed the lid shut. Then I called the police from my phone. "The cops are on their way. We have to turn back. We'll park in the shadows on the street by Jock's lot where we'll be safe. If the guy comes to and takes off, we'll trail him."

"What if he leaves before the cops get there?"

"We'll let the police know we're following him."

She crossed her arms like a spoiled child. "I'm not budging till I have a swig of hard liquor."

I sighed and glanced out my window, rotating my sore jaw from the movement. "Look, there's a bank, a kids' clothing store, and a church. None, to my knowledge, serve liquor. Not that it matters. Nothing's open. *And,* we need to get back to Jock's."

She flipped up the console. "Aha. Here it is." She pulled out a tiny bottle of rum served on airplanes. "Tony brought this home after their last game in Tampa Bay. It never made it into the house. And it's not going to." She guzzled a quarter of the rum and held it out to me.

I was awfully tempted, but liquor was not a friend to my system. I became loosey-goosey in thought, word, and deed. "No thanks."

"Suit yourself." She took another gulp, then wiped her mouth with the back of her gloved hand.

I continued to move my jaw side to side. *Ouch.*

Then again…

"Give me that." I snatched the bottle from her and threw back some rum, coughing as it burned down my throat. My face flamed, and my voice went hoarse. "That'll do," I said, fanning myself.

She took her finger and pulled my chin toward her. "You know your lip is bleeding? And your eye sockets look a bit blue. That backhand he gave you must've been a good one."

I knit my brows together, which was an effort, then flipped down the sun visor and inspected my face. "Terrific."

She dove into the console again and hauled out a small plastic pouch with blue gel inside. "Here." She snapped something, and it made a crackling sound. "Put this on your lip because as of right now it looks worse than your eyes."

"What is it?" I coughed again from the taste of the rum. She leaned over and pressed it to my mouth.

"*Aaah!*" I jolted back in shock from the freezing sensation.

"Don't be a baby. It's an instant ice pack. It'll do wonders for your bruise. The rum should help, too."

We were getting sidetracked, but now she had me curious. "What else have you got in there?" I held the ice pack to my lip and peered down into the console.

She screwed the cap back on the nearly empty bottle, crammed it inside the console, and banged the lid shut. "You'd be surprised. As a mother, slash maid, slash housekeeper, I'm always prepared."

"Yes, you're a regular Mrs. Doubtfire. Now can we go back to Jock's? The guy's probably halfway to Arizona by now."

"Why would he head to Arizona?"

I smacked the ice pack down. "No reason. Just go!"

We pulled up to Jock's condo moments later and parked by the tall streetlight. As feared, the goon's bike was nowhere in sight. I cut Twix an irritable glare. "Happy? He's gone."

"Oops. How was I supposed to know he'd get away? He was out cold."

Oh brother.

The local cops arrived, and I kept it short, ending with the most important detail that the guy had gotten away. No sense confusing them with unnecessary facts.

The uniforms gave us a strange nod. Probably not sure what to make of Twix in her biker outfit and tire chain around her neck. Confirming we weren't in need of urgent medical attention, they called in the incident, hiked back to their black-and-white, and took off.

"That was interesting," Twix said, hopping back into the van. "You didn't even mention Romero."

I slid onto my seat next to her, my stomach stinging from tugging the van door shut. "Why would I? He's not on this case, and he doesn't know every cop in the Boston area."

"Noted." She perched her right leg up onto her seat and twisted toward me. "All right. Let me look at those pictures you pilfered."

I rolled my eyes at her dramatics—which I should've known better than to do because of my tender lids. Then I rifled through my bag. Figuring I'd get to the small stack later, I pulled out all the shots and slapped them in her palm. "Here."

I held onto the photo of the four navy men, at last having a chance to find out if there was anything penned on the back. I flipped the picture over and saw three names. Jock. Vick. Tork. The fourth name, written between Vick's and Tork's, was watermarked and smudged.

I turned the photo over again, putting faces to the names. Then my mind flew back to my discovery on Jock's computer. "Vick and Tork," I murmured. Those were the names mentioned in the email. Were these men more than just navy pals with Jock?

Twix was mesmerized with the photos in her hands, shuffling through them like a casino gambler sorting cards. "Who is *this*?" She swung a picture in the air of Jock on a beach, wearing nothing but swim trunks and a relaxed smile. Beside him was a gorgeous Brazilian-toned brunette in a bikini. Natch. The brunette's arms were fastened securely around Jock's hard abs as if she'd won him at the state fair.

I didn't make a big deal of the picture even though it touched an unsettling nerve. I had too much on my mind with the implications of *this* picture.

"You might want to look at these later." Twix jammed the stack back in my bag, angling over to peer at the photo in my hand. "Wait." She grabbed the picture and studied it, pointing to the man with the carved features next to Jock. "I know that guy."

"You do?"

She squinted at the picture. "Not personally. But I *have seen* him before."

"When?"

She looked off to the side as if pulling from memory, then came back to me. "Remember talking about *Caribbean Gold*, the movie Jock and I were in last fall?"

"Yes." How could I forget?

"This guy in the photo came to Boston Harbor when we were filming. He took Jock aside during one of our breaks and spoke to him. Seemed kind of urgent."

"That was months ago. What would that have to do with what happened last night?"

"I don't know. Nothing? But it was obvious they knew each other."

"Did Jock introduce you?"

"No. And by the look on his face, I didn't want to interrupt what was going on between them." She clutched my arm. "Hold on. What were those names you muttered a minute ago?"

"Vick? Tork?"

She meditated on this for a moment. "*Yeah.* That was the guy's name."

"Which name?" I wanted to be certain we were talking about the same person.

"Vick."

"You sure?"

"Yes." She flipped the photo over, reading the names for herself. "I remember now. Vick. I overheard it when I happened to walk by."

"*Happened* to walk by?" I would've grinned at Twix's choice of words if my mouth had cooperated. "So what happened to him?"

"Beats me. I only saw him that one time, but Jock had definitely seemed disturbed by his visit."

I might've been leaping to conclusions, but I was beginning to think that the photo and the email were connected, and that Jock's disappearance had something to do with his past.

I told Twix what I'd found on his laptop, filling her in on the kite symbol and what it said below. "If last night's attack is linked with Vick visiting Jock at the set, we need to find this man."

"Good luck."

"You have any better ideas?"

She tapped her spiked heel on the gas pedal, fingers drumming the console. "Not at the moment."

"Then unless something else pops up, this is all we've got. And gut instinct is telling me that Vick and/or Tork are tied to Jock vanishing."

She blinked at me as if a sudden thought occurred. "You don't think that Vick was our assaulter, do you?"

"I think we're getting ahead of ourselves. So far, we have two names in an email that match two names on the photo. Then there's the disfigured face. It's possible Vick could've been in a fire since *Caribbean Gold*." I ruminated on this some more. Just because Twix recognized him in this old picture and had seen him on the movie set months ago didn't mean he looked the same today.

I came back to the culprit we'd left behind on Jock's garage floor. "But who's to say that our attacker was Vick and not Tork? The email said, 'It's Tork' as if Vick was warning Jock to be on the lookout for him."

"'It's Tork' could mean anything," she argued. "It's Tork who got his ass stuck in a tire swing. It's Tork who's dating your sister. It's Tork who—"

"I get it. I get it."

"As for size," she said, eyes on the photo, "they both look about Jock's height. The guy on the right, Tork, might be huskier. And who's the smaller guy? His name's been smudged off."

"I don't know." I inspected the photo some more, then summoned up the email. "What about the 823 Hock? I don't have a clue what that means."

"You've never heard of 823 Hock? I thought that place was legendary."

"It sounds like a radio station." I dabbed the ice pack on

my lip, giving her a sidelong glance. "Should I know what that is?"

"Not necessarily. It's an address and name of a place in a dingy part of Cambridge. Tony's grandma used to go to the Hock to purchase a whole beef that she would then freeze during the winter so they had meat all year around."

"So it's a butcher shop."

"Not merely a butcher shop. Remember watching that classic, *Rocky*, after we'd both been dumped by those jocks on the football team?"

"How could I forget? You thought we should take boxing lessons so we could punch out their lights if they ever looked at us again."

"Good times." She grinned at that, then came back to the present. "*Rocky* is one of Tony's dad's favorite movies. Has it playing every time we go over to their house. Whenever Junie wanders into the family room while it's on, she starts slurring, 'Yo, Adrian.' Anyway, Rocky's friend, Paulie, used to work in the plant where all the cows' hides hung on hooks."

I curled up my sore lip and cringed in pain. "Stop. I get the picture."

"I know, it's awful." She frowned and stuck out her bottom lip. "Every time I think of those places, I give Peaches an extra hug. I couldn't imagine that happening to him." She shook her head to rid herself of the terrible thought. "The Hock is no longer in business. Hasn't been for years."

"What's there now?"

She shrugged. "From what I'd heard, the abandoned building was overtaken by homeless people and addicted, PTSD-victim veterans living on the street. But a vet organization eventually came in and moved them all to a proper facility to get help."

She paused. "Why do you think the Hock was mentioned in the email?"

"I'm not sure. But there's something about that address that sounds familiar."

"Tell me you're not heading there now to find out what."

Twix knew me well. But I was in no condition to do any more snooping tonight. I'd be lucky to make it up the front steps of my porch. I slid the photo back in my bag with the others and painfully straightened in my seat. "Right now I want to go home. I've got things to sort out."

Chapter 11

It was eleven-thirty when I made it through the front door and flicked on the lights. My body was aching, the ice pack had lost its effectiveness, and my face felt like it had been smashed with a cast iron frying pan.

Yitts was curled up into a ball on the beanbag chair. Just as well. I didn't think I had the energy to pick her up for a cuddle. I should've run a hot bath with a helping of lavender and lemongrass essential oils to soothe my aches and pains, but I was too wound up to sit in a hot bath. Plus, I wanted to address what I'd learned so far.

I tripped into the kitchen, disposed of the single-use ice pack, and slung my bag onto the table. I pulled out the pictures I'd pinched from Jock's and spread them out, studying the collection that had the four men in a variety of groupings and poses. Huh. There were even a few of Jock with a younger-looking Captain Madera from the Love Boat. No missing that debonair face.

There was a shot of Jock and Tork arm wrestling at a table in a mess tent, their names scrawled on the back. One picture had the smaller guy running backward, flying a kite, about to trip on Tork's foot that had clearly been extended as a prank.

I slid my gaze back to Tork in the first shot that I'd taken from the frame. Though dark and heavyset with bushy eyebrows, he had a devil-may-care grin on his face. The look of a class clown or a practical joker.

I examined the names in order again on the back. Jock. Vick. Smudged name. Tork. Now that I looked closely, the first letter of the smeared name belonging to the smaller guy appeared to be a Z. Zack perhaps? I went back to the kite picture and flipped it over. Zeek was written on the back. Aha. Smaller buddy was Zeek, not Zack.

I spotted a less jovial shot of Jock, Vick, and Tork. It looked as though the three men had been thrown off guard when the picture had been taken. Their smiles weren't as broad, the situation looking less relaxed. Jock, of course, appeared as solid as ever, yet still tense.

Squinting through my haze, I noted again the similar features on Zeek and Tork. Brothers or cousins, perhaps?

I set my elbows on the table and rested my chin in my hands, scanning the pictures as a whole. Okay. What did I have so far?

First, there was an email with the names Vick and Tork. Not much on its own, but paired with the pictures of the men, this raised my antennae. Second, judging by the photos, Vick and Tork were Jock's navy friends. Vick had even visited Jock on the movie set, though, according to Twix, it hadn't been a cheery call. Third, the guy flying the kite was named Zeek. He was also the fourth navy pal. I didn't know if noting him was important, but the fact that he was flying a kite—and a kite was in the email—made him significant. Lastly, our attacker had a scarred face and hairy arms.

What I didn't know was whether Vick or Tork, or someone else entirely, was our assaulter. Wait a minute. Hairy arms! I scrutinized the pictures again. Most were taken from a distance except the one of Jock and Tork arm wrestling. Tork definitely had hairy arms.

When it came down to it, lots of guys had hairy arms. Heck, I've waxed men's arms, chests, backs, you name it. Our assailant could've been anyone. But there was a bothersome feeling that he was staring up at me from the batch of photos.

I zoomed in on Tork again, trying to find a facial feature that was similar to our attacker's. But there was nothing in the shots that gave me a clue that Tork was the same man. Still, something inside kept telling me he had to be. Perhaps it was the seemingly dire email from Vick, despite Twix's ridiculous ideas of what *It's Tork* meant.

If Tork *was* our attacker, when had he become a fire victim? Had he been a navy firefighter with Jock? Had all three? Had there been a fatal mishap?

I went back to thinking about the kite in the email. Four points on a kite. North, south, east, and west. Four men. A kite flies high. Navy flags fly high. What about the kite colors? Did they come into play? How about the names? What did they all have in common? Four letters. Again, four men. Plus, Jock, Vick, Zeek, and Tork all ended with *K*.

I dug deeper, mulling over the word *kite*. Hmm. Interesting. This four-letter word *began* with a *K*. Was any of this significant? Or did the kite represent a summons, sent in an email when one was in trouble? It contained an address, after all. Judging by Jock's reaction when he'd seen it, I'd say yes. Had Vick been the one in danger? He'd signed the email. Or had that been a ploy by Tork?

I felt like I was going around in circles when what I really needed was help from someone who knew Jock's background in the navy. Someone who would give me straight answers. One person came to mind. I zeroed in on the photo of Jock and Captain Madera.

After our cruise last fall, the captain had insisted if I ever needed anything, to just call. Well, time to collect. He could enlighten me on Vick and Tork. If he knew Jock, surely he knew the others.

My spontaneous side was eager to jump on this idea and pick up the phone. But if Madera's evenings were as busy as I remembered them on our cruise, now would not be the best time to reach him. I'd have to wait until morning.

In the midst of all my contemplating I'd forgotten about the Hock.

I reflected on what Twix had said about the place. Was

there any significance to that location? I couldn't help but note that it was another four-letter word ending in *K*. And again, I had the feeling I should've recognized the address. There was a connection escaping me, not because it had been a meat-packing plant or a shelter for homeless people, but for another reason.

I stared at the pictures, trying to recall something that might've been crucial. The beating I'd endured must've killed neurons in my brain because I couldn't stay focused. I forced myself to think harder and was so immersed in my search for clues, I flinched at three abrupt knocks on the door. I swept the pictures into a pile and limped to the window.

The streetlight shone down on a motorcycle parked in the driveway. The lights I had blazing inside like Rockefeller Center filtered onto the porch, outlining a man standing on the other side of the door.

A lick of panic washed through me. A biker had almost killed me tonight. Had he followed me home? Maybe he was here to finish what he'd started a few hours ago. I calmed down, asking myself if a killer would go to the trouble of knocking on his victim's door. Okay, maybe I didn't know the answer to that question. Didn't mean it couldn't happen.

I squinted at the figure and centered on the man's familiar sexy stance, the attitude in his posture in part due to his broad shoulders and muscular thighs. *Whew*. It was Romero. The hour of night and the way he raked his hand through his hair warned me this wasn't a social call. Maybe I did need to worry. Maybe the Cambridge police had notified the Rueland police of the attack tonight.

I opened the door and hesitantly gave a crooked, bruised-lipped smile. He didn't smile back. He looked from my head to my toes and slowly back up to my face. Reaching over, he tugged something from my matted strands and held it up in the air between us.

"Glass in your hair. Swollen lip. And two black eyes." He came closer and took a whiff. "I'm no baby expert, but something smells like spoiled formula."

Why did he have to be so bloody observant? I went from patting my sore lip to brushing my top where remnants of Lambert's spit-up remained.

Romero waited for an explanation. When one wasn't forthcoming, he lowered his arm. "During our conversation earlier, you said everything was okay."

I took the one-inch fragment from his hand of Jock's wrecked ship and set it on the window ledge. "That was at five o'clock, half a lifetime ago."

"Uh-huh. Then I get a friendly call from the Cambridge PD, alerting me of two female Rueland residents mixed up in an assault that strangely enough occurred at an address I'd been to a mere twenty-four hours ago."

He exhaled a sigh, controlling his anger, then cupped my sore face and kissed the tip of my nose. "I know I'm going to love hearing details, but we need to talk." He took me by the hand and led me to the sofa. "You'll want to sit down for this."

I knew it had to be bad. Otherwise, the lecture would've continued. Romero could have a field day on the calamities I got myself into and the aftermath that transpired.

I sat with a dull thud on the couch. Romero tossed his leather jacket on the beanbag chair, then lowered himself on the coffee table in front of me, and rubbed my hands in his. I warmed from his touch, even if unnerved by his gentle gaze and rapid tension in the air. He looked from my eyes to my hands and back into my eyes.

I drew in a deep breath to quell the numbness struggling to surface. "Do you want to go back to talking about the glass in my hair?"

He didn't laugh or even crack a grin. "Jock is dead."

That was it. No preamble. No joking.

With everything that had happened tonight, my mind was in a fog, and I wasn't absorbing those three words. "Why are you here? And why are you riding that motorcycle again?"

He looked me deep in the eyes, his low, husky voice, commanding, strained. "Valentine, Jock is dead."

"No." I tore from his grasp and leaped off the couch. "No, he's not!"

He turned and watched me pace the floor. "There was an explosion late last night at the Hock, an old meat-packing plant in Cambridge. Jock's body was pulled from the wreckage today."

"An explosion? An accident, you mean?"

"A bomb. There's no doubt. It was murder."

"No!" I screamed. "You're wrong!"

He wasn't having any of my denial. He grabbed me by the shoulders and brought me in for a hug, holding me close, rocking me tenderly. "I know you cared for him, but it's the truth."

Nothing he was saying made sense. I broke loose and fanned myself, gasping for air. I couldn't breathe. I kept inhaling, but I couldn't exhale.

Romero hustled into the kitchen, slammed cupboards and drawers, and came back seconds later with a paper bag. "Breathe into this."

I tore the bag from his hand, rammed it to my face, and breathed in and out, concentrating on this simple act. Minutes passed, Romero by my side.

"That's right." His tone was gentle, his touch on my back, comforting.

He *was* right. About more than I wished to admit. I *had* cared for Jock. At times, more than I should have.

Romero's voice softened as if he was also adjusting to this news. Even with the animosity between him and Jock, Romero had always respected him and appreciated his professional skills and merits. "I'm sorry." They were simple words, yet coming from a man with such strength and integrity, they held a fierce amount of weight.

I pushed past him and stood there, my legs wavering, a flood of emotions from grief to fury to fear running through me, making me at once hot and cold.

Jock had been a mix of a lot of things. A mystery, a hero, an idol, a symbol of hope and inspiration. Someone with a life most aimed to aspire to. For me, he'd been a colleague, a companion of sorts. A pain in the ass at times, yet a trusted friend.

I hiccupped back a sob that had bubbled up my throat, the realization hitting me that I loved Jock. Not in the way I cared for Romero, but my feelings for him were strong. What would life be like without him coloring my days, teasing me incessantly, making me feel respected, admired?

Spots blinded my eyes. I blinked hard, forcing the dots away while keeping the tears at bay. *No.* There was no time for tears. I had to find the person responsible for Jock's death. If I didn't, I'd never forgive myself. I'd been at his place when he'd been attacked, and I'd done nothing to stop it. Nothing that made a difference. What had I been thinking, plunging a stupid earring into a thug's wrist? Like that was going to bring down a guy built like a refrigerator.

The shame flowing through me rose from my lungs to my throat, nearly cutting off my airway again. *Oh God.* What if this wasn't over? What if other people died? Maybe Jock was the intended victim last night, but Twix and I had been attacked, too. What if the killer wasn't done?

I wobbled on my feet, choking and gasping, swiping my hand across my runny nose. I shoved the bag up to my face again, inhaling long and deep.

Romero evidently sensed that my emotions were all over the place. He guided me to the couch and gently set me back down. "Take a few minutes. I'm not going anywhere."

I lowered the bag to my lap, blinked through the tears, and gave an arduous sniff. It was an effort to think logically, especially for someone who resorted to impulsive acts, but critical times depended on rationale. I couldn't save Jock. I knew that now. It was even hopeless to think I could make a difference moving forward, but I had to try. I'd never live with myself if I didn't.

Unexpectedly, I recalled Holly this morning saying Romero had to leave for what looked like another homicide. So this was the real reason for the bizarre phone call he'd made earlier. "Checking in" to see if I'd heard about Jock's murder. I took a shaky breath. "When exactly did it happen?"

"In the wee hours after he disappeared last night."

"How do you know it was Jock? It could've been someone else, and you're mistaken."

"We're waiting on the lab to come back with dental records, but everything else matches the description. Height. Stature."

A fleeting thought went through my mind that Romero had put out a missing persons alert after all before the usual forty-eight hours. Otherwise, why connect Jock to the dead body of a guy discovered at a random explosion? But I cut him off, not appreciating his efforts. "That could be *anyone!*" Not true. Men weren't built like Jock de Marco unless they were direct descendants of Thor. I was hurting inside, but I needed details. "What else did you find?"

Romero shook his head, likely not wanting to revisit the scene he'd witnessed. "Between the debris from the explosion, the fire and smoke damage, and the collapsed building, a number of things were hard to determine."

"Try!" I shouted. "I need to know."

He wore his patience like a soldier, his manner professional yet soothing. How many times had he dealt with hysterical witnesses and delivered tragic news to a loved one's family? He, himself, had been the victim of losing someone he once thought he'd spend the rest of his life with.

"The ID unit is still there, collecting evidence, but there were some clothes left in a corner." He inhaled and steadied his gaze on me. "His phone was also there, and a fancy watch, both crushed beyond repair."

No wonder I couldn't find Jock's phone. As expected, he'd had it on him.

The gravity of the situation crashed down on me, and from somewhere deep inside, I realized what Romero was saying was true. Jock was dead. I couldn't escape the truth.

A fresh tear rolled down my cheek. Followed by another. And another. I couldn't remember much after that except I knew I'd wept into the night, and Romero was by my side when I awoke the next morning.

"You want coffee?" He removed his arm from around my shoulder, worked out the kinks, then peeled away the paper bag that had somehow stuck to my face. He took a good look at me and dabbed the drool that had becomingly dribbled out of my blistered mouth, adding to the beautiful picture I must've made.

I swept the back of my hand across my stinging eyes, blinking through smudged mascara and tear stains. "I don't drink coffee, remember?"

He gave me a rueful smile. "Thought you might want to try."

"Will it bring back Jock?"

He rubbed his unshaved jaw, staring at me in concern. "Afraid not." He got to his feet and motioned to the kitchen table. "What's with the pictures?"

I stood, then doubled over from the muscle pain in my gut. *Bugger.* I hobbled over and explained what happened last night at Jock's, giving him details I'd omitted sharing with the Cambridge police, most importantly the contents of the email.

"You went back to Jock's after I advised you to stay out of it?"

"You asked if I *got* your advice to stay out of it. I said *loud and clear.*" *Valentine, you're so brazen you could run for mayor.*

He blew out a sigh accompanied with a look like he wanted to throttle me. "I'm the only cop I know who has a girlfriend who gets beaten up on a regular basis. People are going to talk."

"What will they say?" I wasn't trying to be cute, but at this point I was willing to do anything to lighten the mood.

His piercing eyes darkened to a midnight blue, making his black lashes appear thicker, his expression more dangerous. I tried not to stare at the transformation, but it was something that never failed to amaze me.

Embarrassed that Romero still had the power to fluster me, even at a time like this, I blinked away from his stare and concentrated on spreading out the photos. "As you can tell, Jock was in the navy with these guys." I pointed to the shot that I'd removed from the frame. "This guy next to Jock is Vick. He's the one who sent the email before Jock disappeared."

He took the picture and studied it. "Vick."

"Yes. Twix recognized him in the picture as a guy she'd seen with Jock."

"Twix. The other half of the dynamic duo." He dropped the photo back onto the table. "Why doesn't it surprise me she was involved in this?"

I ignored the attitude. "Since she knew Jock and wanted to help, she went to the condo with me."

"So I heard." He scratched his brow like he was restraining himself from shouting. "Who else did you involve in this scheme?"

"No one." I did a small shrug. "Except for Gibson."

"Who's Gibson?"

I could've gone into a long story of how Gibson's second workplace had towed my car down the mountain last fall after Romero and I had been stuck in the Berkshires on another case. But I thought it prudent to stick to the present situation. "Gibson is Mrs. Shales's grandson."

"Mrs. Shales?"

"My parents' neighbor. He also happens to be a computer whiz."

"An-n-nd?"

"And he helped me crack into Jock's laptop."

He put up his palms. "I don't want to hear this."

"Then why'd you ask?"

The vein in his neck twitched, and he muttered something under his breath that sounded like *God help me*. Then he went back to examining the photos on the table, shuffling a few here and there. "When did Twix see this guy, Vick, with Jock?"

"He came to the movie set when they were filming *Caribbean Gold*. And whatever it was that he told Jock caused unease, even alarm."

He stopped skimming through the pictures and tilted his head at me. "That was, what, last September, October, and you think that *that* conversation is linked to Jock's death?"

"I'm almost certain."

"Interesting theory. And where is Vick today? Bringing back my Bonnie to me?"

"Huh? You lost me."

In typical Romero fashion, he did the widened cop stance, hands on lean hips. "It's an old Scottish folk song. 'My Bonnie Lies over the Ocean.' You heard of it?"

"If I say no, are you going to sing it to me?"

He relaxed his pose. "My point is, is this Vick still in the navy?"

"I don't know. But I think he might be a witness or someone you need to follow up on. He looks like the right size to be Jock's visitor and our attacker, but the assailant also had horrible scars. The Vick Twix met didn't."

I pointed to the photo he'd discarded. "Which leads me to this guy on the right. He was also mentioned in the email. I think he might be the one responsible for Jock's disappearance and therefore probably his death and the explosion. His name is Tork."

Was it the outcome of last night's incident that had my mind playing tricks on me, or did Romero's wide shoulders tense? "Tork?" He snatched the picture again and turned it over, seeing the names on the back for himself.

"Yes. I have a feeling he's the one who assaulted Jock...and me. Remember I told you that the brute was possibly wearing a mask? He wasn't. I think his disfigurement came from a fire." I took the picture from him and inspected it again, taking in Tork's dark features. "There's also the hairy arms."

Romero gave a slow, somewhat dubious nod. "Right. The hairy arms. Which, may I add, I also have." He shoved up his sleeve to point that out—as if he needed to. He might've known every curve of my body, but every inch of his hard, glorious physique was ingrained in my mind.

"I know." I coughed, focusing. "But his are...hairier. As a beautician, I notice these things."

"Hairier. As a beautician..." His voice trailed off as if

once again he shouldn't be surprised by the words that flew out of my mouth.

"Yes." I slid the photo onto the table and searched the others. "See for yourself in this picture of him arm wrestling with Jock."

I paused, deliberating on what I'd discovered so far. "There's also the kite."

"What kite?"

"The one in the email. It was colorful. The kind a kid flies at the park."

His back stiffened. "There was a kite like that spread on the ground at the bombing site."

"What?"

"Pretty darn depressing. The gutted-out building was a smoldering mess of black and gray. Collapsed beams. Rubble everywhere. Then outside, spread on the road was that kite in all its vivid glory." He tightened his lips. "Seems someone's playing games with us."

"I think the kite may be part of some type of alert. Maybe it's a navy thing. When Jock got the email with the kite symbol, he leaped into action. He knew something bad was coming."

Romero considered this, then leaned over the table and took a few close-ups with his phone. "Listen to me. You need to back off. You don't know who you're dealing with."

"It's a bit late for that."

He shoved his phone back in his pocket, went over to the beanbag chair, and slid his leather jacket out from under Yitts who'd curled on top of it sometime during the night. "I've got to go." He moved in for a tender hug, holding me like I might break. "You going to be okay?"

I shivered under his touch yet clung to his compassionate embrace. "I will be. But I need to see Jock for myself."

His chest heaved up and down. He pulled us apart, frustration carved on his face. "What's that going to prove?"

"I don't know. Closure maybe." The hollow ache inside from news of Jock's death resurfaced. "Jock was an important part of my life. I have to say goodbye."

He opened the front door, turned to face me, and shrugged into his jacket. "I've got to head to the morgue in a few hours. I'll let you know when. You can meet me there."

Chapter 12

First thing I did after Romero left was call Captain Madera. He had to know something about Vick and Tork and maybe more about this whole nightmare.

After some static, I finally got through, the sorrow in Madera's voice genuine when I told him about Jock. I informed him about the email from Vick and asked if he knew him or Tork or Zeek. What he revealed left me speechless.

Tork and Zeek were brothers, as I'd suspected, but Jock and Vick were as close to them as blood brothers. Then Zeek had tragically been killed by a landmine about a year after enlisting. The others were all there at the time. When Tork went to save Zeek, another ground explosive maimed his face.

"That incident was one of the reasons I chose to work in friendlier waters on a cruise line," Madera said. "Unfortunately, after that, I lost touch with a lot of the sailors."

Weighed down by this disturbing news, I thanked him and said goodbye. Knowing that Tork had lost a sibling and had been burned and scarred for life didn't make any of this easier, but now I knew that he'd been our attacker. The only thing I couldn't guess was his motive for the assault and whether the past was connected to the present and Jock's death.

I gave one last sad look at all the pictures, then gathered them together and shoved them back in my bag. If anything, I'd have to dig deeper to discover the truth.

Before I did anything else, I headed into the bathroom and showered. I couldn't remember the last time I'd slept with full makeup on after a crying bout, but it wasn't a pretty sight. That, mixed with not one, but two burgeoning black eyes and a swollen lip gave me a striking resemblance to Rocky Balboa.

"Yo, Adrian," I drawled to my bruised face in the partially steamed-up bathroom mirror.

I attempted to hide the black eyes with a dusting of light makeup and concealer, but even with my skills as a beautician, only so much was possible. Good thing I didn't have to work today because I didn't have the energy to care. Who was I trying to impress, anyway?

I swirled my hair back into a half-assed bun, which did nothing to improve my appearance, then suddenly remembered the piece of glass that Romero had pulled from my strands.

I plodded into the living room, lifted the glass off the window ledge, and stared at it with an aching heart. Was there any point in fixing Jock's ship? It seemed like an unnecessary burden. Why torture myself?

I knew the answer to that before I even slid it into my bag with the other chunks of glass. I was grieving the loss of Jock. Rebuilding the ship would give me purpose and maybe even help me come to terms with his death. Plus, once I was done, I'd keep it in the shop in honor of him and all he stood for.

I was slipping into khakis and a light-knit tan sweater when the loud racket of a car motored down the street. A moment later, the noise died, and there was a *hop hop hop* sound up my front porch steps, followed by an impatient knock on the door.

Now what?

I snapped the button on my khakis, traipsed to the door, and flung it open.

"What happened to you last night?"

Phyllis. Naturally. Who else would be hopping around in a kimono with her face powdered white and chopsticks dangling from a top-knot in her hair? Only thing different on her today was that she'd swapped her yellow kimono for a pink one.

She stood in her wooden flip-flops, hands on hips, glaring at me as if I'd committed a mortal sin. "That's two nights in a row you didn't show up at the Geisha Gap."

I barely had a chance to collect my thoughts when Max tripped up the steps behind her, arms open in apology. "I tried to stop her."

I looked from Max to the white behemoth behind him that Phyllis drove to the vision in front of me. I drew in a breath, mentally willing myself not to get emotional. "I was busy, Phyllis. Sorry." So much had changed since last night, but I needed to think soundly, especially when sharing news of Jock's death was imminent.

Phyllis shimmied into the house like a snake inside a wet suit. "You're not sorry. If you were sorry you would've made an appearance. Doesn't matter anyway. They had to cancel last night's event."

"Why?"

She hurled her arms up in the air. "How should I know? There was some accident on Hock. Had the whole street cordoned off."

"Hock?" I stiffened.

"Yes, where the Geisha Gap is. They said the old meat-packing plant down the road exploded. There was dust and debris everywhere."

Of course. Now I knew why *Hock* sounded familiar. Instantly, I recalled the slip of paper sitting on my desk that she'd scrawled the Geisha Gap address on. Figured Phyllis was training to be a geisha in a Japanese restaurant near a former meat-packing plant.

Unfortunately, I now realized there wasn't a connection from the Geisha Gap to what had happened to Jock. I was looking for something that wasn't there. Still, I asked if she'd seen anything.

"Like what?" Phyllis demanded. "Falling rocks? Or did you think Dumbo flew by?"

"Speaking of Dumbos..." Max muttered.

I blinked from Max to Phyllis. "I thought you were taking the drums to the Geisha Gap after work yesterday."

"We were. Had to reroute. Cops wouldn't let us anywhere near the place. So the drums are back in the basement." She gave a gloomy head shake. "At least I got in more practicing. I was on fire last night, too, playing the skins like nobody's business."

"Skins?"

Max leaned against the doorframe, arms folded across his chest, his expression cynical. "Phyllis's favorite slang for *drums*. Honestly, I've got more material for The Idiot Files than even Hollywood will want."

I whirled back to Phyllis, grimacing in pain from the movement but more worried how she'd interpret Max's remark. No need to worry. She was waddling into the kitchen, food clearly the next thing on her mind.

"Good thing we don't need to bring my drum set back for tonight," she shouted through the wall. "The guy who lets us use his equipment doesn't do gigs on Sundays, so his drums will be all set up for my ceremonial extravaganza."

"Your what?" I was going to need a Tylenol from all this shouting.

"You know," Max chimed. "Like when the show-stopping elephant act comes on at the circus."

Phyllis poked her head around the corner, searing Max with a furious look. "It's not a circus act, and I'm not an elephant."

Max slid his gaze to me, eyebrows up as in *wanna bet?* He pushed off from the doorframe and closed the door behind him.

"Main thing is," Phyllis went on, slamming cupboard doors, "the road will be open by tonight, so traffic will be able to drive down Hock." The banging of jars signaled she was in the fridge. "*Stuffed peppers!*"

I flinched from her shriek and winced again from the painful motion. "Yes. By all means, help yourself."

The microwave sounded a second later. Didn't matter. Truth was, I couldn't have cared less whether Phyllis ate my next meal. I had no appetite anyway.

Max eyed me with suspicion. "Not that I don't want to focus on the boob in the other room, but you want to tell me what happened to you?" He moved in closer and studied my face. "Not only are you moving like a troll, but you did a crappy job hiding those two bloodshot black eyes. Furthermore, you look like you had your hair done by said boob."

His eyes scanned my outfit. "Plus, you're wearing tan. I mean, *tan!* You *never* wear tan. You always say it blends in with your skin tone."

First it was Twix, criticizing my brown top from last night. Now Max. What was it with everyone and my wardrobe? Couldn't a girl dress casual once in a while?

Max creased his eyebrows in a thoughtful manner. "Next you'll be wearing flats. *Tan* flats." He puffed out air when I didn't respond. "Are you *trying* to disappear?"

I sighed. A part of me *had* disappeared. Maybe subconsciously, that was the reason for my lackluster outfits. I knew I had to share the devastating news about Jock, but I wasn't emotionally or mentally prepared.

I waited for Phyllis to return to the living room, then I took a measured breath and explained what happened. "That's what the accident on Hock was about," I concluded, wringing my hands. "The explosion happened sometime late Friday night."

Max plunked himself in the beanbag chair, blinking vacantly, no words coming out.

Phyllis licked the plate clean. "Do you have any more yogurt?"

I gaped at her, tempted to pound her to rid myself of all the anxiety and sadness I'd experienced the past few days.

"Phyllis, are you at all aware of what I said? Jock's dead."

She gave a short sniff, then wiped her red-circled lips with the back of her hand, smearing a thick scarlet streak across her cheek. "I'm not deaf. You're wrong, that's all."

I counted backward from five to one, giving myself time to cool down before responding to my ignorant cousin-a-thousand-times-removed. "Wrong about what?"

"Jock being dead. He's not."

Max swept his gaze off the floor, and we shared a skeptical look before I cut my stare back to Phyllis. "After everything I told you in the last five minutes, how can you say Jock's not dead?"

"Because I know. Jock wouldn't let that happen."

"You mean become a victim of violence? Phyllis, I hate to break this to you, but regardless of prior notions you may have had about Jock, he wasn't a god." I'd been first in line, trying to convince myself of that, too. "Yes, he had an impressive background. He was strong and a force to reckon with, but unfortunately, some things are out of our control."

"Well, I don't believe it. He even gave me a ride to the Geisha Gap the other night."

"What other night?"

"I don't know. Friday. Before you went to the ballet. We left work at the same time."

There were occasions when I'd look at Phyllis, wondering if we lived on the same planet. She didn't need to tell me her every move—and Lord knew I didn't tell her mine—but we'd worked together all day yesterday, and not a peep about this. "What happened to your car?"

"I got as far as York Street, and I got a flat. Jock came around the corner in his Porsche and gave me a lift. Said he had to go to the restaurant anyway."

"What for?"

"I don't know. Maybe he was ordering take-out. Even called the garage for me. Arranged for them to fix the tire and bring the car to me when I finished my training for the night."

This was just another example of how decent Jock was, but I didn't want to harp on it anymore. Romero was right. I had to face reality. We all did. "I'm going to the morgue as soon as Romero calls," I told them.

Max blinked like it was the only thing he could manage.

Phyllis plopped the plate on the coffee table with a clatter, making us both jump. "Does that mean you won't be coming to my extravaganza later?"

My heart felt as heavy as it had last night, and now I had to deal with Phyllis's dumb questions. "No, Phyllis, I won't be—uh, actually…yes, I'll be there."

"You will?" She seemed as surprised by this decision as me.

"Yes. What time?"

"Nine o'clock sharp. Back of the Okiya Corral restaurant on Hock. You see? There's a silver lining to everything." She wiggled her way out the door and hopped down the porch steps.

Max pushed off from the beanbag chair. "Why would you go to her thing tonight when you need time to grieve over Jock? I mean, there's mourning"—he dragged his gaze from me to Phyllis struggling to sit behind the wheel—"and then there's mourning."

He was right. Did I really want to spend my night watching Phyllis thrash the daylights out of an innocent set of drums? "The other day you were trying to convince me that I wouldn't get free entertainment like this anywhere else."

"True." He shrugged. "Maybe this *is* what you need. But I smell a skunk. What do you have planned?"

Trust Max to get to the heart of things. "Nothing bizarre. I'm exploring the explosion site for myself. Since it's close to the restaurant, I might as well kill two birds with one stone." I felt an ache in my throat at the memory of Jock teasing me with those exact words a mere forty-eight hours ago.

"That won't bring him back."

"I know."

He pulled me close, and we clung to each other for a long moment, his heavenly cologne comforting me in a way I had never appreciated before. "Things won't be the same." He backed up, never looking so sad.

"No, they won't."

"I better go. I want to say something funny, but there's nothing left in me to say."

The miserable thing was, I knew how he felt.

The morning wore on. Romero had called and told me to meet him at the morgue at eleven. I drove to the address he gave and stood outside the old-fashioned, two-story brick building, eyeing the archaic arched doorways that shrouded two sets of garage doors. Looked like something a police wagon in Al Capone's day would've puttered through.

I tightened my grip on my shoulder bag and limped into the building, my stride painful, my hands sweaty. I took a ragged breath and patted my knotted stomach. Lord only knew how my legs carried me from the car to this point.

I peered down at my three-inch, brightly beaded and stitched toe-ring cork sandals. I'd decided I'd prove Max wrong and not wear flats. But it didn't matter what I had on my feet. If this unbearable heaviness that came over me was what free-falling off a cliff felt like, that was one thing I could scratch from my bucket list.

Romero met me in the hall of the cold, gray-walled morgue, a look of concern adding to the tension lines on his ruggedly handsome face. "You all right?"

My clenched insides must have added to the frightful look on the outside. Not having anything for breakfast except for a glass of juice didn't help either. Throwing up would've felt better than this. I put that out of my mind, stuck out my chest, and gave him a thumbs-up, not trusting myself to say anything that would show I was a wreck inside.

"They'll likely ship the body back to Argentina."

I nodded. I hadn't met Jock's family, but I couldn't imagine the horror they'd feel, learning of their only son's death.

We stopped outside a closed door, and Romero rested his hand on the doorknob. "The pathologist's report came back. Jock's body was badly beaten. Rope burns around his neck confirm he was strangled before the place went up in flames. Cause of the explosion was a manually detonated bomb."

I peered up into his eyes, meeting his sorrowful look. As long as I'd known Romero, he'd always been a cop first. But in that moment, I could tell I meant so much more to him. If he could spare me the gruesome details and of what lied ahead, he would.

I followed him into the room, trying to control my quivering insides. There was a faint smell in the air of preservative chemicals mixed with a smoky yet sickly-sweet odor I wished to forget.

Dizzy from the smell, I lagged behind, groped for my tiny bottle of Musk oil, and dabbed the floral scent under my nose. *Whew.* I could do this. I pressed my lips together, packed the bottle back in my bag, and ordered my feet to move forward.

The autopsy technician said a few words to Romero, acknowledged me with a grim smile, then showed us to a table positioned left to right that had a covered body stretched out on top. I looked down to the left of the form and saw a few sprigs of hair poking out from under the end of the sheet.

After giving us—or more likely me—a second to adjust to our surroundings, the technician pulled the sheet back to the waist. He waited a second—I presume to make sure I didn't faint—then turned and went over to a computer.

I looked from the attendant back to the corpse in front of me and gagged. I forced down a shaky swallow, gagging again, and again. I rubbed my arms, ordering myself to get control. I'd insisted on seeing Jock, right? Tell that to my body breaking out in a sweat and my tonsils that were acting up.

Romero wrapped his arm around my waist, helping me to balance myself or keep me from falling to the floor. "You don't have to do this."

I put up my index finger to say that I did. Though no words came out, he understood. He gave me a nod and a moment to reconcile what I was seeing.

Though I was a sweaty mess, I approached the table and gaped in shock at Jock's once overpowering figure, badly scorched and bruised, a shadow of the man he once was. His beautiful dark hair had been charred, his face terribly burned, his strong jawline the only thing that remained. I dragged my gaze from the rope burn on his mangled neck down to his collapsed chest and tattoo on his arm before I fled the room, gasping for air.

I staggered out into the hallway, nearly blinded from specks coloring my eyes. I didn't notice I'd been running until I was bent over by my car, retching orange juice and last night's stuffed pepper. I sensed Romero hustling to my side. A second later, he smoothed my back while I vomited. Lovely. Another romantic moment with the man of my dreams.

Swiping my damp forehead, I focused on the ground, willing myself to finish puking. Through the blur of tears that always accompanied it, I had an instant vision of Jock's rope-and-anchor sculpture that had been sitting on his sideboard cupboard beside the glass ship that Twix had broken.

I hadn't been able to place where I'd seen that image before, why it seemed noteworthy. Yet how could I have forgotten about Jock's tattoo? That symbol had been an important part of his navy days, so significant that he had a carving of the image.

I took heavy breaths, that vision replaced by the picture of Phyllis at work yesterday, talking to the girl with all the tattoos. Phyllis had reportedly told the girl to go home and wash them off, as if that were possible. There was still something about that that was plaguing me. The name Hock had also nagged me and had come to nothing. But I had a feeling the tattoo was important.

In the midst of this, I thought about Jock's life in the navy and the tragedies he'd seen. Tork had been part of that life, and hadn't *he* survived an unspeakable tragedy? Seemed this guy was invincible. For whatever reason, had he killed Jock?

Romero cleared his throat, likely having enough of the show before him. "You going to be okay?" He pulled out his phone that had been buzzing in his pocket. "It's the crime lab. I'm needed back at the station."

I rubbed my hand across my nose and straightened, avoiding Romero's eyes. "Yes. Go ahead. I'll be fine."

"You sure? You look a little green around the gills."

If I'd been feeling perky, I would've made fish lips and sent him off with a kiss. All I could work up was a green-gilled *yes*.

"Good. Looks like another long day. Half my team is at Jock's, dusting for prints. The other half is on Hock, collecting evidence. Whoever detonated that bomb knew what he was doing, clever son-of-a-bitch." He pressed a tender kiss on my forehead and jogged toward a motorcycle a few rows over.

"Wait!" I called. "You haven't explained about the bike." He wasn't going to either. Next thing I knew, he donned his helmet, roared the engine to life, and tore out of the parking lot.

Chapter 13

It was well after noon, and I had things to do. Since the police were carrying on the investigation at Jock's, I was staying clear of his condo. Ditto the Hock…for now. I'd wait until tonight as planned to check it out, especially if the road was closed until then as Phyllis pointed out.

Given that I needed to sanitize the shop, I decided to head there first. I needed the distraction, plus, there was Jock's ship to fix. I wasn't fooling myself. This was going to be worse than putting Humpty Dumpty together again. But I had to try.

I pulled into the parking lot at the back of Beaumont's and ran into Max and the Japanese empress loading the drums from the basement into her trunk.

"What's up?" I shut my car door and picked up a drumstick that rolled toward me. "I thought you didn't need to lug your drums back to the Geisha Gap tonight."

"I'm not." Phyllis took baby steps from her car that had all four doors open to the shop's glass door. "I'm returning them to the store. I won't be needing them anymore."

Max looked at me, trying to hide a grin. "You want to come with us and watch Phyllis ask for her money back on the skins?"

I slid the drumstick on Phyllis's backseat. "Tempting, but no thanks."

He finished ramming the snare drum into the trunk and dusted off his hands. Meanwhile, Phyllis moved with the pace of a snail and hopped back into the shop.

The grin crept up Max's cheek. "Watch this." He pulled out his phone and tapped the screen. "I'm timing how long it takes her to trek downstairs, grab the next piece, and then hop both flights back up. Last trip, it took five minutes and twelve seconds, and the only thing she had in her hand were the cymbals." He laughed. "Guess what's left to bring up?"

"I don't know. A foot pedal?"

He could barely contain himself. "The bass drum. That should add another five minutes."

"You could go down and help her, you know."

He looked taken aback. "And miss seeing her burst a seam wriggling back up to the landing? Where would the joy be in that?"

When I didn't respond, he searched my face. His expression sobered, the seconds ticking by while he considered his next words. "Should I ask how it went?"

I fingered the strap on my shoulder bag. "It went."

"Do you feel better now?"

"No. How are you able to put on a cheery face?"

He looked at the door Phyllis had entered a moment ago. "I'm opting to be with *her* today, aren't I? You know this next harebrained scheme will be a comedy show in itself." He lowered his phone to his side. "Also…I'm choosing to believe what she said."

"About what?"

His eyes softened as they met mine. "Jock."

"What, that he's alive?"

He lifted one shoulder, hesitant to hold the stare. "Yeah."

"They call that denial. I should know. It took a while to accept the news myself."

We were both silent for a moment. This was uncharted territory for us, losing someone so dear, coming to terms with the reality of never seeing or interacting with that person again.

"I'm not going to ask what he looked like," Max said. "If he *is* gone, I want to remember him as the hunk we all knew and loved."

I gave a small smile. "I can appreciate that."

He held up his phone to me. "Two minutes and counting."

I rolled my eyes at his wit, which wasn't the brightest thing to do considering my bruised and swollen lids.

We rearranged things in Phyllis's trunk to make room for the bass drum when Austin trotted out the back door of Friar Tuck's and tossed a huge black garbage bag into the Dumpster.

"Hey, Valentine. Max." He gave a timid salute, probably because I looked like I'd gone the distance in the ring. "Uh, sorry to hear about Jock."

Max and I eyed each other, then I gave Austin a cautious *thanks*, wondering what I'd missed. "Um, Austin, how did you know about Jock?"

He scratched his head under his felt crown. "Saw the news coverage on the old meat-packing plant." He shivered. "I didn't know Jock had died until this guy came in this morning and told me to give you this condolence card." He patted his medieval tunic and then his back pockets. "Oh, right. It's in the bakery. Hold on." He put up his finger, signaling us to wait, then shuffled back inside.

Max watched Austin disappear, then turned to me with a frown. "Who'd be giving you a condolence card already?"

I didn't know, but I wasn't crazy about the uneasy feeling spreading through me.

"*I* know." Max's face lit up. "Probably Mrs. Benedetti. She must've heard it on the news and, being we're closed Sundays, she must've popped into Friar Tuck's and told Austin to give you the card when he saw you."

I listened to Max's theory, the anxious feeling climbing to my neck. "Austin said it was a *guy* who delivered the card."

"So? Mrs. Benedetti has three sons. Maybe one of them took the morning off from breaking someone's toes—or whatever it is they do in the Mafia—to deliver the card."

I was contemplating my own theory when Austin exited the back door, a small white envelope in hand. "Here it is." His face looked woeful as he handed it to me. "I always admired Jock, you know? Whenever he came into Friar Tuck's, he made me feel important. Never talked down to me like some customers. Even encouraged me to join a gym. I kinda looked up to him...like an older brother." His bottom lip quivered, and his voice croaked. "I'll miss him."

I patted his arm, and Max nodded in agreement. We both knew what Austin meant about Jock. The guy had left his mark. Which brought me back to the envelope in my hand. "Austin, can you tell me what the man who gave you this looked like? And did he have hairy arms?"

"I couldn't get past his face to look at his arms," he squawked, his nimble body shuddering. "He was wearing a freaky mask, like it was Halloween and he was Freddy Krueger." He shuddered again and turned to go. "Wish I could be more help."

He didn't know how much help he'd been. We watched Austin shuffle back inside the bakery, though I wasn't sure how I was still standing. I had an icky sensation inside, and my limbs were trembling. Worse, I knew without opening the envelope that Tork was on my heels. Only thing I couldn't comprehend was why. Jock was dead. Why come after me? Because I could finger him for Jock's murder?

"Well?" Max elbowed me. "Open it."

I took a deep breath to steady myself, then peered down at the envelope. There were no rips, no smudge marks except for a bit of icing sugar, compliments of Austin. I gave the envelope a feel, a sniff, and then held it up to the light.

"You going to marry it or open it?"

I sliced Max a stony look, then peeled back the flap and slid out the card.

Blank.

"Flip it over." He nosed over my shoulder.

I waited until he caught my peeved glance. "Golly, why didn't I think of that?"

"Because you're not clever like me." He smiled like the imp he was.

I flipped the card over and faced a colorful sketch of a kite. At each of the four points was a letter. T represented north. V, south. J, east. Z, west. And there was a red X through each letter except for the T.

I swallowed a hard lump, my muscles tense. What did all this mean? Each person had been, or was about to be, eliminated except for the person who represented the T? Pretty easy to guess that was Tork. V and J had to stand for Vick and Jock. Z for Zeek.

"What's the purpose of this?" Max asked, interrupting my thoughts.

My mind raced as I put the pieces together, but I stalled for Max's sake and went into more detail about what had happened last night.

"You wasted time going to your parents' to learn where Gibson works?" He raised a palm in the air. "You could've looked him up on the internet."

"He's an employee at a computer shop," I said. "Why would his name be on the internet?"

"You can find everything on the internet." Max clicked away on his phone, then thrust it in my face. "See? Workplace. The Computer Store."

I pushed his phone away. "Thanks. I know that now."

"Okay, so you saw the kite on Jock's screen, and, through photos, have connected him to three other men from the navy, one who was badly burned."

"That's the gist of it."

"And you think the kite symbolizes something."

"It could mean a lot of things, but I believe it was an alert the other night."

He furrowed his brows, a look of concentration encompassing his face. "What about the fact that a kite represents destiny? That it's been used for experiments in aerodynamics, scientific research, and even generating power."

I stared at him slack-jawed. "When did you become an expert on kites?"

"Had one as a kid. Was fascinated by them." He looked up past Friar Tuck's creaking revolving donut, his gaze faraway. "And if you dream about them, it symbolizes freedom."

I slipped the card back in the envelope. "I'll remember that next time I dream of a kite." Which, with everything happening lately, wasn't far-fetched.

I slid the envelope in my bag when the back door of the shop banged open, and the bass drum bounced onto the pavement, Phyllis a step behind.

Max peeked at his phone and then at me, a twinkle in his eye. "Eight minutes and fifteen seconds."

"Uhhhhh!" Phyllis bent forward to catch her breath. "That's the last of it."

Max stopped the rolling drum before it hit Phyllis's car. "Aww, Phyll, I was just about to come down and help."

"Yeah, right." She wiped her sweaty brow, taking off a patch of white gook that left a streak of natural skin tone beneath.

Max shrugged with an air of innocence, then shoved his phone in his pocket, picked up the bass drum, and plopped it in the trunk. "We're ready to roll." He gave me one last look, mischief in his eyes. "You sure you don't want to come to the music store with us? I don't know if I'll be able to contain myself when Phyllis asks for a refund."

I came back to the reason I was here. "You'll have to. I need to clean the shop. If I recall, *somebody* spilled black tint all over the place."

Phyllis straightened her spine, catching a second wind. "If I were you, I'd make the dingbat clean it themself."

"Yes," Max prodded. "Why don't you get the dingbat who made the mess clean it herself."

"I tried. She's too busy playing drums and dressing as a geisha."

Phyllis's jaw plunged to the V-neck of her kimono. "There's someone out there stealing my gig?"

Oh boy. That black dye must've seeped into her pores and fried her brain cells. "Go, okay? I'll see you tonight at the restaurant."

"Don't be late," Max said. "I'll save you a front-row seat."

"Nope. Under the exit sign will be close enough for me."

They took off in Phyllis's big beluga, and I locked myself in the shop. I trudged down the hallway, flicked on the lights, and flopped my bag on the counter in the dispensary.

I filled a bucket with disinfectant and soapy water and went to work, scouring sinks, counters, and equipment. Then I got on my hands and knees and used every bit of strength I could muster to rid the ceramic tile of black stains.

I let the floor dry, drained the bucket, and turned my attention to repairing the ship. With careful hands, I pulled out the bundled cape from my bag and all the glass chunks with it.

Drat. I wouldn't be able to restore this jigsaw puzzle. I couldn't even remember what the darn thing looked like except that it resembled a pirate ship more than a naval ship. I googled some images and found one that looked similar. Close enough for me.

I went through a pile of tissues to dry my tears and half a bottle of glue to reassemble the craft. It was a labor of love, and I bombed miserably, struggling with bits of glass to form the tall mast and winged sails. I finally decided I needed help, so I dug into my reserves and used a tint brush as the mast, and my colorful eight-pack of clipper attachments to prop up the sails.

An hour later, I stepped back and tilted my head judiciously at the finished product. *Valentine*, I thought, *your work ought to be in the Museum of Fine Arts*. Ha. Who was I kidding? It looked no more like a ship than Phyllis looked like a geisha. But it was the thought that counted. And in some small way it brought me closer to Jock, reminding me of the adventures we'd had.

While the glue was drying, I traipsed downstairs and hauled Saturday's laundry out of the dryer. I folded towels, thinking I could've asked Twix to join me in cleaning the shop, as she often did, and assist me in rebuilding Jock's ship. But last night's ordeal was enough stress on a mother of two tots. Then there was Peaches and his Village People getup to contend with. Twix was probably at this moment slathering him in lotion. I didn't want to disrupt that.

I lugged the towels back upstairs, stuffed them in everyone's cupboards, and took a long, deep exhale. Satisfied everything was once again sparkling, I slogged back into the dispensary and shook out my cape in case I'd missed any glass bits to add to my work of art. The swooshing sound of the cape was followed by *pinging* on the floor.

I looked down and spotted several green-and-white pebbles rolling to a stop. I went down on one knee, clasping the counter, accidentally tipping my bag onto its side. Several more pebbles trickled out of my bag, and I caught them before they, too, bounced on the ceramic tile. Where'd these come from? I collected the ones off the floor, adding them to the ones in my palm, and fingered the two-tone bits.

Holy smokes. These weren't pebbles. They were some type of pill. But whose?

I retraced my steps to…*yikes*! *That's* what that tinkling sound was last night during our brawl with Tork. These pills must've spilled out of his jacket, and I'd unconsciously swept them up with the glass before we'd fled. I'd been so worried about staying alive I hadn't noticed them. Question was, what was Tork on?

Wait a minute. I examined the pills closer. I'd seen these before. I fingered the smooth coating on one of the tablets when it hit me. My mother and Tantig had been reviewing my great-aunt's pills yesterday. These looked like one of Tantig's medications.

I flipped open my bag and zipped the meds in the inside pouch. I didn't know what this was all about. And I wasn't sure if there was any connection between the pills and Jock's murder. One thing I did know, I couldn't waste more time hypothesizing.

Coiffing my mother's and Tantig's hair was next on my list before driving into Cambridge to check out the explosion site. Then there was Phyllis's crowning or whatever it was that I'd be witnessing.

I carted the newly fashioned ship to Jock's station and set it on the counter as gently as if it were a newborn baby. Then I grabbed my bag, switched off the lights, and rushed down the hall.

I'd verify if Tantig was taking the same pills as a two-hundred-and-fifty pound killer. Then I needed to find that killer and keep myself from getting dead in the meantime. It was a tall order, and if I had a choice, I'd rather paint my toenails dangling from a chandelier. In the grand scheme of things, it'd be less effort.

Chapter 14

My mother and great-aunt were waiting at the kitchen table like two wet cocker spaniels, their hair washed and towels draped around their necks. Doing my best to mask my limp, I walked from the shadow of the hallway into the kitchen.

My mother looked at me in alarm, her face pale. "What happened to *you*?" She leaped to my side and all but pulled out a magnifying glass from her apron pocket.

This was tricky. Lying about my less-than-stellar appearance would only get me in more trouble. Of course, telling the truth had proven to be a mistake in the past. The resigned look of dread on her face was all the confirmation I needed. The truth would have to wait.

"You were beat up, weren't you?" she blurted before I had a chance to speak.

"Uh, actually—"

She inched closer. "Bruised lip, painful walk…and look at your eyes."

I blinked sorely. "I'd look at them if I could see through them."

"Is that a joke? You look like those pandas at the zoo."

"Well? Their black eyes are cute."

"On pandas, they're cute. On humans, they're shocking. I knew it," she went on, following me to the table. "The moment you left yesterday after telling us Jock was missing, I said to Tantig, 'That girl is going to get herself in trouble.'" She bobbed her head at my great-aunt. "Didn't I say that, Tantig?"

Tantig wasn't stirred by my mother's emotional display. "Who-hk cares?" She cut to the chase, as always. "I don't need my hair-hk done."

"Of course you do." Thank goodness for the diversion. I plunked my bag onto the kitchen table and pulled out my supplies. Several green-and-white tablets rolled out along with everything else, stopping directly in front of my mother.

Oops. Guess I had more of those damn pills in my bag than I thought.

My mother leaned over the table and picked up a tablet. "What are you doing with Tantig's pills?" She looked from the pills to my battered face, her expression turning suspicious. "Start talking."

Oh boy. "They're not Tantig's. They're…they're… Phyllis's."

"*Phyllis!* What's she doing taking antidepressants?"

"*Antidepressants.* Why is Tantig taking them?"

"They're temporary since her heart scare. Dr. Stucker prescribed a handful. They're only to be taken when needed."

We both glanced at Tantig sitting in her chair, cool as a cucumber. She needed antidepressants about as much as I needed another pair of sparkly earrings. "Has she taken any?"

Worry puckered my mother's brow. "No. It's hard to tell if she needs them." She redirected the conversation back to me. "What's this about Phyllis? How'd her pills get in your bag?"

"Uh, I suppose some dropped inside when she was popping one at work yesterday." I fingered gel into Tantig's hair and combed her waves into place. "The truth is, Phyllis has, uh, been more irritable lately, having these outbursts of anger. And…and she's losing touch with reality." Now *that* was true.

My mother nodded in understanding. "Mary Ann Ganolli implied this. Said Phyllis was clothed like a Japanese geisha."

"Right down to the black hair and white face."

"Poor Phyllis." My mother made *tsk-tsk* sounds, shaking her head in sympathy.

"Yes." I tried to sound concerned. "I think the pills are temporary for her as well. Probably once she's done dressing like a geisha, she'll stop taking them."

I switched the blow dryer on high and finger-dried Tantig's hair, putting an end to the ridiculousness spewing out of my mouth. My mother busied herself at the kitchen counter, which indicated she had forgotten about my condition and more likely was focused on Phyllis's.

Thank the Lord for small miracles.

The hour went by quickly. I styled their hair, slid on my cork sandals, and thought I was home free from further probing about my appearance. I was wrong.

My mother stuffed some large bills in my bag for the hairdos, patted it shut before I could refuse, and put her index finger under my chin, a warning not to speak. I swallowed, unsure of what was coming next but wise enough to keep quiet.

"God gave me two daughters." Her voice was unwavering. "Don't you dare make it one."

Just what I needed to hear. My throat tightened, and a flood of tears mounted inside. Before I knew it, wet drops rolled down my cheeks, dripping onto my plain tan top.

My mother gently embraced me, then yanked a tissue from her apron pocket and pressed it into my palm.

This wasn't like me. It was much easier to choose flippancy over tender emotions. If I allowed myself to think about the reality of Jock's death too much, it'd be even harder to soldier on. Unfortunately, the woman standing before me could get information out of a stone.

"You know how Jock was missing?" I said between sniffles. "There was an explosion in Cambridge late Friday night, and Jock was the victim in that blast. He was murdered."

A look of horror crossed my mother's face. "Oh, dear, I'm so sorry." She stared into my bloodshot eyes, taking a moment to absorb the news. "You know who's responsible?"

"I think so." I swiped my runny nose with the tissue.

"And this is the reason you got into a fight?"

Fight was putting it mildly. "More or less."

"Wait here." She turned her back, passed Tantig who was still at the kitchen table, and dashed down the hall.

Tantig looked at me, and I looked at Tantig. "What's a Jock?" she asked.

I wiped my tears and blew my nose. "Jock was my employee, Tantig. You met him on the cruise last fall. He passed away."

She lowered her lids to half-mast and made a thin line with her lips, signaling she'd heard enough. At times, my great-aunt might be oblivious to her surroundings, but she knew when silence was preferred over words.

I looked past her to my mother who hurried from the spare bedroom into the hall, pinching a six-inch pin in her fingers. "Here." She pried my bag from under my arm and horizontally wove the pin on the inside rim of the fabric.

"What's this?" I inspected the cute pin that had a purple-gemmed cat at the end.

"My old hat pin." She patted my bag, making sure it didn't stick out. "I gave some hats to the church for a skit the kids are doing, and I didn't want anyone stabbed from a pin."

I snapped my mouth shut, realizing I was gawking at her. "Which still doesn't explain why you're giving it to me."

"It's in case."

"In case of what? I find myself needing to secure a hat?"

She looked at me like she was dealing with a dumbbell. "It's no secret you've brought down crooks with your beauty tools. This hat pin is sleek, sharp, and can do a lot of damage if stuck in the right spot." She adjusted my shoulder strap and hushed her voice. "You can add it to your arsenal. It's already in a handy location."

My mother, the beauty weapons' pimp. I raised my brows so high in shock, my lids hurt.

"I figure if you can't beat 'em, join 'em." She gave me a gentle push out the door. "Just *be* careful."

My insides were still in turmoil over everything that had happened since Friday night, but I told myself I needed to eat something before this evening. I was determined to see justice done for Jock, and I could use all the fortification I could get. Plus, I needed something in my belly before stomaching Phyllis's affair.

Maybe fries would be good. I peered at the dashboard clock. Gosh! Four-thirty already. Fries would definitely be good.

I rolled into Burger Brothers, owned by four hot young brothers who'd won dozens of awards for their mile-high burgers and fries. What the heck. I'd get a burger as well. What I didn't eat, I'd give to Yitts.

I pulled into the drive-thru, ordered a Diet Coke with my meal, and advanced to the pickup window. I was staring into space, thinking of the night ahead, when I heard a familiar growl and low whine of a motorcycle. I looked straight ahead at the quiet traffic on Montgomery and saw the bike responsible for the noise. The driver slowed to a stop, looked my way, then sped by.

Suddenly, I recalled Candace's insistence yesterday that I'd been followed by a guy on a motorcycle. Then a biker showed up at Jock's condo last night while Twix and I were there. Since *that* biker was Tork, was this him today? Had he trailed me yesterday when I left my parents'? Had he been tracking me now?

Milo, the second-youngest of the burger brothers, handed me my meal. I thanked him and just about ripped off his arm as I flew out of the drive-thru.

I kept a left-handed grip on the steering wheel, wolfing down fries with my right. I was so high on adrenaline, I swerved around cars, ran a red, and took Clairmont on two wheels. I was proud I hadn't lost sight of the biker.

If it were Jock's bike I would've recognized it in a heartbeat—I think—since his Harley had a long extended front. Every other bike looked the same to me. This wasn't clothes or fashion. We were talking a piece of metal on two wheels.

I gulped my soda and put it back in the cup holder when another motorcycle cut out in front of me, almost causing me to veer into a telephone pole. What in the world! Was this guy insane? I had a death grip on the wheel and muscled back into my lane. The biker angled his head toward me, waving me to go away. Of all the—

I gritted my teeth and floored it, ready to bump this jerk off the road. In a flash, he took a sharp right and disappeared down Oxford.

"Good riddance!" I let out a breath and eased up on the gas, calming my rattled nerves.

Tork veered right a block ahead, drove five miles south on Aspect Boulevard, and passed the old dump. By now, we were on the outskirts of town. I stayed a safe distance behind him, gagging from the faint stench of ammonia and sulfur that still filled the air from the old landfill. I closed my window before I upchucked my fries. One throw-up a day was enough.

Two miles further, Tork pulled into a storage site comprised of six long rows of blue-roofed metal sheds. He cruised down the fourth row and disappeared from sight. I followed him as far as the lot, then parked and ran to the start of the unit where he'd turned. Bag tight to my side, I peeked to my right around the corner and saw him near the far end, his back to me as he dismounted his bike and took off his helmet.

Simultaneously, a black sports car pulled up from the other end and stopped beside Tork's bike. Tork nodded to the dark-haired guy getting out of the car, and they both disappeared inside a shed. Clearly, Tork thought he'd lost me back on Montgomery, or he'd underestimated my chutzpah. Fool.

Several minutes later, they emerged. Tork carried a large duffel bag and unzipped it in front of the man. They were facing the other way, but I could see the guy pull a handgun out of the duffel bag, bring it up to his face, and examine everything from the barrel to the grip. Then he set it back inside the bag and tossed the bag in his trunk.

Holy cow. What was this all about? Was Tork gunrunning? Had Jock been onto him?

How was this connected to the email from Vick? No one had located him, as far as I knew, yet he was the key since he was the one who sent the email that brought Jock to the Hock. Had Tork done away with him, too? I was thinking this through when a hand came around my face and clamped my mouth. In one swift move, I was spun around and nailed to the wall.

"Ro-m-ro!" I cried through a muffle, my heart ready to leap out of my chest.

"*Shh!*" He removed his hand from my mouth.

"What are you *doing* here?" I panted, my whisper anything but shushed. I shook loose from his hold and looked from his wild dark waves down the length of his toned body. He was clad in the same black leather gear he'd worn earlier. Then it hit me. "You were that idiot on the motorcycle, waving me off the road."

He arched an eyebrow, his cop eyes daring, his tone dangerous. "Idiot?"

"Well? Were you trying to kill me?"

He curled his fingers around the neck of my top and hauled me away from the corner of the unit. "I was trying to keep you and your *reckless* nose from arriving at this point."

I dropped my bag to the ground, beyond incensed. "Obviously, you and your *hot-headed* nose failed miserably." I was close to crossing the line, and Romero knew it.

Like the sage cop he was, he held back from commenting on something he'd be sorry for. I probably could've learned a lesson or two.

He pressed his hard frame into me, straddling his hands high on the wall above my head, his stubble grazing my cheeks, his breath whispering on my neck. "God only knows why you're turning me on at this moment. You're hell to reason with, you're interfering with an investigation, *and* you ran a red back there."

The electricity between us was fierce, and I could feel in his touch that he was fighting for control. How dare he make me feel like he could have me on my back in a millisecond. Liquid heat ran through me at the thought. I felt even hotter thinking about his anger.

Collecting himself, he pushed off from the wall, scooped his hand under my elbow, and ushered me toward the parking lot. "You've got to leave. *Now.*"

I shrugged out of his embrace for the second time and went back for my bag. "I'm not going anywhere until you tell me what's going on. How are you involved in this?"

"Look, I haven't got time to explain. I'm working a case. A bike's required for speed."

"On gunrunning?" Suddenly, I remembered him tensing this morning when I pointed out Tork in the pictures. Now I understood why. Romero's interest in him was because the guy was dealing in arms. This must've been separate from Jock's murder.

Madera's story about Tork and the landmine that had disfigured his face came to mind. I quickly brought Romero up to date, sharing that Tork was definitely our assaulter and most likely Jock's murderer.

"Why didn't you tell me this earlier? Like at the morgue?" Then, as if recalling how gutted I'd been at seeing Jock's lifeless body, he took a heavy breath, holding back from furthering this line of questioning.

We heard yelling, and Romero poked his head around the corner. "*Shit.* We've been made." He thrust me toward the parking lot. "*Go.* Get in your car and *take off!*"

I recognized the sounds of Tork's bike and the sports car roaring to life. I ran like the devil in my cork heels, every inch a strain on my battered body. I made it to my car, fell inside, and ducked toward the passenger seat.

I gasped for air, my lungs burning, my mind racing on

what to do next. I couldn't leave Romero alone. Jock had already been murdered. What if Romero was killed, too?

I wasn't considering he was a tough-assed cop who carried, at a minimum, one gun and who had far more skills than those outlined in a police handbook. But there were *two* of *them*.

The roar of Tork's bike was deafening as it zoomed by, the sports car on its tail. I didn't hear any gunshots, and I deduced the two men were anxious to flee the scene.

My heartbeat thumped erratically, but I took a brave breath, poked my head up, and peered through the windshield. Amid the swirling dust in the air, I spotted Romero leap on his bike, rev the engine, and skid out of the lot.

Damn. I fumbled in my bag for my keys, my hands shaking violently.

Romero disappeared along with the other two men. Meanwhile, I ransacked my bag, flinging tools left and right. Giving up on my key search, I whacked my palm on the steering wheel, banging my head back on the headrest. By now, the motors were a distant sound, and here I sat. Romero was right. I *was* reckless. And foolish. And cheeky. Good thing I had cute shoes, or my life would be a total sham.

I lowered my gaze from the windshield to the ignition. Dangling from the key slot was my glittery *V* keychain. Abso-bloody-lutely fantastic. I'd been in such a hurry to spy on Tork, I'd left my keys in the car. I smacked my forehead with my palm. Now what? Everyone had fled.

I shoved everything back in my bag and peered down at my fast-food wrapper. The sensible thing to do now was to go home, eat my burger, and get ready for tonight's mission.

I was far from looking forward to Phyllis's event, and my stomach was in knots about being anywhere near the Hock, especially if Romero was on Tork's trail. But I had to push forward regardless of what was in store because before the night was done, someone would pay for Jock's murder.

Chapter 15

I sat on the kitchen floor and hand-fed Yitts pieces of my burger, polishing off what I could stomach. My body was aching, my mind, drained. All I wanted to do was bury myself under the covers. The only way I could see myself watch Phyllis blend in with a bunch of geishas-in-the-making was if someone were holding a gun to my head.

But a promise was a promise, a saying I was paying for in spades. I'd already let Phyllis down twice before. Plus, there was Max to consider. He'd been shouldering this farce all along. And he had a point. Good or bad, Phyllis's show would be entertaining. It'd also be a distraction.

Yitts crawled onto my lap, expecting more.

"You just ate half my burger." I got to my feet, opened a new pouch of salmon-flavored cat food, and dumped some in her bowl.

Yitts crunched on her meal, and I hiked into my bedroom. I didn't know how I was supposed to dress for tonight's event at the Geisha Gap, but since that wasn't my top priority, I decided to dress in honor of Jock.

I went through my drawers and pulled out the black fitted boatneck top and 3/4-length black tights. "That's right, Jock," I sang, trying to sound carefree. "I'm dressing like Catwoman again. You better come and stop me."

Maybe I was losing touch with reality, but if Jock heard me, his sensuous lips would twitch up into a grin while his sexy gaze raked over my body. The thought gave me shivers.

I stopped dressing, waiting for a reply, knowing I'd get none. For a moment, my throat was too tight with anguish to move, anger seizing me. Anger at Jock for leaving this world. Anger at the person responsible for this tragedy.

I unfurled my hands, realizing I'd curled them into fists. Then I took a deep swallow and pushed on. I had to. My commitment to Jock's memory depended on this.

I tugged out my shoddy bun and brushed my hair back into a severe, sleek ponytail. Catwoman or cat burglar? Either was fine, considering I *was* planning on breaking and entering.

I slid on my black sparkly ballet-type shoes and did a plié, testing the foam soles. Perfect if I needed to make a fast getaway from Phyllis's gig…or anywhere else.

After doing a few stretches to limber up my tense body, I said a short prayer for insurance purposes. Let's face it. I wasn't built like a Greek Amazon, and I wasn't a warrior like Joan of Arc. I was a beautician who flung a few beauty tools in self-defense. If the good Lord couldn't help me, nobody could.

The Okiya Corral was a red-brick restaurant, boasting a green awning over the front door and an orange neon sign above scrawled in Japanese. It was situated on the corner of Hock and Pheasant in Cambridge, half a block south of 823 Hock—the ex-meat-packing plant.

An alley that wound around the Okiya Corral separated the restaurant from a string of buildings that led to the old plant. The Geisha Gap was at the back of the restaurant. Its entrance was at the side in the alley, noted by the smaller green awning over the door.

It was closing in on nine, and Phyllis's white behemoth was parked on Pheasant. Apparently, I had the right place.

The darkening sky was hazy from remnants of dust and particles from Friday's disaster, the smell of soy sauce, horseradish, and smoldering wood ripe in the air.

Except for the brightly lit restaurant, the area was still, spooky. Fast-food wrappers, soda cans, and cigarette butts littered the road. Down the street, crime scene tape and police pylons surrounded the three-story shelled-out meat-packing plant—the source of the smoldering smell.

I locked Daisy Bug after finding a spot on Hock and dropped my keys in my bag. By the turnout at the Geisha Gap, I presumed I wasn't the only fool roped into viewing this sham.

I tapped my ballet shoes on the ground and focused on the damaged building down the block, ignoring the scratchy sensation scaling my neck. Well? What was I waiting for? I still had time before Phyllis's event. And the Hock wasn't coming to me.

Warning bells clanged inside me, making me more anxious, but I wasn't about to reconsider my actions. I had to investigate and see if there was any evidence that would explain Jock's murder and bring his killer to justice. My next thought was irrational, but deep down, I wouldn't be able to help myself from still looking for Jock, too.

I took a moment to fight the gruesome vision that jumped to mind of Jock's burned body on a slab at the morgue. I squeezed my eyes tight, willing it to pass, remembering him as the overly muscled hunk I knew. Finally, the burned version of him faded, and I felt my shoulders come down in relief. Swallowing the worry of what lie ahead, I gripped my bag tightly and plodded down the street.

I slowed my walk, noticing a narrow, dented door at the rear of the plant, hanging half off its hinge. With the stealth of a cat, I crawled on my hands and knees under a steel fence, and snaked around steel drums, forklifts, and other scattered equipment to get to the door.

Inside was a mess of broken glass, rubble, collapsed beams, and destroyed gear from the former plant. I shuddered and tiptoed across the debris to the center of the room, surveying the gutted area for clues, finding nothing more than a few small piles of tattered clothes.

Then I heard a slight *crackle* as if someone else was stepping on glass, and I saw a moving shadow outside.

My ears pricked up in alarm, the sight sending my pulse into a frenzy. Though the crime scene had been sealed off, anyone could get inside if they really wanted to. Hadn't *I* entered without permission?

Shivering in fright, I scanned my surroundings and hurried over to the corner where I'd entered and hid under a small counter tipped on its side. I crawled into the triangular cubby no bigger than a doll's house and curled into a tight ball. I held my breath and peeked from underneath the cabinet across the ashes and crud on the floor in the direction of the shadow.

Slowly, a pair of legs came into view on the far side of the room, the echo of footsteps on the floor, chilling. It felt like I was in a horror movie and the next victim to be slaughtered. *Dear heavens. In a slaughtering house yet.*

Blood pounded in my temples, panic building at an alarming rate. *Think, Valentine. Concentrate on identifying the person. Use your senses.* Yes. That was it. Concentrate. The prowler. Was it Tork?

If I could just see his hairy arms or scarred face, but it was impossible. The sun had already set, and I was crouched so low I couldn't view anything higher than his baggy pants, the bottom of his long, tattered coat, and shoes that looked worn and outdated.

The stride was deliberate, as if searching for something in the room. No discernable smells from this distance other than odors from the burned-out building. He paused, and his feet turned in my direction.

My heart stopped cold. I took thin breaths, closing my eyes for a millisecond, willing myself to keep dead still.

What was he looking for? Despite what Twix had shared about a vet organization aiding in moving homeless vets to a facility, was it possible some were still using this building as a shelter? Was this why Tork first came to the Hock? In that instant, it occurred to me that I didn't know if he was homeless or struggling, but this would've tied him to the scene of the crime.

I scanned the bits of ragged clothes left with the rubble. Had Tork returned for something? What if he camped out here all night? How would I escape? Worse, what if he'd followed me here?

My thoughts were all over the map, but I could link him to Jock and the fight at his condo on the night of the explosion. Naturally, he'd want to eliminate his only eyewitness. Of all times. Why didn't I listen to Romero?

The intruder took measured steps in my direction, each tread reverberating in the empty room. The suspense built as he neared, and I didn't think my heart could take any more.

Out of nowhere, he slowed, turned, and walked to the center of the room. Then he bent, and I spied a frayed knit hat on his head as he picked up something small off the ground. Something I'd missed? And what about the cops? Hadn't they swept through the place?

Seemingly satisfied with his discovery, he picked up his pace and exited from where he came.

Whew. My mouth felt like sawdust, my hands and legs trembling beyond control. I waited a solid five minutes, then crawled out from my hiding spot and ran for my life back to the Okiya Corral, jumping at unidentifiable shadows that seemed to follow me.

I finally stumbled to the corner of the alley and stooped over and gasped for air. Then I twisted around, making sure nobody was on my tail. The street was still, the only noises coming from inside the restaurant.

Convinced I was alone, I straightened up, heaved my bag over my shoulder, and took a final calming breath. Where did I go from here? If that prowler was Tork, he may or may not have realized I was there.

I peered up at the neon Japanese sign. Right. Phyllis's gig. Might as well get this over with. Maybe it'd give me time to plot my next move.

I staggered down the alley to the door for the Geisha Gap. Six feet beyond the entrance were two barred windows I would've needed a stepstool to get to, a stack of wooden pallets, garbage cans, and a Dumpster. Inviting or what? Didn't matter. After my spine-chilling experience at the Hock, I mounted the two steps to the door and walked inside, feeling as safe as if I'd come home.

Going by the lotus clock on the wall, I was half an hour late, and the festivities were already in full swing. Oops. Phyllis would have a cow. Main thing was I showed up. More than I could say for Max who was suspiciously absent.

I threw some money in the donation box and bowed several times to the petite geishas who welcomed me in the foyer. They were lined up in a row and looked identical in height and size except each wore a different-colored kimono. One woman, in blue, took a dainty step forward and asked who I was here to see tonight.

I swallowed back a cough. *You mean this wasn't anonymous?* I smiled faintly at each of them, imagining how different Phyllis was going to look stacked up beside them. Not only was she a head taller than these ladies, but our clumsy geisha-in-waiting had them by a good seventy pounds.

"Please?" The lady bowed again. "The name?"

It seemed like a bag of cotton balls filled my mouth. The words *Phyllis Murdoch* wouldn't come out.

"Ahh…" The lady gave a perceptive nod, her face lit up like a Japanese lantern. "I understand."

"You do?" If she knew, why was she being so nice?

"Yes. You are here for Rini."

"Rini?"

"Yes. It's Japanese. We give a name to all our girls at the Geisha Gap." She pronounced her words with thought. "Rini means *little bunny.*"

I looked around, waiting for the punch line. "I think

there's a mix-up." I spoke slower, adding a smile to my words. "I'm here to see Phyllis Murdoch."

"Yes, yes," she rushed on. "You've come to the right place."

The door behind me burst open and Max charged in, out of breath.

"What happened to *you?*" I asked, relieved at his appearance, albeit late.

He pulled me aside and raked his hand through his streaked blond hair. "I've been running errands for Madame Geisha all day, but I'm *done* with this charade. First, it was take notes on her training. Then it was cart her drums here. Then return them to the store." He huffed out air. "You don't want to know how *that* turned out."

He was right. I had enough on my plate.

He gave a high-pitched peep, typical when he was irate. "The guy at the music store told Phyllis if she and her drums didn't vacate the premises, he'd call the cops."

"And?"

"And Phyllis said he didn't know who he was talking to. The guy looked her up and down in her kimono and smeared painted face and said he was talking to an obviously mentally ill woman."

"Oy."

"Oy is right. Phyllis smacked him on the head with her cymbals. It pretty much went downhill from there."

Max looked so flustered, I felt an instant pang in my chest for him. "So why are you late?"

"Take a guess. I've been smoothing the waters with the music store, convincing the guy to *not* press charges. Phyllis, being Phyllis, and not recognizing the damage she'd done, took off in her car, complaining she had to go home and touch up her makeup before tonight. I was about to call an Uber, but I ran into a neighbor at the store who offered to give me a lift home." He swiped the perspiration off his forehead and expelled a sigh. "Phyllis owes me big time for this. You know she could've gone to jail?"

"People, people," the tiny woman urged. "Please."

We hushed our voices, and I made a face at Max. "Speaking of Phyllis, why didn't you tell me she had a new name?"

"And ruin the surprise?" He got over himself and chuckled mischievously. "Forget Hollywood. I could make a mint filming my own Idiot Files production. I can see the caption now. IT'S A BULL! IT'S A BUNNY! IT'S PHYLLIS MURDOCH!" He swept his hand in the air, as if displaying an imaginary sign. Then he dropped some money in the donation box and hauled me toward the three steps on the left leading up to the party room. "Come on. I don't want to miss seeing what our geisha does next."

Chapter 16

Roughly one hundred people faced a small stage at the front of the room. On the stage, ten geishas-in-training served tea to their models—if that was what the ten elderly Japanese men were called. Each model sat at a tiny bistro table for one, nodding politely to their particular trainee as she waited on them.

There was an aisle down the middle of the audience. Guests made good use of it, going back and forth to the bathroom like bladder draining held more appeal than sitting through the extravaganza.

Max and I angled out of the way for one gentleman heading to the bathroom. Then Max pointed to an empty chair near the stage. "I've got a front-row seat waiting for me."

I saw the chair he spoke of. "Go for it."

"Where are you sitting?"

I looked to my left at the sole seat unoccupied by the window. "Right here. Close to the exit."

"Suit yourself." He skipped to the front, and I got comfy in my seat in time to witness a live take of The Idiot Files.

Nine of the geishas treaded softly in their wooden-based flip-flops around their models, pouring tea with expertise and bowing respectfully. Phyllis, the tenth geisha, puckered her lips, barreled around two of the girls, and bumped them out of the way. Then she gave a loud huff. Phyllis-speak for *I can do better than that*.

I looked around the room. This couldn't be what an actual geisha training ceremony was like. Instead, it felt like a westernized production where the trainees were dressed in costume to entertain. Costume play or not, Phyllis was making the most of it.

She mutely poured her elderly model a cup of tea, then took a swat at a fly buzzing around his bald head. Tea sloshed all over the place, and the fly landed on the back of the man's crown.

Phyllis zeroed in on it, wound up her arm, and smacked the guy's head, almost sending him into next week. The fly flew off, tea went *glug glug glug* down the man's back, and the poor soul sprang face first into the table.

Phyllis yanked the dazed model back in his chair, unwound the long obi from around her waist, and circled the guy, flapping the wide belt at the insect.

The crowd cheered and hooted. Clearly, people were getting more out of this production than they'd first anticipated. The only one who seemed to think it was real was Phyllis.

Between swatting at the fly and wiping tea from the guy's back, she ran out of length on the obi and lurched forward. Her arms flew up, the teapot went sailing, and Phyllis landed headfirst in the man's lap.

The volume in the room hiked twenty decibels. Max rocked back and forth in his seat and slid his thumb and third finger in his mouth, giving one of his ear-piercing whistles.

Yep, this was way better than staying home, burying myself under the covers.

Once the crowd settled down, the show moved on to the musical portion. Several trainees began by playing flutes and stringed instruments. Next, three other geishas shimmied onto the stage with decorative fans and sang "Three Little Maids From School Are We."

Phyllis was in the background, moving the drums an

inch here and there, heedless of the musical number in front of her from *The Mikado*. Max turned around in his seat and gave me a grin that said, *Are you getting this?*

Phyllis waited until the three little maids scurried off the stage, then gave an exaggerated eye roll like *they* were the ridiculous ones. She plunked down on the drum stool, emitting a loud whoosh, and nodded to the guy across from me at the back manning the sound system.

All of a sudden, Phyllis pounded the drums in beat to a guitar coming from the speaker system, her head bobbing up and down, the dangly bits from her chopsticks slapping her in the face. *Raa-ta-ta-ra-ta. Raa-ta-ta-ra-ta. Raa-ta-ta-ra-ta. My Sharona!*

Nobody knew what to think. Except Max. He was singing and waving his phone high in the air, flashing the light on Phyllis like he was at a rock concert, and she was in The Knack. "My Sharona. Woo!"

People jumped in the aisles, some dancing, others looking as if they'd fallen into a sinkhole. Max and I were the only two sitting, watching Phyllis, Max getting his jollies egging people on, me trying to keep the tears of laughter back.

Getting myself under control, I took a deep breath and pulled a tissue from my bag. I had to refocus on finding Tork. I tilted my face to the barred window and was dabbing my right eye, when I spied Freddy Krueger staring in at me.

I choked in shock and fell sideways out of my chair, away from the window and the evil grin pasted on his scary face. Nobody thought much of my actions. Everyone was too wound up over Phyllis's performance.

I darted back to the window, but it was empty, the only thing visible through the bars, a dim view down at the alley. I knew I'd seen Tork. He must've stood on a garbage can to look inside, but where did he go? I scooped up my bag and dashed out the door into the alley, panting, looking both ways.

Like a shot, a motorcycle engine revved to life. I spun to my right and spotted in the darkness a sole headlight aimed my way, the revving escalating. Tork! The bike burst into action, picking up speed, the whining engine deafening as it drew near.

The air was thick with the smell of burning rubber and fear—my fear. I stood paralyzed, unable to lift my feet to run for help. How ironic was that? In ballet shoes, and I couldn't even raise a bloody leg. This was it. Tork had found his eyewitness, and now I was going to die.

I gathered every ounce of willpower and forced my legs to move, but I wasn't quick enough. Tork barreled by me, thrust his leather-clad arm out, and punched me in the face.

A *crack* resonated between my ears, and the force of the blow sent me flying back in midair. I landed hard on the wooden pallets by the Dumpster, moaning, my limbs at funny angles, blood gushing from my nose.

Get up! Get up! a voice screamed inside. *What are you made of?*

Sugar and spice, I replied to the inner voice, bobbing my head like a broken doll, praying nothing was broken.

Screw sugar and spice! Get up and fight! Your life depends on it!

Drool seeped from the side of my mouth, I was seeing triple, and blood from my nose was pooling onto the ground. If I could just get back to the safety of the restaurant…

I spit on the cracked asphalt in defiance. No! The voice was right. I had to get up and fight! I was doing this for Jock. I couldn't quit now.

Taking a breath for courage, I gave my mouth a furious swipe and clawed my hands in the air for something to grab onto.

I lurched for a garbage can, but it tipped over. I reached for another. The second can spilled on top of me, covering me with a slurry of sushi, coffee grounds, and chicken scraps. Pushing back nausea from the putrid smells, I crawled past the trash and blindly swatted the air.

Tork squealed his brakes at the end of the alley, swerved around, and raced toward me at full throttle. He let up on the gas at the last moment and kicked up dirt, skidding donuts in the alley, making a game of this. Taunt Valentine Beaumont, then run her over.

A sharp spasm shot down my spine, but I refused to let the pain overtake me. I stumbled to my feet, my bag miraculously still on my arm, and gripped the back of the Dumpster handle to steady myself.

Tork circled around the Dumpster, trapping me, plowing his tail end repeatedly into the garbage cans. Still woozy from the blow, I fell on my ass, and he zoomed down the alley.

I watched him retreat, fighting to stay with it, my foggy head struggling to retrieve something that felt important. Suddenly, it dawned on me. Tork wasn't in baggy pants or a grungy long coat, and he was wearing boots, not shoes. But that *had* to have been him I'd seen earlier at the Hock.

He disappeared from sight, yet the unmistakable sound of his idling engine persisted. He wasn't done with me. Guaranteed.

I rolled my head toward the restaurant, the barred windows grimly staring down at me. Why wasn't anyone helping me? Couldn't they hear the commotion outside?

The pounding music to "My Sharona" reverberated in the alley. Of course. What could be heard over Phyllis's drumming?

I swallowed in terror at being all alone. After the past two assaults from Tork, I was pretty sure I wouldn't come out of this alive. Everyone knew: three strikes, you're out.

No! I wouldn't let that happen. With a shaky hand covered in blood, I gave a backhanded stroke across my face, an iron will rapidly overpowering me. I fought angry tears blurring my vision and staggered to my feet again. I was certain I could make it inside the restaurant and call for help, but instead of escaping this maniac, I was determined to catch him.

I gulped for air through the clotting blood in my nose, suddenly conscious of my bag swinging from my arm. I peered inside. I had to have *something* that would end this once and for all. My gold aerosol can of hairspray was sitting on top, the purple-gemmed hat pin next to it, catching my eye.

The motorcycle continued to rev around the corner, urging me to move quickly. In a panic, I pulled out the hat pin, praying this would work. I wheedled it through the pinhole on the hairspray can's actuator valve and gave it a firm twist so the pin was sticking out at a ninety-degree angle.

I hobbled into the alley, laid the can across the ground with the pin aimed straight up in the air. Then I ripped off two pieces of nail tape and taped the can in place.

Vroom. Vroom. Vroom.

My heart was in my throat, and I couldn't feel my legs. If my plan didn't work, I'd be dead. No two ways about it. I hitched my bag over my shoulder and stood rooted to the ground two feet in front of the booby trap.

The bike roared to life, and Tork appeared around the corner, aiming straight for me. My pulse was out of control, my hands sweaty with fear. I was petrified and in danger of losing my life, yet there was nothing I could do different. This was for Jock.

Tork advanced on me, picking up speed, swifter this time. I remained steadfast in place, gritting my teeth, staring straight ahead at him, tears staining my cheeks. Hard to say who was psyching out who, but at the last second, I dodged for the wooden pallets, and Tork drove over the trap.

The pin sank into the tire, the can exploded into a ball of fire, and the bike swayed and skidded across the alley. Tork was thrown from the bike a split second before it burst into flames.

I was fighting for air, struggling to my feet, thinking it was all over for Tork. But he shook off the haze from the crash, tore off his helmet, and strode over to me, looking mean and ugly.

He yanked me to my feet by my ponytail, swung me around by my hair to disorient me, then slapped me hard across my bloody face. "You tried to burn me!" he screeched, his tone unbelieving.

My bag went flying, and I cried out for help, but even to me my voice sounded weak.

He lifted me off the ground, choking and shaking me, his grip merciless, the frenzy evident on his frightening face.

I could feel the life draining out of me. I flailed my arms, gasping for air when all of a sudden Tork was hammered on the head. I had to be in a coma because I thought he'd been hit with a wooden flip-flop.

"Take *that*!" Phyllis shouted, hopping on one foot. "And *that*." *Whack. Whack. Whack.* "That's my cousin you're trying to kill. You better think twice before you lay another hand on her."

Before I blacked out, I rolled my gaze to my captor's face. Something seemed off—no doubt, the result of being brutalized by Phyllis—but I couldn't pinpoint what.

He dropped me like a hot potato and, without looking back, sped down the alley.

"And *stay* away!" Phyllis barked, clenching her flip-flop in the air.

Max rushed to my side and pulled me to a sitting position. "*Valentine!*" he screamed in my ear. "*Say* something."

Just what I needed. I jerked from his shriek, holding my head in pain. "I'm fine," I said through a cough. Then I spit up blood.

"You sure?" He brushed bits of sushi rice off my shoulder, then waved a hand in front of my face. "How many fingers am I holding up?"

"Six."

"Smartass." He let out a sigh of relief and helped me to my feet, scrutinizing me more closely. "I hate to tell you this, but I think your nose is broken."

I touched my nose. It was swelling at an alarming rate. "*Yow.* I think you're right."

A dozen or so people from the festivities had come out to see what the excitement was all about. Some gave a low whistle of astonishment at the blazing bike. Others shrank back in fear.

A worker from the restaurant in a white shirt with sleeves rolled up to his elbows held the door open wide. "Please, everybody. Come inside."

"Yeah." Phyllis tugged down her kimono that had ripped from her ankles to her thighs. "I'm not done with my solo."

Max tilted his head from Phyllis, sliding on her flip-flop, to me. "Yes. Phyllis isn't done with her solo."

I shifted my gaze from Max to the restaurant worker holding the door, something niggling at me. The employee was Asian like his counterparts and was no one I knew. Then what had me transfixed? I shook my head to clear my mind, but all that did was hurt my brain. *Darn.* Something was pulling at me, and it felt huge.

In the dim light from the alley, I studied the guy some more. My gaze ran down the length of his body and back, stopping at his left forearm, which was stretched across the open door. Then I spotted it. The tattoo on his arm. A compass or a dragon. Didn't matter what.

As if struck by lightning, a moment of understanding hit me, the implications so profound, it left a clanging in my chest.

"Go ahead," I said to Max, collecting my bag and a few things that had fallen out of it. "I need to get in touch with Romero."

"First, can we finish watching Phyllis play all three stooges in her *Comedy of Errors*? At least till the cops get here?"

I nudged him toward the door. "I can't. It has to do with Jock."

He spun around, all humor gone from his face. "What about Jock?"

"He's alive."

"*What?* You mean Pooh-Bah, Lord High Everything Else, was right all along?"

"Max, Phyllis doesn't resemble the grand Pooh-Bah."

"She certainly doesn't resemble any of the Three Little Maids Are We!"

I gave him a shove. "I'll fill you in later. Right now I've got to talk to Romero."

"Okay." He pulled a hunk of crab meat out of my hair and flung it on the ground. "But if you're not inside within five minutes, I'm coming back out for you." He reluctantly left me alone and followed Phyllis and the crowd back inside.

Before I got too comfortable, I glanced both ways down the alley. Looked like Tork was long gone. Chicken. Probably scared by the whining sirens in the distance.

I glimpsed at the smoking bike, then pulled out my phone. "Jock's not dead," I said to Romero when he picked up.

"What?" I could hear a sigh on the other end, one that implied Valentine was at it again. "Look, you're still in shock. Less than twelve hours ago, you saw the badly burned body of a man you cared for." He paused as though reflecting on something. "Why do you sound stuffed up? You catching a cold?" He waited a beat, his next words measured. "And why do I hear sirens?"

I dabbed a tissue to my bleeding nose, trying to overlook the throbbing from the break. "I'll get to that later. You have to listen to me. I think Jock's alive."

"I heard that part. What makes you so sure?"

"The tattoo." I relived that moment in the morgue where Jock was laid out, head on the left, feet on the right. "His right arm was under our noses, right? Though it was burned, it had the remnants of a rope-and-anchor tattoo."

"So?"

"Jock's tattoo was on his left arm, not his right." Now I knew why thoughts of the tattoo girl from work yesterday were plaguing me. It was Phyllis's comment to her about washing off her tattoos that led me to thinking about the *placement* of tattoos.

In that moment, I recalled spotting a marking on Tork's hairy arm when he'd pinned me to the garage door Friday night, something I hadn't given a second thought to because of the poor lighting playing tricks on me, plus, I'd been struggling to stay alive. I couldn't tell what the image was, yet I'd bet my last tube of lipstick it was also of a rope and anchor.

"You're sure about this."

"Absolutely. The tattoo proves that the person on the table at the morgue was not Jock. If he was dead, why was Tork at his place last night? Jock's death means Tork has won. He's already gotten what he wanted."

By the silence on the other end, I could tell Romero was mulling this over.

"Unless Jock isn't dead," I went on. "And Tork knows it. Maybe he came by looking for Jock again and was shocked to find Twix and me there instead. That has to be it."

I speculated some more. Was that the reason he delivered a card to Friar Tuck's? Was the kite meant to scare me? Alert me? Or was he trying to find out if I knew more about Jock's whereabouts by following me? I had to hang onto hope that my theory was right, and Jock was alive.

"If that wasn't Jock in the morgue," Romero said, "then who was it?"

"Vick."

"Vick."

"Yes. It all ties together. Vick sent Jock the alert in the first place that Tork was coming. Plus, he was the same size as Jock. Twix noted that when she'd seen them together at the movie set. On top of that, Vick and Tork both had the same tattoos on their right arms."

"Right arms. And you know this because?"

"A friendly card from Tork that had a depiction of a kite. He and Vick were paired as north and south on the kite's points."

"Am I supposed to understand this?"

I shrugged as if he could see me. "Doesn't matter. It was a link to the tattoos being on the same arms."

I could visualize a lick of steam piping out Romero's ears. "What *does* matter is you were withholding evidence."

I sniffed, trying not to get indignant from his tone. "I was going to give you the card. I just didn't have a chance."

"Beautiful." Sirens wailed from several blocks away and were hard to ignore. "You want to tell me where you are?"

I was about to share what had happened in the alley when a reeking cloth came around my mouth. I tried to scream, but I couldn't. Everything went black.

Chapter 17

I didn't know how long I'd been out. The room was dim, the air musty, and my butt was cold from sitting on a concrete floor. Several crude light bulbs hung on wires from the ceiling, and the walls were bare of windows.

My hands were tied behind my back, and my feet were bound in front of me. I suspected it was still Sunday night since blood continued to seep from my nose, saturating the cloth muzzling my mouth. My best guess was that I'd been dragged to a basement of a building or a cold cellar not far from the Okiya Corral. Though I had no proof. With no way of seeing the neighboring buildings or even the neon sign from the restaurant, it was impossible to gauge my location. Plus, the sirens I'd heard earlier had died.

I took a shallow breath. The gag tied at the back of my head restricted my airway, my injured nasal cavity making it worse. Suffocating to death was foremost in my mind, a terrifying thought that had always haunted me. I struggled to picture happy thoughts to tamp down the panic, like being in a jewelry boutique or playing Beethoven's 8th Sonata, which I still hadn't cracked.

A clattering sound brought me back to my predicament. Through a fog, I stared at Tork's back about fifty feet away. He faced a makeshift table of boxes and crates and was going back and forth cramming weapons into duffel bags and other containers.

I wished Jock were here, that he was indeed alive. However, maybe I'd been wrong. What if my theory on the tattoo had been way off?

It hurt like the dickens to focus, so I stared dully at Tork as he shed his leather jacket and tossed it on a heap of cartons. He prattled to himself, checking guns and orders. Wouldn't want a crook to get the wrong weapon.

I gulped back a sob and cranked my head to my right where my bag sat six inches away. I prayed nothing had been removed from inside. Hopefully, Tork had been more interested in binding and gagging me so he could get on with his illegal business before he killed me. The impact of that thought was like a cuff to the head, and out of nowhere a tear from each eye rolled down my cheeks, adding to the choking sensation from the bloody, wet gag in my mouth.

The reality was I knew little about the person I was dealing with or what was driving him. The reality of *that* made me hyperventilate. I breathed in and out, swallowing thickly, trying to put a lid on my fear. I had to stay in control before Tork noticed I'd come to. I ruminated on what I'd gathered about him, hoping that might help.

First, there was losing his brother and maiming his face. Had that contributed to his mental instability? Maybe he'd left the navy and fallen away from society, then gotten himself into trouble, and was now gunrunning to stay afloat.

Then there was the medication he'd been taking. Likely a result of PTSD from exposure to combat and the disaster he'd experienced. All this, a fifth grader could've guessed. What I needed to know was how would I come out of this alive. I didn't want to die just as I'd figured out Jock could still be out there, blood flowing through his strong veins.

I should've listened to Romero. He was right about Tork. He may have been tormented, but the son-of-a-bitch was clever.

The numbing possibility that I was going to die raged inside me. It was obvious to me now that Jock had discovered Tork's dealings. Jock had fought with him and tried to stop him. There was no way I was sitting back without fighting, too. I was already a dead man walking. I had nothing to lose by going out in a blaze of glory.

I waited for Tork to pack a new crate. Once I heard the clacking of guns set on top of guns, I moved past the pain in my limbs and wiggled inch by inch until I was positioned with my bag behind my back. I fiddled with the opening with my tied hands until I gained access to the interior. *I beg you, Lord, give me the right tool to cut through this rope.*

I stretched my right hand farther into the bag, swallowing a grunt from the pain of the rope burns on my wrists. Sweat trickled down my forehead into my eyes, panic getting in the way of concentration.

I closed my eyes against the prickling sweat and worked through the sting on my wrists. Finally, my fingers tapped something smooth and long. A blade. Thank goodness! My German-made scissors. The highest-quality instrument I owned.

I gripped the cold metal in my hand and almost squealed with relief, putting to the back of my mind the salesman's warning to never use these on anything but hair. I tugged the scissors out of my bag, and my flat iron shifted, hitting the ground with a *clink*.

Tork whipped around a crate to see what was going on. Before he caught my eye, I slumped forward and lowered my lids, biting down on my gag to keep from moaning. He had to believe I was still unconscious. *Had* to.

He cursed to himself, then twisted around and continued with his task. Amid his clicking and clacking, I coaxed my thumb and fourth finger through the ring holes on my scissors and snipped at the rope. The twine wasn't super thick, but the angle was tough, the knot tight, and a waxy coating on the cord made cutting a challenge.

Minutes ticked by as I grappled with the rope, every muscle in my body tense. Added to that, I was fighting dizziness, my stomach was roiling from anxiety, and *ouch!*

a fresh sliver in my thumb. Physically, I didn't think I could take much more.

I pep-talked my way through the last snip, untied the rope, and gripped my scissors by the handles like a weapon. I may never use these on hair again, but if they saved my life, it'd be worth it.

Tork made a call on his phone, said something about the shipment being ready and that he had one small matter to take care of. I knew without asking what that matter was. He wandered around the far side of the room while he spoke. Every time his back faced me, I reached forward and hacked at the rope at my feet, using my left hand to help untie the cord.

I didn't know who I was fooling. I'd never split it in time, and I didn't want to risk dropping the scissors and gaining his attention.

Tork hung up, slid his phone back in his pocket, then wandered over to me. My hands were back where he'd tied them, my scissors poised. He kicked my foot and barked out a laugh. "Wakey, wakey."

I slowly lifted my chin, faking grogginess. With my aching skull, it wasn't all fake.

"It's time to say bye-bye cruel world."

"Uuf-faa-hff."

"What's that? You want to say something?" He crept closer, an aura of smoke surrounding him, the same smell I'd noticed last night when he'd attacked Twix and me.

I nodded helplessly, it hitting me that the smell was from the explosion at the Hock, not from a campfire as I'd originally thought. Tonight's explosion added to the smoky stench.

"Hey. I'm not such a bad guy. I'll let you have your peace before I shoot you, even though I shouldn't. It's all Jock's fault I have to vacate the premises. If only he'd joined me with this venture, things would be different."

He scrutinized my face. "Then *you* came along, poking your nose where Jock left off. It was kind of fun turning the tables and following you around, seeing where you'd lead me. But good heavens, girl, you drive like you're in the Indy 500. You need to learn to obey signs."

He shook his head in disgust, moving on. "You've also got to learn when enough is enough. My beatings would've sent any other female to the hospital by now. But you keep coming back for more. You're either too stupid to live, or you're tougher than I give you credit for."

I sank my teeth into the gag, fighting to let his insults roll off my back since I wasn't in a position to retaliate just yet.

"But blowing up my bike was the last straw. Now the area is crawling with cops again, and I have to figure out how to get these damn guns out of this building without being seen." He looked around and grunted. "I had a good operation here, too, partnering with the owners of the Okiya Corral."

What? So he had other business with the restaurant?

Suddenly, I recalled Phyllis telling me Jock had given her a lift to the Geisha Gap Friday night before the ballet. Maybe he'd been worried about Phyllis, but suppose he'd been poking around the Okiya Corral, asking questions. And what about the restaurant worker with the tattoo, holding open the door earlier after the bike explosion? My mind was still fuzzy, but I was sure he was the same guy in the black sports car who'd met Tork at the storage units.

"Abandoned buildings are the best," Tork said, bringing me back. "No one suspected a thing, only being two units away from the Hock. And those homeless vets were a good cover. Everyone focuses on them, don't they? Better than dealing with real crimes. Of course, Jock put a kink in things, getting them moved to that facility in Boston."

Jock had organized that move?

He shook his head. "Always the hero, that boy. But now there's you to deal with, and it seems I have to kill another person." His smirk was evil, his laugh, thin. "One bombing a week is enough, don't you think?"

I was thinking a lot of things. Top of the list, how to get out of this predicament.

"Your perfume, by the way, was a dead giveaway last night in Jock's garage. Trained firefighters have keen sniffers, darlin'."

I cringed inside. I was so used to my fragrance, I never smelled it on myself.

"Problem now is," he turned toward his crude setup, "I don't know which gun to use on you. I've got an Uzi, automatic rifles, handguns, shotguns. You name it. I've got it. Do you have a preference?"

His psychotic humor was more frightening than his scarred face, which, as he turned back to me, seemed more distorted. Was it the dim shadows playing tricks on me? Or had Phyllis left a permanent mark? When she went on the attack, she took no prisoners.

"Speaking of weapons," he said, "I'd heard Jock worked for a beautician when they were making *Caribbean Gold*, but I didn't know how ingenious you were until you crafted that explosive. I almost thought the old master-at-arms had taught you a thing or two." He chuckled at that. "Next time I need a bomb made, I'll call on you. Oh wait. You'll be dead."

Tears were streaming down my face, and I was helpless to wipe them away. I squeezed the scissors behind my back, keeping my untied hands in place. I was near the end of my life, and at this point I just wanted it to be over.

"Aww, don't cry. You think I cried when that cub Zeek got his head blown off?" He took his arm and wiped the back of it across his hairline, avoiding touching his scarred face.

"He made that unit a better place, the s-o-b. Turned us all into brothers." He held out his right arm and shoved up his sleeve, the faint rake marks above his inner wrist from yours truly still visible. "Talked the four of us into getting these tattoos."

I looked through the hair on his arms. So Tork *did* have a rope-and-anchor tattoo.

"Called us the Flying *K*'s, linking our names to a stupid kite. Can you believe it? Kid was obsessed with them.

Obsessed with having it be an alert if one of us was in trouble. Obsessed about caring for his brothers. Dumb, stupid kid."

A stubborn tear squeezed out of his eye and detoured down his craggy skin, dripping to the ground. He spun away, shaking his head in what I could only deem was remorse. "What kind of dreamer comes up with shit like that? Huh? *Tell me.*" His voice cracked, and he kicked a stray light bulb on the ground, shattering it into a million pieces.

I jerked back, worried he was working himself into a state, the memory of his brother Zeek resurrecting painful emotions.

He paced the floor, stopped short, then strode over to where he'd tossed his jacket. He fingered through the pockets, tugged out a pill bottle, and snapped off the lid. After prying pills into his gnarled mouth, he stuffed the bottle back in his coat.

My skin crawled at his unstable behavior, yet there was an ache in the back of my throat that was hard to suppress. Here was a man, a veteran, who'd served his country and lost everything in the process. His brother had been killed, and he'd been scarred and maimed for life.

Twix had called Tork a monster, and though his appearance was frightening, I couldn't imagine what it'd be like to have people afraid to even look at you. I'd seen a lot in the beauty industry, and my goal was always to make people feel better about themselves. But this went way beyond physical appearances. This was something I could never fix.

Though my heart hurt for this tormented man, he was a murderer, and in my head I knew he had to be stopped. I was next on his list to kill. After me, then who? I fought with everything I had inside to remain still, unmoved.

He turned his attention to the table, presumably deciding on which weapon to use on me. Letting out a huge sorrowful wail, he took his arm and swept all the weapons onto the ground, the sound of the clattering guns, deafening.

That was when I lost it. I hiccupped a loud sob, panting through my muzzle, wriggling on the floor to get his attention back on me and away from the guns.

He whirled around. "What is it? Can't you see when a man's down?"

"Fuf-fah."

He gave a terse sniff, then sauntered back over, dangerously subdued as if he'd donned a new personality. "I feel sorry for you. I really do. You idolized the wrong man."

"Foo-fff." Anger bubbled inside, trumping the anxiety eating away at my gut. I snorted out my nose like a bull, splattering a big clot of blood onto the floor. It was pathetic enough that Tork mistook my anger for sorrow.

"I'll give you a chance to say your final words. Will that make you happy?"

I nodded.

He took a step closer, looking me over, the slits of his eyes watery, unnatural. I recoiled inside from his appraisal but forced myself to act cool. There was no escaping, and hell could freeze over before I backed down from his stare.

"To tell you the truth," he said, "I don't think you'll be missed. Let's face it, dumplin', who'd want a specimen like you?"

"Whaff?" He was one to talk! I'd never sink so low to criticize *his* features.

"You're a disgrace to the female species. You've got sushi in your hair, chicken innards on your pants, and you're covered in grime. And I haven't even gotten to your face."

He gave a throaty chuckle. "If there's a man out there who loves you, God help him."

I'd had enough of his insults. The terror and fury inside me had swelled to a point that I was shuddering violently. I made the mistake of twitching my feet, and a piece of rope sprang away from the knot and flopped onto the floor.

Our gazes immediately dropped to the semi-hacked twine, then locked back onto each other.

"What the—" He glanced from my face down to my

arms where they curved behind me. "What have you got back there?"

He rushed at me, and out of sheer determination to live, I brought my bound feet up and kicked him hard in the crotch. He grunted and doubled over, falling to his knees. After spitting out a string of swear words, he took in a breath, then lunged for my neck.

I worried this would be the last move I ever made, but I had no choice. I swept my freed arms over his head, clenched the scissors in both hands, and stabbed him between the shoulder blades.

He arched his spine, howling in pain, his gnarled mouth open like a dead fish.

Hardly believing what I'd done, I dragged my hands back as fast as I could and caught his left ear with my nails. Swiftly, a soft latex covering came loose and peeled off in my fingers. A mask!

Screaming in shock, I shook the mask away, the warm underside slimy from my abductor's sweaty skin. I dared to stare into his face and realized his true identity.

Jock's assailant wasn't Tork. It was Vick! The guy in the photos who struck me as a thinker. The guy Twix had seen at the movie set. The lines around his mouth were softer than in the navy photos as he'd gained weight. And I wouldn't be much of a beautician if I didn't notice the crappy job he'd done of darkening the hair on his head and arms. All this in an effort to resemble Tork?

Nausea flowed through me and I panicked, scared I'd vomit with the gag in my mouth.

Instinctively, I swept my hands behind my head, fumbling to undo the cloth. But it was too tight, and I couldn't get my clammy fingers to cooperate.

Vick staggered to his feet, jerked the scissors out of his back, and growled like a beast in pain, his true face contorted into that of a real monster. I hopped away from him, but it was pointless. He raised his arm, scissors high in the air, and plunged them at me.

Suddenly, the loud crack of a gunshot echoed in the

room. The noise stunned me, and I leaped back, my teeth cutting into the cloth. Vick dropped the scissors to the ground with a *clank*, a glazed look in his eyes as he plummeted flat on top of me.

A gut-wrenching shriek exploded from deep inside my throat, cut short by his weight, knocking the wind out of me.

The sound of footsteps approached while I lay dazed, wheezing scraps of air. The sound stopped at our feet, and I squinted up at a large masculine form looming over us in a knit hat and a long, grimy coat, tucking a gun at his back. The light behind his head caused a ring like a halo. Was this it? Was I dead and this was heaven?

The figure leaned over, grasped Vick by the scruff of his neck, and flipped him onto his side next to me, checking for a pulse. That was when I saw my hero's worn, scraped face.

Jock!

He frowned at the still body, the sadness in his eyes like nothing I'd seen before. Taking a heavy breath, he stuffed his hat in his coat pocket, his hair spreading over his collar, then gently helped me to a sitting position. "You okay?"

"Uff." My heart thudded.

I watched him kick my scissors out of the way with his scuffed shoes. Then I inhaled a shaky breath, relief flooding me that it was all over.

Hold on. Jock in grimy clothes? A frayed hat? Scuffed shoes? Those shoes. I'd seen them before. But where?

Everything was scrambled in my head. One too many punches. Then slowly it came to me. That was Jock surveying the explosion site earlier tonight. I'd seen the clothes and shoes from my hiding spot under the counter.

I was an emotional wreck, blurry-eyed and spent, the puzzle pieces still unclear. But I'd figured out that much. All I could manage was another muffled moan.

Jock untied my ankles, lifted me to my feet, and cradled his arms around my waist. It was a moment of quiet before the storm. I clutched his lapels, trembling, yet couldn't help but turn to look at Vick spread out in a pool of blood on the floor. No matter what else he'd done, he'd once been a good friend of Jock's, a brother-in-arms. He'd been a victim of war like so many, and he'd suffered from PTSD. This had to hit a fellow vet like Jock hard.

I forced my gaze away from Vick and patted Jock's well-defined chest and biceps, making sure he was whole, fighting to catch the exotic scent of his cologne, craving the comfort it gave me. But I couldn't detect much past the garbage smell stuck to me, thanks to my broken nose.

My legs quivered under me, and every muscle in my body felt bruised. I was beyond pitiful. Yet I clung to him, afraid if I let go, he'd disappear again.

An army of footsteps pounded into the room, Romero holding everyone back by his sudden stop. Our eyes connected through the commotion, the rumbling voices, and approaching sirens in the background. His stare compelling, powerful, intimate.

A lump formed in my throat from the intensity this man projected, and my heart knocked in my chest, his presence taking the remaining chill from my bones.

He gave me a moment with Jock, watching closely as Jock untied the gag from around my head.

Thank you, I signaled with my eyes, gazing up into Jock's face, forcing myself not to let emotion overpower me. Truth was, there were no words to describe what I was feeling. I'd almost been killed in cold blood, yet I'd survived thanks to this man.

Jock took his large hands and, by way of saying "You're welcome," gently brought my head forward, sinking his lips in my hair. An intimate gesture that couldn't have been easy for Romero to watch. He'd already lost someone he once loved. Was history repeating itself, only this time was he losing that person to another man?

I locked my gaze back on Romero, but it was interrupted by the lights and paramedics rushing into the room, followed by Max and Phyllis.

"Where is she?" the geisha Godzilla boomed.

I blinked back a tear, the joy at seeing my employees

overwhelming me with new emotions, the revelation tonight about Phyllis, startling. From what I knew, my cousin had never helped someone in need. Yet she'd neglected her own safety earlier in the alley and had come to my rescue.

Max tiptoed up to Jock and me, gave Jock a warm pat on the shoulder, and handed me my phone. "You forgot this."

I was grateful Max didn't comment on my worsened condition. I nodded, too choked up to say anything, my numb mouth tricking me into thinking I was still gagged.

The EMTs got a pulse on Vick and strapped him onto a stretcher that was brought into the room. Jock's chest visibly compressed, and he gave a short hand-to-mouth cough, clearly relieved, fighting a world of emotions.

A second gurney was rolled in, meant for me. Evidently, I had no idea how appalling I looked. In fact, I felt surprisingly euphoric. Both men in my life were here and sound. I was in one piece. And I had no broken bones. Well, maybe I had a broken nose, but everyone had a little break at some point in their life, didn't they? Far as I could see, I was a walking miracle.

Romero made a path through the crowd and aimed straight for me, shoulders tense, a stern tilt to his mouth. He and Jock exchanged a brief but meaningful look in passing. If my eyes had been any more swollen, I might not have noticed.

He took me in his arms and held me for a long moment, his grip overprotective like he'd never let me go, his normally deep voice a tad unsteady. "You had me worried." He placed a kiss on my hairline, then peered down into my face, a mix of fear and admiration filling his eyes.

His rugged jaw twitched, an indicator he wanted to say more, but he held back, the hard-headed detective remaining in control. "Good thing Max found your phone and told me you'd been at the restaurant. Plus, we were lucky the alley explosion was called in when it was." He took a deep breath, blowing it out slowly. "Of course, then it was a matter of spreading out and finding you."

He looked at Jock in his homeless gear, then back at me. "I'm sorry I didn't get to you first."

Under normal circumstances, I would've swooned at his vulnerable manner, no matter how tough he chose to act. But at the moment, I was determined to ignore those feelings. It was the look he and Jock shared, making me feel like the village idiot.

The worry and rage I'd suppressed from the beginning of this whole ordeal exploded like a volcano, and the impetuous side of Valentine Beaumont let loose. I released myself from Romero's embrace and gave Jock a swat across the chest. "How could you let me think you were dead?"

He folded my hand inside his large palm, the understanding in his voice apparent. "I had no choice. I had to stay missing to sort things out. As odd as it sounds, I was trying to save my tortured friends while protecting you."

Humph. I swung my gaze to Romero. "You knew about this?"

He put up his palms and shook his head. "Up until you called, I thought Jock was dead. You've got my word on that."

The paramedics ushered me to the stretcher, but I wasn't done venting. I had my voice back, and I was making good use of it. "I have more questions…" I ground my teeth, allowing the EMT to strap me to the stretcher. "Don't you *dare* think this is over!"

Romero slipped out a sigh and placed his hands on his hips, head tilted at Jock. "I don't know about you, but I think I liked her better when she was gagged."

Chapter 18

I was told Romero had been in and out of Rueland Memorial all night, checking in on me between cases. This had made my heart swell. But between me being drugged and in surgery, we hadn't spoken.

Jock brought me a huge bouquet of red-tipped pink roses Monday afternoon, his appearance warming me from the toes up. The scruffy look was gone, the neat stubble was back on his chiseled face, his chestnut hair falling in shiny waves. He was dressed in stylish black pants and a white polo shirt, the pink flowers in his hand adding to the beautiful picture.

"Hey." He'd uttered one word, but boy did it hold a lot of meaning.

I sat up in bed and gave him a feeble smile. Compared to Jock, I looked like the walking dead. My cracked ribs were dressed, my bandaged nose had been put back into place, my eyes were more black than blue, my bruised lips were swathed in ointment, and because I was still dehydrated, I was hooked to an IV drip.

The warm feeling quickly evaporated when three nurses scurried into the room after Jock and sashayed to his side, all but feeling up his biceps while asking if there was anything they could do for him. Honestly. *I* was lying in bed half dead with tubes sticking out of me, and I didn't get so much as a *How are ya?* Jock enters a building, and suddenly staff are coming out of the woodwork.

He winked at me, then gave the flowers to one of the nurses. He thanked her ahead of time for finding a suitable vase, then closed the door after them. They swooned out in the hallway as if they'd met Thor in person. And...I had to admit, maybe they had.

Jock strode to the bed, leaned over, and placed a soft kiss on my forehead, the only spot that wasn't bruised. "What?" He obviously saw the cynical grin on my face.

"For your information, vases usually aren't part of hospital property."

He looked over his shoulder to the glass window. "I'm sure they'll find something."

"Naturally." More evidence of Jock's magnetism.

He gave me a good long stare. "Doc said you'll be released later today."

I inhaled his quintessentially aromatic scent that was blessedly back. "I can't wait. Hospitals are for sick people."

His sexy gaze roved down my wounded body and landed back on my tender face. "Yeah, you don't look sick."

"Thanks." I feigned a lighthearted voice, but I knew he caught the act.

He sat on the edge of my bed and took my hand in his.

"Ouch." I pulled my hand back and pressed my thumb. "Had a sliver."

Without reacting to the irony of that, he gently grasped my hand again and put my thumb to his mouth. One kiss from his luscious lips and, never mind relieving the pain in my thumb, every nerve in my arm went on high alert. Swallowing in disbelief at this man's unceasing powers, I slid my tingly hand from his clasp and propped myself higher on my pillows.

He waited until I was comfortable, then gave me an affirming nod, his voice low. "Thank you for everything you did to try to find me."

This was a huge statement for Jock. He didn't strike me

as someone who needed anyone for anything, yet his words were heartfelt. "You're welcome."

I'd had time, lying in the hospital, to think about what Jock had gone through in the navy, losing friends to war, mutilation, and even mental illness. Until the past few days, I hadn't stopped to consider the weight he might carry. "How is Vick doing?"

"Under the circumstances, good. He's got a long road ahead of him, but I'm confident he'll get the help he needs."

Silence lingered in the room, the only sound, one of the machines making a quiet, steady beep. I wanted to ask questions, but I held back because of the sorrow that filled his eyes. Without a doubt, this nightmare had affected him.

"First," he said, as though struggling internally, "you need to know I would never allow any harm to come to you. I'd been trying to find Vick and stop him. I wanted to get him the help he needed." He made fists with his large hands, his tone regretful. "I thought I could reach him without involving the police, even after I knew he'd killed Tork. But this was worse than any combat I'd ever faced. In the end, when it came down to Vick or you, I had no choice but to shoot him."

I cast my eyes down, unable to look into his penetrating dark stare. "I know." He'd done the right thing regarding Vick, and I couldn't have him feeling bad over my present state. I'd chosen to become involved because I cared. None of this was his fault.

I batted my eyelashes, though it hurt like the devil, and turned my head sweetly from side to side. "But don't you like the look? I resemble Phyllis's last makeover." I pursed my lips, picturing the poor woman after Phyllis had finished with her. "Scratch that. Her eyes were more black."

He chuckled in agreement. "Good thing you're tough."

I choked on the words. "Me? Tough?"

"Yes, you. I'd go as far as to say the glitter and froufrou are a guise. You're actually Wonder Woman when you set your mind to it."

"I do like her tights." I smiled brightly, glad we could laugh about things.

He grinned, studying my face, the corners of his eyes drawn down in regret. "When you hired me, I never fully told you why I moved here. Guess it's time you knew."

I sat up a little taller, the feeling that what I was about to hear would be tough.

"Vick and Tork were both from the Boston area. Likely why they'd bonded and had become friends in the navy. I met them when I joined the firefighting team. Then when Zeek joined up, he, too, became part of the group."

His face turned grim. "After Tork lost Zeek and disfigured his face, he went off the deep end and dropped out of sight. He was suffering from PTSD, but I had no idea to what extent. He was drifting and often seen at the Hock with a group of other homeless men, many of them drug-addicted vets suffering from the same disorder. I'd tried to stay in touch, and I wanted to help get him and the others off the street. After my tour of duty ended, I thought the best way to do that would be to move closer."

He tightened his lips, taking his time before continuing.

"That was all long before *Caribbean Gold* and before I first walked into your shop. Then last fall, Vick came to me on the movie set. Told me he'd been doing some digging on Tork. Found evidence he was dealing arms with criminal organizations. Vick was adamant about it and said our friend had to be stopped. He knew about Tork's condition, too, and how he'd been living. Ironically, Vick himself had become addicted to drugs, and somewhere along the way, he'd stumbled onto the perfect spot near the Hock, which turned out to be where he set up business."

I shook my head, taking this all in. "He looked pretty intense in the pictures."

Jock narrowed an eye. "Pictures?"

I reached for my bag sitting on the nightstand, pulled out the stack of photos and the wrecked frame, and plunked the whole clump in his palm. "Sorry, Twix and I sort of commandeered these when we went back to your place, looking for clues." I peered sheepishly into his face. "The picture frame seemed to have dropped."

"Uh-huh." He pinched the bent frame between two fingers and held it in the air, his butterscotch-brown eyes challenging mine. "Seems I'm also missing a glass ship."

"Uh, yeah. It kind of broke when we found the picture."

"*Kind of? Sort of?*"

"But I fixed it. You're going to love it." I wasn't betting on that.

I also wasn't volunteering news about his ripped duvet. Two confessions a day were plenty. "Don't worry. If you don't like what I've done, I'll pay for a brand new one."

"I'm not worried." He set the frame on the nightstand and flicked the photos back and forth in his hand, his smile devilish. "I know you'll pay."

Gulp. If there ever were a promise, *that* was it.

He looked down at the pictures, his gaze shifting from the first photo to the next, the muscles around his mouth strained. "Zeek was a dreamer, always coming up with ideas like the Flying *K*'s and our tattoos." He glanced down at his left arm sporting the image of the rope and anchor. "He and I had these on our left arms, the other two, on their right. All for the memory, Zeek said, from our tour of duty together in the navy."

That much about what Vick had said was true.

I had a sudden recollection of the kite card Vick had delivered. I rifled through my bag, plucked it out, and held it up to Jock. "A gift from Vick to me."

Jock examined it carefully. "Vick had played his role of Tork to a *T*. Marking a red *X* through all the letters except for the *T* furthered the illusion that Vick was a dead man himself."

Exactly what I thought. I stuffed the card back in my bag.

"Zeek looked up to Vick and me," Jock said. "Used to get tired of being the butt of his big brother's jokes. Followed Vick around like a puppy. Idolized his every word. Vick loved him like a brother, too. Never had any siblings of his own. Said he'd kill himself if anything ever happened to the cub. We were a tight family unit in those days."

Jock kept the emotion out of his voice, but the underlying threads of sorrow were there. He came back to the photos, pulling out the one where Zeek was absent, him and the other two looking somber.

"Zeek took this after we found out we were due to go on a dangerous mission. Wanted to capture the look on our faces." He blew out air at the stupidity of it. "Tork, Vick, and I had a few years on Zeek. We'd been there, knew the risks. But Zeek was this wide-eyed kid. Everything to him was a ride at the fair. Two days later, he was blown away by a landmine. Lost his life before it even began. Tork tried to get to him to save him but was hit by another ground explosive."

I cringed, listening to Jock's story. It sounded so much worse coming from him than from Captain Madera.

"After Tork got out of the hospital, he left the navy and went into hiding. Depression hit him hard. Didn't want anything to do with anybody."

"But you had the code. The kite…if he needed help or was in danger."

"You got it. And in some way, Tork wanted help. Time went on. After my tour of duty, I went home, as I'd once told you, because my mother was sick. Once she was on her feet again, I eventually landed back on American soil. You know of my other work history, but when I got the signal from Tork, there was no question. I moved here to help my buddy."

I was astonished, impressed, and yet saddened by his account, and for once words failed me. I sat there, leaning forward, bruised and speechless, my bag between my legs, waiting with a heavy heart for him to continue.

"Tork was in bad shape," Jock said. "But I'd also been watching and trailing Vick. He'd made some bold claims about Tork leading up to this point. And when he'd finally told me about the gunrunning, things didn't add up. Tork was a jokester. He teased his brother incessantly, but he was the softest of the four of us. I couldn't see any logic in what Vick was alleging. And I found no proof of my own."

I snapped my mouth shut, realizing too late it had been hanging open. "So what happened the night of the ballet?"

He took a deep breath, his jaw clamped tensely. "Vick claimed he'd put all the pieces together. He'd called, then texted me during the evening, ruining the plans I'd had for us."

I felt my skin heat at that remark but didn't allow myself to think of what those plans entailed. I knew Jock had been agitated from the time he'd picked me up Friday night. It now made sense why.

"When we got back to the condo, I saw Vick's alert. Then he texted, claiming he was at the Hock. Said Tork had figured out he'd been digging into the arms deals and was afraid of being turned in. Vick, scared for his own life, was certain Tork was going to kill him, then come after me, eliminating everyone who knew about his activities."

"But it wasn't Vick in trouble. It was Tork."

"Yes. Tork was trying to straighten out. Hell, he'd been doing so much better lately, it'd given me the freedom to go on our cruise. He'd also been doing his own digging. All along it was Vick who'd been dealing in arms. Vick had so many people convinced it was Tork he'd even rigged up a mask as part of the charade. I believe he killed Tork sometime while we were at the ballet, but we may never know exactly what occurred before he showed up at the condo."

This was mind-boggling. "What happened when you stepped outside?"

"It was dark, and he started throwing punches. At first, I thought I *was* wrestling with Tork. That mask was so damn lifelike, and Vick had gained weight in the last year, so he was as heavy as Tork. But then I realized Vick wanted me to think I was fighting Tork, since Vick was supposedly at the Hock, possibly even dead."

He paused, reflecting on his words. "Vick wanted me out of the way. He knew I was onto him and the whole affair. If anyone saw him—like you did—they wouldn't be able to identify him. We exchanged blows, and I tried to reason with him. But he was too far gone. He'd suffered the loss of Zeek like the kid had been his blood brother. Blamed himself for not keeping him safe on that mission. I think there was even a part of him that blamed Tork."

By the tight muscles in Jock's neck, I could tell he was reliving that nightmare as clearly as if he were standing on war-torn ground.

"I told him to straighten himself out. But the guy was on so many prescription drugs he needed more help than what I could give."

"So you fled."

"I needed to find Tork. I gave Vick a cuff to the temple, and he lost consciousness long enough for me to fade from sight. I made an anonymous call to the cops. Said there was someone prowling in the neighborhood. Thought the sirens would rouse Vick and he'd take off, leading me to Tork. I didn't want to deal with the cops. I had to handle things on my own, and I wouldn't have been able to do that if they'd been involved."

My own experience with the police had told me that was true.

"After the paramedics took you away yesterday, Romero filled me in on what happened to you after I vanished. I had no idea you'd left the bathroom and were in the garage, or that Vick had attacked you. I headed up the fire escape at the back of the building that leads to a secret entrance to get you. But when I heard Vick's bike peel out of the lot, I rushed back down, hopped in the Porsche, and went in pursuit."

Noble to the end. "Where did you go?"

"The Hock. It was where I figured Tork would be if I could get to him in time. I didn't know Vick was dealing a few doors down."

"But when you got to the Hock, Tork was there, dead."

"That's right. After I discovered him, Vick showed up. We finished what we'd started at my place. He threatened me, said he'd made a bomb. During our struggle, he detonated it. The place went up in flames, and Vick took off. I switched into some old clothes left there by a homeless person so I could go after Vick unnoticed. I failed to save Tork and Zeek, but maybe I could still save the last of my three friends."

"Why do I suspect Romero comes in at this point?"

He blinked away the moisture in his eyes, staying in control. "The body you saw at the morgue was Tork's. Because it was burned beyond recognition, the cops could only rely on dental records to identify him, which took time. While I was involved in this and trying to save a mentally disturbed friend, Romero was looking for evidence to arrest a gunrunner and murderer."

He gave my hand a squeeze, waiting for me to meet his gaze. "Romero did not lie to you. You know that, right? He honestly thought I was dead."

I did know that, but it was reinforcing hearing it from Jock.

"We had different goals, yet we were after the same person, both of us, in the meantime, trying to keep you safe. It was bizarre that the events intersected on the night of the explosion."

I managed a weak smile. "Where were you staying through all this?"

He gave me a look that implied some things would forever be kept a secret. Okay. I could deal with that.

I processed everything he told me, but there were still a few strings untied. "What about last night? That was you who'd snuck into the Hock. I saw you from under a tipped cupboard."

"I knew you were there. I caught a distant whiff of your perfume."

Again with the perfume. *Was* having a keen sniffer a firefighter's trait? I'd have to check this with my father. "Why didn't I smell *your* cologne?"

"Wasn't wearing any. Wouldn't give myself away. Tip for future reference."

Smart-arse.

"Truth is, I wanted to approach you, but it was vital I found Vick before he hurt anyone else. I hoped I could still reach him. I even put the kite out at the Hock after the explosion. I'd had mine packed in my saddlebag for weeks, then switched it to the Porsche's trunk, thinking the time was near where I might need it. When I spread it out, I thought if Vick saw it, he might come to his senses."

This was all very much like Jock, cryptic from beginning to end. "Just so you know, not long after I left the Hock, I realized you weren't dead."

"Oh? How did you come to that conclusion?"

"The tattoo at the morgue. Wrong arm," I spouted, pretty pleased with myself.

"I'll have to buy you your own Sherlock hat. It'll look cute once the swelling's gone."

I ignored the flattery. "What was it you picked up off the ground when you were there?"

He placed the pictures on my nightstand, the humor in his voice gone. "Vick's meds. He was popping those things like candy. I knew he was nearby, and I wanted to find him. It was a long shot, but I was hoping he'd turn himself in."

He got up from the bed and turned to look out the window. "Vick was an intellectual, a planner. But the mind is a funny thing. Zeek's death and Tork's disfigurement did a number on him. Couldn't get his life back on track after that disastrous mission."

Centering on me again, he leaned in and swept a piece of hair off my shoulder, his hand lingering on my gown. "I owed you an explanation."

We locked eyes, and I reached up and placed my palm on his large, powerful hand, the feeling of life pumping under his skin warming me, the bond between us stronger than ever. "Thank you for that."

It wasn't easy being solemn with Jock. The sexual banter, the jokes, the flippant remarks were what made us work. But I'd come to learn there was a part of him that I needed to take seriously. He was a man with many layers, and this, perhaps, was the most vulnerable I'd ever seen him. "By the way, you might want to let Captain Madera know you're still in one piece."

He grinned, removing his hand from my shoulder. "We've talked. He's wondering when we'll visit him again."

I carefully avoided eye contact as memories of our hot cruise resurfaced. Acting busy, I reached back into my bag, withdrew his keys, and dropped them in his hand. "You might be needing these."

"Always good to have a few sets." He winked. "By the way…" He squinted at me, curiously. "You wouldn't happen to know why my dining room light is shorting out, would you?"

"Ha!" I exclaimed almost too quickly. "What do you think? I was swinging from the chandelier?"

"No. But now that you mention it, were you?"

I gave *him* a look that implied some things would forever be kept a secret. He could deal with *that*.

Work Tuesday turned out to be the best medicine for me. Things were steady, I was moving slowly but feeling human, and the customers were a delight. I'd dressed in slim jeans, royal-blue strappy, peep-toed ankle boots, and a blue-and-white, vertical-striped, off-the-shoulder, poufy blouse with pirate sleeves that cuffed and flared at the wrists. My hair was curled down my back, and I'd opted for blue glittery earrings. I'd gone long enough looking like wallpaper. Today, the sparkle was back.

Jock had spent the rest of Monday arranging a remembrance service for Tork. Today, he was at a preliminary hearing for Vick. Max and Phyllis were toeing the line and weren't squabbling as much as usual. I spent a good part of the morning peering from one to the other, wondering if I *had* died and gone to heaven.

I'd just slammed shut the money drawer after the first wave of clients had filtered out of the shop when Phyllis bustled up to me at the sales counter in a long-sleeved white crop top and green slacks. "I need your advice."

Phyllis? Asking *me* for *advice?* The chance of that happening was akin to me dressing like a geisha and parading around town, twirling a paper umbrella on my back. I glanced from her lightened hair down to her extra belly that had jiggled to a stop over her waistband. At least the outfit wasn't as outlandish as the kimono, chopsticks, and wooden thongs, which had miraculously disappeared. "Don't tell me—you want to bring the drums back in to practice."

She gave a dismissive wave with her hand. "I'm *done* with *that* gig. Nobody appreciated my talents as a geisha. Would you believe, my rendition of 'My Sharona' came in dead last?"

Sounded like they'd been graded, but I wasn't about to ask questions. "I'm sorry, Phyllis. Your version of that song will forever be etched in my mind." It was the truth.

"Yeah, they were a bunch of sticklers. Who wants to serve tea their whole life, anyway, wearing a kimono and shuffling around in wooden thongs? You know I got blisters from those things?" She swung her spongy sandaled foot up at me to demonstrate, almost knocking me in the teeth. "And here I learned about the Geisha Gap when I visited the Okiya Corral food truck at the multicultural fair. Like I didn't have enough to worry about *that* weekend. Never. Again."

I backed up from Phyllis's swinging foot and glanced at Max who was at his station, creating a loose herringbone braid in a woman's hair. I had to give him credit. He was artistically outperforming himself and paying no attention to us.

I pushed Phyllis's foot down. "You said you wanted advice?"

"Oh. Right. Since that girl came in with the tattoos, and then there was all that business with Jock and the tattoos, well, I was thinking maybe *I* should get a tattoo."

Max gave a high-pitched snort, no doubt meant for Phyllis. So much for paying us no attention.

I tried not to roll my eyes, but the urge was strong. "Phyllis, you hate tattoos. Why now?"

"I don't know!" She threw her hands in the air, her frustration evident. "Everyone's got them."

"If everyone had lice, would you want that, too?"

She puckered her lips, thinking this through.

"Phyllis, that was a rhetorical question. My point is, just because lots of people have tattoos doesn't mean *you* should get one."

She reached for my sleeve, yanked it up, and twisted my arm left and right. "Do you have any?"

"No." The thought of getting a tattoo made my brain bleed.

"Why not?" She bulged out her eyes. "Don't you like Jock's tattoo?"

Why did I know that was coming? "On him, it's fine." I wrenched back my arm and pulled down my sleeve. "They're not for me. But if you want one bad enough, then get one."

"Really?" She jerked back, surprised at my response.

Max, having had enough of missing the party, fixed an elastic around his client's braid, slapped a magazine in her hand, and trotted over. "I think you should get one, too, Phyll."

She narrowed her gaze on Max and folded her arms across her chest. "Now I *know* I shouldn't get one." She cut him an even shrewder look. "Where are *your* tattoos?"

"*Moi?*" Max spread his hand on his chest. "My body's a temple. I wouldn't mark it up with ink blots. But as that's clearly not the case for you, what have you got to lose?"

Phyllis missed the insult in that statement and examined her arms with new eyes. "Yeah. Maybe you're right."

"Of course I'm right." Max helped her push her sleeve up to her elbow. "You have so much going for you all that's missing is a tattoo." The look he slid me inferred he really wanted to say, *You have nothing going for you, might as well get a tattoo.*

I shook my head at his craftiness. I could tell Phyllis was

buying his theory, but she was misguided if she thought this truce was going to last longer than a day.

"What kind of tattoo should I get?" Phyllis asked Max.

He tilted his head from side to side, chin out, considering all the options. "I don't know. First things that come to mind are a horse, a cow, and a hippo. Maybe you could combine those somehow."

"Those are all animals!"

"So? You want a genuine likeness, don't you?"

On second thought, this truce wouldn't last longer than an hour.

"I want something that speaks to the unique things I've done."

"Ohhh. Why didn't you say so?" Max counted on his fingers. "There's the bowl of fruit you wore on your head on the cruise. And don't forget the Scottish caber toss. You could have a log tattooed on your thigh. Or what about a tambourine circling your knee?" He thought some more, the glee on his face infectious. "Maybe you should get something from this latest endeavor. Perhaps a tattoo of your smiling face made up like a geisha."

Phyllis wasn't buying any of these ideas. "I'm thinking more a symbol."

"You mean like the cone for a dunce cap?"

Phyllis bunched her hands into fists. "*No.* I mean the symbol for people."

"Ah. The male and female signs. You want the circle with an arrow pointed out."

Phyllis looked like she was going to clobber Max. "That's the *male* symbol."

"What's your point?"

She puffed out air. "I don't know. This whole idea is giving me a headache."

I gave Max a stern look, then turned to Phyllis. "You don't have to decide today, Phyllis. You want to make the right decision. Remember, it's forever."

Her back straightened at that, and I sensed this thought put a kink in her plans.

"Yes," Max chirped. "Take your time. I'm here to help if you need me."

Oh Lord.

After giving Phyllis a brotherly pat on the back, Max returned to his client. Phyllis ignored *her* next client and went to search images of tattoos on her phone. Right when I thought she'd turned over a new leaf...

The day almost cruised by without incident until Candace sauntered in, shoving Max's departing client out of the way. She came to a halt in the waiting area, legs wide, arms crossed. She was wearing shiny red tights, red spikes, and a red-sequined tube top. Her black roots had been bleached blond, her hair was poufed out like an angora rabbit, and her lips and nails were painted red.

"If it isn't Strumpet Barbie," Max said. "Or is it Hump-it Barbie? I always get those two mixed up." He faked a concerned voice. "What's wrong, Candace? Did someone steal your street corner while you were playing *Little House on the Prairie*?"

She looked accusingly at both of us. "What makes you think I was doing that?"

Max spoke up, keeping what I'd told him about Candace's latest getup a secret. "There was a front-page spread in the *Rueland News* of you dressed like Laura Ingalls. Surely, you must've seen it."

Candace huffed at Max, then swung her head at me. "I came by to see if it's true."

I rolled my eyes so far back into my head I could almost see where they fixed my nose. "If what's true, Candace?"

"That you broke your schnoz." She stared at the white bandage across the bridge of my nose. "Guess it *is* true."

I had nothing to hide. "Yes. The doctors did reconstructive surgery, and now my nose is perter and cuter than ever."

"Bully for you. If you had *my* nose, you wouldn't have needed surgery."

"She's right," Max said. "Candace has poked her nose in so many affairs, it's hardened like a rhinoceros's."

Candace shot Max daggers, and Max crossed his fingers at arm's length to ward her off. I'd once seen him do the same thing to Phyllis, but aimed at Candace, it held more spite.

I sized up her red outfit. "Why are you dressed like a lobster? What happened to the black frocks? The granny loafers?"

Candace quivered from head to toe, her jiggly boobs almost falling out of her top. "I couldn't *stand* it any longer. Dressing like a frump was *not* good for business."

"True," Max said. "Hookers would never make a cent dressed as frumps."

"I mean the *hair* business, you nincompoop."

"What about Hoagy?" I asked. "What does he think about this reformed look?"

"Hoagy and I are through. I was more woman than he could handle. So as of now, I'm a free woman."

Max pushed her out the door. "Wonderful. The drunks at the Wee Irish Dude will be happy to hear that."

Candace tripped onto the sidewalk, and Max dusted off his hands, then backed me into my office. "Now that we've gotten rid of one kook, let's discuss another."

"What are you talking about?" I had an inkling I knew.

"The you-know-who being your you-know-what."

"You want to speak English?" I would've drawn this out forever if I could, but the you-know-who would be back any minute from picking up her afternoon snack.

"You know what I'm talking about. When were you going to tell me?"

"Tell you—"

"That Phyllis was related. Wait. Forget I asked. I already know the answer to that."

I avoided his stare, then exhaled a sigh. "Sorry, Max. It was one of those things better kept a secret."

He crossed his arms over his toned chest and leaned back on my desk. "To tell the truth, I've known for a long time."

"What? Why didn't you ever say anything?"

He shrugged. "I figured you'd tell me when you were ready."

Max was probably the most perceptive person I knew. Of course, Romero was no slouch in the perception department either. "You're not mad I kept it from you?"

"As if. I would've done the same thing."

I poked my head around the corner of the office, making sure we were still alone, then swiveled back to Max. "What about The Idiot Files and Hollywood?"

I expected him to give me one of his impish, wise-guy retorts. Instead, he shot me a rueful smile, his hazel eyes soft. "I decided to give Phyllis a break. It's not every day I witness her being human, or even half human. But I'm keeping the files on hand. You never know when I might need them."

I gave him a thoughtful nod. "Good to know you'll be ready."

Phyllis stomped into the salon and marched past my office door, a submarine sandwich in one hand, a bowl of dripping soup in the other.

Max gawked from Phyllis, leaving a trail of chowder on the floor, to me, his ears perked in his scampish way. "I'm always ready."

The week went by, and by Friday night it had been five whole days since I'd seen Romero. He'd checked in, asked how I was feeling, but his absence told me something was up.

I'd had almost a week to come to terms with his involvement in the case. I'd even gotten over him not disclosing any information to me during the investigation.

Romero was a tough cop with the highest sense of honor. It couldn't be easy leading a squad of men and fighting crimes, all while attempting to restrain an imprudent girlfriend from getting involved in things she shouldn't. But he did his job with diligence and expertise, and his team valued his principles and trusted him beyond measure.

As for me, he'd been right. Vick and his cohorts had been people I didn't want to fool with. There was a lesson in there for someone willing to learn. I smoothed the bridge of my nose, wincing from the memory the break evoked. Hell, why were lessons always painful?

I wasn't sure how much longer I could go mentally or physically without staring up into Romero's swarthy face, running my fingers across his unshaved jaw, feeling his toned hands stroke my skin, hearing his caught-off-guard burst of laughter. But Jock had a point. I was more Wonder Woman than I gave myself credit for. I could be strong despite the froufrou and sparkle. I could handle anything that came my way. Even if it meant separating my heart from Romero…if that was what he wanted.

I locked up the shop, put Daisy Bug in drive, and headed home. Tomorrow was a new day. If Romero was in my life, great. If not, I'd survive.

I pulled into my driveway and spotted his truck at the curb. Romero sat on my porch steps wearing an unbuttoned plaid shirt over a dark T-shirt and jeans, elbows resting on his knees, head hung low. Swinging from his index finger was a shiny square metal ring that seemed to have him mesmerized.

He raised his chin, and our eyes fastened on each other. *Oh no.* I had an immediate sinking feeling in my gut. My head didn't feel so well either. I shut off the ignition, and the keys dropped from my instantly shaky hands. I reached down to get them and bumped my forehead on the gearshift. *Youch.* I massaged my forehead. Boy, was I stupid. Today was the first day my body felt mended, and I almost looked like a normal person. Now this!

I swallowed the lump in my throat and, bag in hand, angled out of the car. I tugged down my dress and sauntered up the walkway. "Greetings." No harm trying to sound cheery.

I waited for a reply, but I couldn't overlook how tight his lips had gone. *No.* I was wrong about all this. I wasn't

Wonder Woman. Romero was here to say goodbye. The grim look on his face said it all. That irresistible yet frightening look. I wasn't ready to cut this gorgeous man from my life.

I looked for the dangerously sexy signs that he was playing with me, the dilated pupils, the expression that said he was stripping me without one touch, the sensual grin on his lips. I couldn't detect any of it.

"You're looking well," he finally said.

Looking well? He seemed so cold and distant it brought a sudden throb in my chest. I gulped back the pain that gripped me and wore my best smile. "You coming inside?"

He got up, and I noticed a take-out paper bag behind him. "Yeah. I've had a hankering for Szechuan chicken. You hungry?"

"Sure," I said, an unsteady ring to my voice.

"Good." He held out his palm, offering the square ring that had him mesmerized. It was my glittery hooped earring I'd worn the night of the ballet, the one I'd used to stab Vick. "Lab came back with the test results," Romero said, "confirming Vick's blood on the earring."

He pulled something out of his shirt pocket. "I believe this is also yours."

My hat pin! Mind you, the straight stem was now corkscrewed, but I'd take it. I did a tiny shrug and slid them both in my bag. "All's well that ends well. A-heh."

He wasn't amused. He clutched the take-out bag, grabbed my hand, and waited for me to unlock the door. Then he followed me into the house.

Once the door was closed, he ditched the food, tugged my hand back, and twirled me into his arms. Banging me against his firm chest, he took a second to absorb the look in my eyes, then pressed his full lips on mine.

My heart skipped a beat in confusion at the urgency of the kiss, but I wasn't asking questions. The bruising around my mouth was gone, and I was hungry for more than Szechuan chicken. If this was my last night with Romero, I'd make it a good one.

He steadied his feet from the impact of the embrace and, with his lips still on mine, he dropped my bag to the floor, wrapped his hands under my butt, and hoisted me onto his powerful thighs. In a rush, he backed into the door, devouring me with his passionate kiss.

My heels clunked to the mat, and my dress rode up my legs. I didn't want the kiss to end. Once it was over, he'd leave. He'd say his farewell.

At the moment, his roving touch indicated he wasn't going anywhere. His kiss deepened, his tongue thrashing wildly with mine. He squeezed my breasts, stroked my face, then propped me higher onto his hips. I felt his heart pounding inside his chest, his desire obvious.

He reluctantly ended the kiss and put me down but didn't break the gaze. His hands cupped my face, his fingers laced through my hair. His stare moved from my eyes to my mouth and back to my eyes.

"*Damn* it." He tore his hands away, his tone serious.

"Sorry?" I was catching my breath, my skin still tingling from the kiss.

"God knows I tried, but I couldn't do it."

"Do what?"

He raked his hand through his thick mane. "Focus on work. Keep you at a distance."

I frowned, confused by his words. "Why would you want to—"

"To what? Keep you at a distance?"

"Yes. You told me you hearted me." Sure, it was said with a tube of cream on my arm instead of with words, but the sentiment was there. "Aren't I cute anymore?"

"You're exasperating!"

"Am I cute and exasperating?" I asked it with a high lilt to my voice, hoping to ease the tension.

My question caught him off guard. "If you were any cuter, I'd wrap you up and carry you in my back pocket."

I brightened. "Then I can take being exasperating."

He shook his head like I didn't get it. "I thought I was going to lose you. When I got to that hideout and saw the guns and the blood running down your face, and the broken nose and gagged mouth—"

I moved him along, gesturing with my hand. "Okay. I was a mess. But I didn't die."

"You could have. Before Jock's involvement, we suspected we were dealing with an ex-military, supplying weapons to arms dealers. But all we had were names. When you mentioned Tork as the guy who'd attacked both you and Jock, it struck a chord. Yet we couldn't find the real Tork."

He let out a long sigh. "I knew it was going to get ugly. Further complicating things, there were inconsistencies on the disfigured face. Seemed Vick was using the mask at will. But *you*, going off half-cocked, making your own explosive." He crossed his arms as if he couldn't get over it. "Who am I dating? A beautician or a mini Albert Einstein?"

I flung my hands on my hips. "My hair's not anything *like* Albert Einstein's."

Romero rolled his eyes. "God save me."

"Well?" A chill rushed through me from the memory of that night in the alley. "I told you I wouldn't give up looking for Jock until I found him. A promise is a promise," I concluded, stalwart in my decision.

The mood suddenly changed, and Romero's eyes softened as they met mine, his tone low. "Would you have looked that hard for me?"

There it was. The question that hadn't been asked. It was abrupt and out of nowhere. Yet I knew this had been playing on him. "I would've looked harder...because...I love you."

He let that sink in.

"And when you get down to it," I added, "you're not easy to love."

The thoughtful look turned into a wicked grin. Scoundrel. He liked that he had me on my toes.

He threw his hands in the air. "Why did I have to fall in love with a woman who a) doubles her beauty tools as weapons, and b) acts before she thinks?"

I calmed my pitter-pattering heart at the romantic claim.

"Because a) you think I'm cute, b) you like a challenge, and c) you wouldn't want me to change."

"I'm not asking you to change, but on occasion could you think before you act?"

"I did think. Do you suppose I whipped out my can of hairspray without devising a plan? Even Vick said I was ingenious, rigging that explosive."

"Great. Comforting to know you were getting insight from a mentally disturbed murderer."

Well, when he put it that way. Truth was, I'd never been more scared than I'd been when Vick rushed at me with my own scissors. Mercifully, things had turned out as they had.

Vick and his cohorts would be put away for a long time. And thanks to Jock's initiative for the homeless and mentally disturbed vets, Vick would get the help he needed. Fortunately, I'd come out of this with no permanent scars.

Ending the conversation and bent on lightening the mood, I picked up the tasty-smelling take-out bag and swung it under Romero's nose. "This is going to get cold."

He followed me into the kitchen and watched me dish out the food, a sexy grin on his face. "When I was sitting out there, waiting for you, I was thinking of the funny things I love about you."

I shifted my gaze to him without moving my head, wary of what was coming next. "Liiiiike?"

He chuckled in his low, soft way. "Like how you say *Excuse me* after you sneeze."

"Everyone says *Excuse me* after they sneeze."

"Yeah, but you say it even when you think no one is around."

He reached over and gave my hair a playful tug. "And you keep me on my toes. If anything were to happen to you, I might do something desperate."

I quit spooning rice onto the plates and teasingly arched my eyebrows. "Like Romeo and Juliet?"

He belted out a laugh. "More like *Romero* and Valentine."

I coughed at his remark, hiding a smile, then handed him chopsticks from the bag. "If we're going to move forward, we'll have to work on that humor of yours."

He slid his chopsticks under my dress strap, tugged me closer, and bent his head at my neck, his stubbly jaw tickling my skin. "That's not all we'll work on."

Other Books in
The Valentine Beaumont Mysteries

BOOK 1

MURDER, CURLERS, AND CREAM

Valentine Beaumont is a beautician with a problem. Not only has she got a meddling mother, a wacky staff, and a dying business, but now she's got a dead client who was strangled while awaiting her facial.

With business the way it is, combing through this mystery may be the only way to save her salon. Until a second murder, an explosion, a kidnapping, death threats, and the hard-nosed Detective Romero complicate things. But Valentine will do anything to untangle the crime. That's if she can keep her tools of the trade in her bag, keep herself alive, and avoid falling for the tough detective.

In the end, how hard can that be?

BOOK 2

MURDER, CURLERS, AND CANES

Valentine Beaumont is back in her second hair-raising mystery, this time, trying to find out who had it in for an elderly nun. Only trouble is there are others standing in her way: hot but tough Detective Romero, sexy new stylist Jock de Marco, and some zany locals who all have a theory on the nun's death.

Making things worse: the dead nun's secret that haunts

Valentine, another murder, car chases, death threats, mysterious clues, an interfering mother, and a crazy staff.

Between brushing off Jock's advances and splitting hairs with handsome Detective Romero, Valentine struggles to comb through the crime, utilizing her tools of the trade in some outrageous situations. Question is, will she succeed?

BOOK 3

MURDER, CURLERS, AND CRUISES

In her third fast-paced mystery, beautician Valentine Beaumont and her madcap crew sail the high seas on a Caribbean "Beauty Cruise." When a bizarre murder takes place onboard, Valentine finds herself swept into the middle of the investigation.

If things aren't bad enough, her mother is playing matchmaker, a loved one is kidnapped, drug smuggling is afoot, a hair contest proves disastrous, and a strange alliance between tough Detective Romero and sexy stylist Jock de Marco rubs Valentine the wrong way.

Will this impulsive beauty sleuth comb through the catastrophes and untangle the mystery, or will this voyage turn into another fatal Titanic? With Jock and Romero onboard, it's destined to be a hot cruise!

BOOK 4

MURDER, CURLERS, AND KEGS

In her first action-packed mini mystery, beautician Valentine Beaumont is stalked by an escaped felon she once helped put behind bars. As she strives to stay one step ahead and stop this maniac before he kills her, she stumbles onto a dead body, unearths secret plots, struggles with family obligations, and is tackled in more ways than one.

With a string of beauty disasters, two sexy heroes, a ticking clock, and a little help from her friends, can Valentine solve this case before the killer gets his revenge, or will this be her last?

Murder, Curlers & Kegs is book 4 in the Murder, Curlers series and the first in Valentine's shorter-length mini mysteries.

BOOK 5

MURDER, CURLERS, AND KILTS

A weekend visit to Rueland's multicultural fair turns sour when beautician Valentine Beaumont comes face to face with a corpse wearing a kilt. What's worse, she learns the victim was a target of foul play, her #1 nemesis is on the case, and no one is who they seem.

Despite warnings from hot, hard-headed Detective Romero to leave things to the police, Valentine sets off to snag the killer. While on the case, she crashes into sexy, Herculean stylist Jock de Marco, rattles an old foe, wrestles with family issues, and tangles with secretive clan members.

Will Valentine catch the murderer before she becomes the weekend's next target? Or are her fair days numbered?

What's Next in
The Valentine Beaumont Mysteries

Make sure you're subscribed to my newsletter for updates on Valentine's next mystery.

www.arlenemcfarlane.com/signup/signup5.html

Also, you won't want to miss Valentine's next hilarious, crime-solving adventure when she teams up with three other sleuths in

A Killer Foursome Mystery

Book Club Discussion Questions

Enjoy the banter while you share these questions with your book club!

1. Tattoos have a meaningful role in this book. Do you have any tattoos? If yes, is there a specific meaning behind them?

2. Valentine's best friend, Twix, is always ready to jump in and help Valentine in any circumstance. Do you have a best friend who sticks by you through thick and thin?

3. Valentine rebuilds Jock's glass ship because it's a token of how much he means in her life. Do you keep mementos from people you love?

4. Jock and his buddies called themselves the Flying *K*'s. Have you ever belonged to a friend group/team/sisterhood that had a unique name?

5. When you read the title, what did you think this book would be about?

6. Phyllis learned an instrument for her training as a geisha. Have you ever learned an instrument or a skill specifically for a special performance?

7. If you were a cover artist, what would you add or change to the cover?

8. What would you like to see happen in book 7 in terms of character relationships and storylines?

9. Can you pick out the references from Valentine's previous adventures that were threaded through this story?

10. Do you think the lengths Jock went to to help his friend were justified? Why or why not?

Note to Readers

Thank you for taking the time to read MURDER, CURLERS, AND KITES. If you enjoyed Valentine's story, please consider telling your friends or posting a short review. Word of mouth is an author's best friend and much appreciated. Thank you!

Social Media Links

Website: www.arlenemcfarlane.com

Newsletter Sign-up:
www.arlenemcfarlane.com/signup/signup5.html

Facebook: facebook.com/ArleneMcFarlaneAuthor/

Facebook Readers' Group:
www.facebook.com/groups/1253793228097364/

Twitter: @mcfa_arlene

Pinterest: pinterest.com/amcfarlane0990

Photo credit: Tomas Klein

Arlene McFarlane is the *USA Today* bestselling author of the *Murder, Curlers* series. Previously an aesthetician, hairstylist, and owner of a full-service salon, Arlene now writes full-time. She's also an accomplished pianist and makeover artist. When time allows, she plays publicly and posts makeovers on her website.

Arlene is a member of Romance Writers of America®, Sisters in Crime, Toronto Romance Writers, SOWG, and the Golden Network. She's won and placed in over 30 contests, including twice in the Golden Heart®, twice in the Daphne du Maurier, and twice in the prestigious Chanticleer International Mystery & Mayhem Book Awards. She's also received a Voice Arts nomination for her audiobook, *Murder, Curlers & Cream*.

Arlene lives with her family in Canada.

www.arlenemcfarlane.com